High School Runner

High School Runner
(Freshman)

Bill Kenley

RIVER'S EDGE
—— MEDIA ——
Little Rock, Arkansas
2015

HIGH SCHOOL RUNNER (Freshman)
By Bill Kenley

www.RiversEdgeMedia.com

Published by River's Edge Media, LLC
100 Morgan Keegan Drive, Ste. 305
Little Rock, AR 72202

Edited by Kirk Curnutt
Cover design by Gable White

Manufactured in the United States of America.

ISBN-13: 978-1-940595-22-1

This book is for all the coaches.
Especially Coach Kenley and Coach Patrick.

"And yet I think man will never renounce real
suffering, that is, destruction and chaos.
Why, suffering is the sole origin of consciousness."
—Fyodor Dostoyevsky, *Notes from the Underground*

"We few, we happy few, we band of brothers;
For he to-day that sheds his blood with me
Shall be my brother ..."
—Shakespeare, *Henry V*

DEAD? - A RACCOON EATING RASPBERRY JELLY - DEATH FART - ATTACK - BREAKDOWN - A SECRET - THE START

"Are you dead?" I asked. There was no response. "Coach?" I said.

It was six a.m. and I was still rubbing sleep out of my eyes when I found him.

He reminded me of roadkill—one of the dead raccoons or opossums I often saw on the country roads surrounding our town. I thought of my brother and what he always said when we drove by a bloody lump on the road. *He's sleeeeepy.* Saying that was one of the few things my brother intentionally did to be funny, although he was often funny unintentionally.

Drawn close, fascinated by the awful possibility of a dead man before me, I hovered over coach's body, inspecting him, looking for clues. There were no telltale wounds anywhere—

no holes, no red leaking out of him. It was all like a dream, actually. I know that's a cliché, but it was.

I nearly swallowed my tongue when he farted. It was a high-pitched whine like letting air escape from a balloon. He sat up and rubbed his red eyes with his thin fingers and picked up his big black glasses from where they sat beside him and delicately placed them on his nose. "K1," he said anxiously, a rasp in his throat, "what the hell time is it?"

"What?" I think I said.

"What the hell time is it? Does anyone else know I'm in here asleep?" He quickly rose from the mat. "Doncha have a watch?" he asked. "Did I sleep through school or what?"

"It's about ten after six," I said. "Everyone's here. For morning practice."

Coach glanced nervously around the wrestling room as if witnesses might be hiding in the corners or somehow wedged behind the signs on the walls. The room was empty but for me.

"I mean," I restated, "they're not in here. They're waiting for us. For me … they stopped waiting for you. I had to go to the bathroom and I accidentally came in here. It was dark. I turned the lights on. There you were." I pointed at the spot of drool, or maybe it was sweat, on the floor.

He sighed in relief and covered the lower part of his face with his thin fingers. His brown eyes, so deep brown they seemed black sometimes, stared into mine. He was thinking. This made me nervous. "Sit down," he finally said.

I looked around for a chair. There wasn't one.

"On the goddamn mat," said Coach.

I sat down, avoiding the wet smear.

Coach scooched over on the mat so he was directly across from me. We were both sitting cross-legged. There was a black clock with a white face ticking away behind a black steel cage on the wall. I listened to it, not quite counting the ticks. Neither of us said anything. This went on for some time.

"Listen to me," said Coach finally. Then he bit his lower lip and tilted his head down toward the floor so I couldn't see his face. His shoulders began to hitch up and down. He was crying. "Can you keep a secret?" he whispered.

And that was the real beginning.

But I might as well start at the start. The very start, I mean.

Before that October morning in the wrestling room when my cross country coach became Coach with a capital C. Before Slade. Before Keene and K1 and K2 and Ridgeline and Moats and Leonardo Chavez and Popeye and Squid. Before the hares and the hounds and the gun and the ninja and Victor's and One of Us. Before all that, there was Willie Davis and the day that I, Sherman Leopold Kindle, first understood what I was supposed to be.

WILLIE DAVIS - MY UNCLE - NEW BALANCE MARSHMALLOWS - ROCKY BALBOA - RAW EGGS - THE KIWANIS SUNRISERS PANCAKE BREAKFAST AND TWO-MILE RUN - 110% - THE BIRTH OF A RUNNER

Willie Davis carried at least a hundred and eighty pounds of lean muscle on his five-foot-seven frame. His dark skin was the color of coffee, no milk or cream, and I would've bet my ten-dollar-a-week allowance that Willie had once been a big time college running back or a quick-as-lightning point guard. I never would've pegged him for a runner. Not a distance runner, at least. That was because black people, as far as I could tell, just *didn't do* certain things. They didn't swim, and they didn't smoke anything but menthol cigarettes. They did not farm, drive foreign cars, play hockey, bowl, live in my neighborhood, or run over a quarter of a mile at a time.

Well, Willie did the last of these. Often and well. Actually, I learned later, he was a farmer, too.

The local studs always gathered at the starting line of the weekend 5Ks and 10Ks. I can see them now in their short side-split shorts and silky singlets, seven or eight of them standing in the cool morning air shaking their arms gently, doing strides and high knees incessantly out and back, out and back. As the time to the gun ticked down to five or six minutes, one of the studs would inevitably mention Willie, who was always prominent in his absence at the starting line. I always lurked up near the start, in spite of my uncle's protests that I'd get run over, hoping to stand for just a moment next to the eventual winner.

"Guess Willie's not gonna win this one today," someone would say, or, "Looks like Willie's giving someone else a chance." Then they'd all laugh nervously. But then, as if on cue and at the last possible moment, Willie's beat-up green-and-white Ford pickup would roll in and Willie would get out, dash to the race director's table to pick up his number and some safety pins, and hurry back just in time for the gun. He must've stretched, somehow, in the driver's seat of his truck as he never strained one of his very prominent and hyper-striated muscles. He almost never lost a race.

That's why I still believe there must've been something wrong with Willie on that day. Maybe he'd been in his barn late with a sick calf that was laid out, or maybe he had a little brown-bottle cold caught sitting around the kitchen with his buddies the night before drinking beer. In any case, I refuse to believe that I as a twelve-year-old would've been able to take Willie down at the height of his abilities.

I must say, though, even before my surprise victory I believed running was in my blood. It hadn't yet been proved, but my uncle claimed he saw in me something of himself when I was a little kid, five or six, tirelessly charging up and down the soccer pitch, swarming the ball with all the other kids.

This made me proud and hopeful, as my uncle had been top ten in the state in cross country three of his four years of high school. He had gone on and run at Indiana State on a scholarship, briefly, before he gave it up for cigarettes, motorcycles, and jazz. I didn't know about those other things at age twelve, but I was hopeful about running.

As a boy, I often obsessed over my uncle's trophies. When my twin brother and I spent the night at my grandmother's house, we slept in Grandma's dusty guest room—my uncle's room as a boy. A special job I'd given myself was caretaker of those forgotten trophies.

I kept them properly lined up on their bookshelf. I dusted them and dreamed they were mine. Mostly, they were small golden statues of runners in mid-stride, faceless and with perfect form. I sometimes lined them up and raced them against each other.

My uncle was my first role model. I wanted to be just like him, but it wasn't until I got a pair of real running shoes that the dream started to feel like it could be real.

I got them on my twelfth birthday. They were a pair of gray and maroon New Balance marshmallows, about as good as you could get back then. It was the first real step, symbolic as it was, towards thinking of myself as a runner. The second step was using them. And I used them every morning. Before daylight if I could manage it.

The movie *Rocky* was important to me when I was twelve. Even though Rocky Balboa was a boxer, everyone's favorite scene in the movie was when he was running. It's become a cliché now. Rocky rises in the early morning darkness, he sleepily dons his gray sweat suit and black knit cap.

He cracks a few eggs, swallows them raw, and then, starting slowly, dodging the predawn deliverymen and smoking trash cans in the crowded alleyways, barely shuffling, he makes his way through the dark, grimy streets of Philadelphia.

The music begins. *Bum-bum-ba-ba-bum-bum-bum-ba-ba-bum, bum-bum-ba-ba-bum-bum-bum-ba-ba-bum* ... Rocky punches the air. He's alive now. He's gonna fly now. He keeps running and the music picks up. *Ba-baba-ba-ba-ba-baba–bum bum* ... The sun rises spilling daylight through the streets. Rocky keeps running. Then the music grows larger somehow and, before you know it, Rocky is sprinting. He *is* flying. And nobody's gonna stop this guy no matter how unknown, no matter how poor, dumb, and hopeless he might be. And then he's bounding up the famous steps, those famous steps of the Philadelphia Art Museum where thousands upon thousands, maybe over a million people by now, have bounded up in imitation of him. And then he's on top of those steps, raising his gloved hands in victory, forever a symbol of the spirit of a champion.

Well, I wasn't immune to this. That song had been going through my head for over five years by the time I was twelve. I, too, had the spirit of a champion. And some new running shoes. And my New Balances, mushy as they were, were way better than Rocky's black high-top Chuck Taylors. Therefore, I, too, would eat raw eggs.

The raw eggs part didn't last long. My mom found me out one morning and had me on salmonella watch for twenty-four hours, then didn't buy eggs until she thought I'd forgotten about Rocky. But I did keep running. And I never forgot about Rocky.

I started out running around the block, marveling at how good my size fives felt, staring down at them all the while as I ran. Then I ran around the block twice. Then three times. By the time I lined up against Willie Davis at the Kiwanis Sunrisers Pancake Breakfast and Two-Mile Run, I'd probably logged a long run of nearly a half-mile.

It was a good thing I didn't know how woefully under-prepared I was. It was also a good thing I had no idea how to pace myself. I never would've competed with him had I understood how foolish I was when I matched Willie stride for stride, going through the first mile mark at five minutes and ten seconds.

Sometimes it's good to be stupid. But when I look back on it, it's not my stupidity that I marvel at. The thing that shocks me when I really and truly think back on that day is the astounding willpower of a prideful twelve-year-old.

While I've always scoffed at the concept of giving "110%" as one of the many goofy platitudes some of the dumber football and basketball coaches spout, I believe, somehow, I may have actually done it on that day. Defying the laws of mathematics and my own physiology, I may have given more than one-hundred percent. One thing I know for sure, I never, ever, would put myself through such intense pain now that I'm older and wiser. That 5:10 first mile required of me everything I had and then some. And the thing was, there was a mile still left in the race. But the other thing was, Willie didn't get far enough ahead of me.

As I bathed myself in lactic acid, nearly fainting every step of the way for the last thousand meters of the race, Willie maddeningly kept the same lead of ten to fifteen feet that he'd surged for around a corner just beyond the mile mark. I suppose, savvy racer that he was, he had hoped to break my spirit. He would have with one more good push. He had to have known how close to the edge I was, as I was huffing and snorting like Rocky after his first round with Clubber Lang in *Rocky III*. But he couldn't quite gap me. And when we turned the last corner for home everything changed because I saw, through my bleary vision, my uncle standing on the side of the road.

The surprise on my uncle's face ... I might as well have been the Italian Stallion himself. And then, after the reality set in that the scrawny little scrapper in second place actually was *me*, his nephew, came the joy and the hope.

"Go!" he yelled. Then he started to run alongside me, shouting at me, his arm windmilling as he ran yelling, *Go, go, go, go! Kick! Kick! Kick!*

For just one moment, one magical hallucinatory second, I could've sworn that it was not Willie Davis ten feet in front of me but Apollo Creed himself.

I kicked. And unlike Rocky, I won. I ran a 10:19. My second mile had been even faster than the first. My first negative split effort.

It was a day of firsts. In the finish chute, Willie Davis put his arm around me. It was the first time I'd ever touched a black man. He put his arm around me and rubbed my head, and, in my hazy joy, I had been brave enough to put my arm around him in return. His eyes rolled back in his head from lack of oxygen. I only saw the whites of his eyes and was afraid he might pass out in my arms, then he regained his focus and smiled at me. "You, my man," he said, "are a runner."

As we walked through the chute together, I felt the pleasure of shared effort, which is the pleasure of the runner at the end of a race as he leans on his fellow runners and becomes almost one with them in the delirium of his exhaustion. I felt the pleasure of respect, which was what Willie had given me, and what I had given him since first seeing him at those road races years before. And I felt the overwhelming pleasure, the abject relief, of knowing I was good at *something*. At least on that day, my sense of myself was as solid as the road we'd run on.

THE NEXT YEARS - ADAM KEANE - AN EASY 10:32 - BALL SPORTS - WISHING I WERE A DOG

The years after that race didn't add up to much running-wise. The cross country coach at the junior high school didn't have a clue. He was just a science teacher filling a coaching void and earning a paltry extra five-hundred bucks a year. And worse, he was boring. He had a whistle and a clipboard and, for some reason, that combination bothered me. Also, I thought at the time that the guys on the cross country team were nearly all weirdoes and unathletic sissies.

I would learn after I joined my high school cross country team that much of my intuition was right: runners do tend to be weirdoes and unathletic. They are rarely sissies; I was wrong about that.

Maybe the primary thing standing between me and my destiny was the fact that I, unlike many runners, *was* athletic enough to play on the football, basketball, and baseball teams. The lure of those uniforms, the gladiator helmets and shoulder pads of football, the All-American webbed gloves and billed caps of baseball, the nearly genetic desire of most Hoosier boys (and girls) to wear his (or her) high school's basketball jersey, was powerful. The having of an actual number as you do in ball sports was magical to me.

On top of it all, I had the self-satisfaction, without even running cross country, that I was the best distance runner in the school. It was a sweet denial somehow not to run. Wasting one's talent is, at least at first, a wonderfully luxurious feeling.

Then Adam Keane popped up on my radar screen. I'd heard from a sports-minded math teacher that Keane had run a two-mile cross country race in a time faster than my Willie Davis-driven 10:19. Of course, I shrugged it off, saying that with two years maturity I'd be able to do better—that I simply hadn't tried since that muggy spring morning two years previous.

"But he was on grass!" responded the math teacher gleefully.

The smirk on the teacher's face made me angry, although I pretended not to care. I could've beaten him, I said nonchalantly. But something vital inside me was crumbling.

I went to see a race. Just out of curiosity, I told myself. It didn't help.

Keane was big. Nearly six-feet-tall as an eighth-grader. And not scrawny either. I immediately leapt to the possibility of unfairness—surely he was an idiot who'd flunked a grade or two. Or worse, one of those jerks whose parents held them back so they could be superior due to their advanced age. But neither of those were the case. In fact, he was a better student than I was. And two weeks younger.

Neither idiot nor weirdo nor sissy, he totally dominated the race.

His first mile, up and down hills and around tight cornered turns, his spikes flicking up grass impressively, was just over five minutes flat. I had no idea what I could do except for my 5:10 opening mile and 5:09 closing mile from two years before, but I had a hard time envisioning myself sticking on Keane's shoulder. All I remembered was how bad it had hurt to run a 5:10 and a 5:09. On hard, fast pavement.

Repeating the effort I had given in that last mile against Willie Davis was nearly unthinkable. It had seemed a once-in-a-lifetime experience, as if I would die if I ever went to that place within myself again. But I couldn't help but think that I'd have to visit that oxygen-deprived, vein-popping world regularly to keep up with Keane.

He hung on easily for the win with a leisurely 5:30 second mile that left him looking like he could go one more mile, or one point one more to be exact, the 5000 meter high school distance, without much trouble. He ran that day an easy 10:32. He won by a football field at least.

I was disconsolate. Screw any thoughts of maybe being his teammate and eventually getting a killer scoring five together and smoking every other team in the state. Maybe it was that I didn't yet know what a scoring five was. The way cross country is scored is that the five fastest runners on a team get their places added together and the lowest total points for a team wins. However, I wasn't thinking about being on a team, I was thinking about myself, so I walked away from Keane's performance shocked at my bad luck that such a talent should go to the same school as me. Why couldn't he have gone to Ridgeline, the perennial high-school

15

power just nine miles up the road where all the future state champs in all the sports seemed to go?

I took solace for the rest of the year in the ball sports and my friends on those teams. I wore my numbers with pride. But I knew that when high school came around, I wasn't a good enough football player, or a good enough baseball or basketball player for that matter, to make those sports worth my while in the long run—no pun intended.

As high school approached, I reminded myself that I was born to be a runner. As I twisted and turned in bed at night, thinking and thinking and thinking instead of sleeping, my dog snoring peacefully by my bedside, I regularly replayed Willie's words to me from that glorious day only two years before. "Man, you are a *runner*," he'd said. And running was in my blood, I reminded myself. But for the first time, I felt the pressure that having talent brings. For the first time, without really even giving myself a chance to prove otherwise, I doubted myself.

I was growing up. The monsters of my childhood had disappeared. They had been replaced by even scarier monsters. The Boogeyman, the Werewolf, and the Clown from the Sewer had been replaced by Failure, Humiliation, and Embarrassment.

My first day of practice as a high-school runner could've been better. I learned the toughest, meanest guy on the team—my team captain—hated me. Looking back, though, I should've been thankful. It sounds strange to say, but the immediate and concrete fear is always preferable to the abstract fear—the impending doom and despair that saturates the world when you're not sure of yourself and what you're about. If the fear that dominates your life is real, doing something about it is a lot simpler.

JEFF SLADE/TEAM CAPTAIN - CUSSING - THE "F" WORD - COACH - UNIFORMS - 1, 2, 3, 4, 5, 6, 7 - EAGLES, HAWKS, AND BLUEBIRDS - BOWDEN AND A CAUTIONARY TALE

"Well, fuck me gently with a chainsaw."

Those were the first words that Jeff Slade, my team captain, ever said to me.

The F-word is the filthiest word there is. Everyone knows it. That's what makes the next thing that happened on my first day of cross country practice even more surprising.

Coach, an entirely unknown commodity to me at the time, did not erupt at his senior leader. He did not frown or scold. He didn't even pretend he hadn't heard. No, he smiled and nodded as Slade stared at me after uttering his ugly little rumination. I took this to mean that Coach tolerated the use of the F-word.

I was wrong there. He didn't just tolerate it, he relished it. He cherished it. He used it often himself with a natural-born potty mouth's poetic grace.

Martin Viddstein, I was soon to discover, used curse words the way Jackson Pollock used color—intuitively, emotionally, and with a style all his own. He sprinkled and splattered his rants and lectures impulsively with F-bombs and scatological phrasings. When he was on a roll, it was a glorious thing to hear, almost like music, like jazz—The Bad Plus or Charles Mingus. It was an aspect of him that I enjoyed even when I hated him. Even before the secret.

Needless to say, Coach wasn't your typical coach. And Jeff Slade wasn't your typical team captain. To put it bluntly, they both were probably insane. And I don't mean that hyperbolically. I think, had they been subjected to psychological testing, both would have been found to merit serious observation and medication. Buckets of it.

On the occasion of our first morning practice, a hot August a.m., the sun already pressing down on us at seven o'clock, we sat in a loose circle in our thinnest cotton T-shirts and nylon shorts. The bleached-out school parking lot bounced the slanting glare of the sun up into our faces. I remember sweating just sitting there. I remember feeling like a buttered chicken in a rotisserie.

Coach roared up that day ten minutes late in his rusted red Subaru. There were cartoonish puffs of black smoke farting out the tailpipe.

He screeched to a halt sideways across several parking spots. "Hey, Slade," he brayed in his Boston accent as he shoved his door open. "That li'l bastard"—he said this while pointing at me, although I had not yet formally met the man—"his brother, and the Keane kid are gonna put all you old sons-a-bitches outta business." He smiled. "You better quit smoking them goddamned cigarettes. He ran a 10:20 two-mile … as a *sixth grader!*"

I wanted to correct him as it had been a 10:19 but thought it better to keep my mouth shut and wait to see what happened next. And that, to get back to the start of this anecdote, was when Slade said it.

His long right leg was stretched out in front of him, his left leg tucked under him. He stared across the loose circle of runners right at me. *Well,* he said very deliberately, *fuck me gently,* his eyes hard and glassy, *with a chainsaw.*

The look on his face left no room for interpretation. Slade wanted to kill me.

After smiling approvingly, Coach replied. "Ahh, that won't help. Maybe someone oughta fuck *me* with a chainsaw. Get my mind off of my problems … which are many. Wife kicked me out of the house again, dammit. Slept like shit."

Then, as he was walking back to his car to get something he'd left there, he shot back over his shoulder. "Then again, unless you get faster, you're gonna be the first senior team captain who had to run for the goddamned jayvee in school history. You got three freshmen who're better than you without trying"—He swung open the car door and picked up a pen from the floor then slammed it shut again—"and a few of these other pudknockers have actually put in some miles this summer." He shrugged, changing his mind. "On second thought, maybe someone *should* fuck you with a chainsaw."

The most shocking phrase I'd ever heard. Three times in under ten seconds. Twice by the man who was to be my coach and the other directed right at me from my team captain.

It was all a little mind-bending and I suddenly wished I was six years old, back home barefoot and sitting in front of the TV in my jammies, sticky glazed doughnut in hand. However, by the power of pure social inertia and the relentless nature of time, I was stuck in what was quickly becoming my predicament. Sometimes your destiny feels more like a spider's web than a mountain's summit.

The two of them, I realize now, were perfect for each other. Coach Viddstein was a small, raven-like man with a sharp beak of a nose, small dark eyes, a pair of black chunky glasses he wore about half the time, and hands like a pair of nervous birds themselves.

Slade, birdlike as well, was a nearly six-five stork of a guy. His thin forearms were banded with muscle and thick bluish veins. Those sinewy forearms suggested that he might easily strangle me if he wanted to. And, terrifyingly, he seemed to want to. He had two earrings in his left ear, a golden hoop and a small fake diamond stud. His bleached-blond mullet was so carefully blown dry and moussed that he could've easily sat in on a set with Poison, Def Leppard, or Ratt with nobody the wiser.

It was just after our initial exchange that I thought, after conceding to myself that I'd never be six again—probably never even wear jammies again for that matter—of football, and how I might possibly still be able to switch fall sports. The thought of being pounded into the turf by a rabid linebacker suddenly seemed strangely comforting—predictable at the least.

The football players, who had wordlessly clacked by us in their cleats that morning before Coach's arrival, had sported practice shirts with catchphrases like "The Will to Win is Nothing without the Will to Prepare" and "There is No 'I' in Team." I longed, as Slade's caustic words bounced around in my head, for those kinds of wholesome slogans, that bland certainty. The cross country team's unofficial slogan, by comparison, seemed raw and surprisingly uninterested in athletic performance.

But Coach wasn't about to order us anything like practice shirts with slogans on them anyway. He had no time for such nonsense. "You boys ain't a bunch of Barbie Dolls for me to dress up," he'd say. He was true to his word. We never had an official slogan or matching practice gear. We never had a chant that we did before each race. With Coach it was all about the running and nothing else. Everything else was silliness and distraction.

I would first be confused by, then intrigued with, then embarrassed by, and ultimately proud of the baggy gray cotton sweats our varsity seven warmed up in before each race. A far cry from my junior-high days when I wore my crisp stitched-on number twenty-one in the fall and winter for football and basketball and my sharp-edged nine in spring out on the baseball diamond, Coach's unis, warm ups and racing singlets and shorts, were devoid of our school's name (Pennsgap High School) school initials (PHS) our mascot (the Snapping Turtles—Snappers for short). We didn't even wear the school colors, which were pine green and orange. Instead, we wore white Adidas singlets with three black stripes and black Adidas side-split running shorts with three white stripes. At the start line, we looked like the generic-brand high school cross country team.

The core of it was that Coach hated school allegiances. Actually, I don't think he cared for allegiances of any kind except to the spirit of running and his runners themselves. For us, I came to realize over time, he would've died many horrible deaths.

"We're the goddamned Snappin' Turtles!" said Coach when I asked once why we didn't sport our mascot anywhere on our uniforms. "How can a runner be a turtle, for cryin' out loud!"

The only decoration, if you could call it that, on the varsity warm-ups were black, hand-written numbers in Coach's own hand—1, 2, 3, 4, 5, 6, 7. These numbers were located just under the brassy drawstring grommets on the heavy cotton hoodies, just under the neckline in front. The sweatshirts were all the same size, large, and following every race we swapped according to place.

If you fell out of the top seven, you traded with the jayvee guy who had taken your spot and had to pull on the smelly green and orange nylons they wore. It was a dream bordering on obsession of mine that year to wear the number one at least once during the cool down. But that was Slade's number. At least until proven otherwise.

When Coach came back from his car, he had a clipboard with three different workouts on it. Eagles, Hawks, and Bluebirds were the group designations. You were an Eagle if you'd ever run sixty or more miles in a single week and had broken five minutes for a mile. You were a Hawk if you'd done more than forty in a week and broken 5:30. If you'd never run forty miles in a week, even if you'd gone under five, you were a Bluebird. Therefore, I, along with all the other freshmen, was deemed a Bluebird.

I felt, then as now, that there was an inordinate status drop between the medium and low groups—the leap up from lowly Bluebird to predacious Hawk seemed a touch ridiculous. However, I expressed my intelligence, for the second time that morning, as one often does. By keeping my mouth shut.

"Bowden," said Coach after we'd mostly finished stretching, "you're in charge of the Bluebirds today. Take 'em out on Promise Road. Six miles."

Chris Bowden, an average runner and a kind person, a slightly built, soft-spoken guy with a huge Adam's apple and a mop of black hair, left his privileged place in the circle next to Slade and the other seniors and shambled over and sat down next to me, my twin brother, Adam Keane, and the other two silent, spooked freshmen—Brad "Popeye" Bechtel and Leonardo Chavez. Bowden smiled as he shook my hand.

"You're pretty good, they say." His voice was quiet and smooth, calming even. He nodded at Adam Keane as well, then my brother. "You too, Keane. Kindle Number Two ... all three of you better watch your backs."

He was smiling, but I could also tell he meant what he said.

"All you guys better watch out for Slade. I'll tell you a story on the run today." He made eye contact with all us Bluebirds, each in turn. "Think of it as a cautionary tale."

But I didn't want to hear a cautionary tale; I just wanted to run. And I didn't want a crazy and violent team captain and a cussing coach whose wife had kicked him out of his house. I just wanted to start down the road to my destiny.

This was my first day of practice, mind you, my first formal foray into being what I was supposed to be. Back in the soft glow of my youth I'd decided that being a runner was my future identity. That morning on the parking lot hadn't seemed a very auspicious beginning. In fact, things were going to get a lot worse before they got better.

PROMISE ROAD - "THE HINTERLANDS" - FLOCKING - PEEING IN THE CREEK - SKID MARKS - THE MAN WITH THE GUN - BOWDEN/ STORYTELLER - THE DIFFERENCE BETWEEN CROSS COUNTRY AND FOOTBALL - THE CRAZIEST GUY IN SCHOOL - PLANS TO KISS BUTT

As we made our way through town on that first day of practice, out toward the farm roads where we did much of our training, Bowden kept his silence. Seven runners, Bowden, the five freshmen on our team, and a chubby and slow kid named Sydney Porter, aka "Squid," slowly plodded out, sweating, soaking up the heat bouncing up off the bone-white pavement.

As we ran farther and farther out, the houses crept back from the road. They looked lonelier, smaller, and rougher in appearance than the quaint little homes we'd left behind in town.

It should be said, rural to me as a kid always somehow equated to immorality—dark goings on out in the sticks, murder and incest. I think the movie *The Texas Chainsaw Massacre* had a lot to do with this perception. Not that I'd actually seen it.

As the road grew narrower and the sidewalks disappeared, the cars that passed us, although fewer in number, seemed to have slight regard for our safety. They blasted hot air into us and their tires kicked up dust and small rocks, causing us to edge off the road when they hurtled past. After ten minutes or so of slogging, we were truly into farmland.

Out here in what we would come to call "The Hinterlands," the road deteriorated. Brittle crumbling edges narrowed the tarmac and small volcanic-looking potholes ran down the center. Promise Road was straight and flat with four black, tarlike strips disappearing into the hazy distance, seas of green fields on each side.

The tires of pickups and cars made an ominous ripping sound as they blasted past us. When vehicles weren't threatening us, invisible waves of humidity ebbed and flowed from out of the emerald fields on both sides like hot wet ghosts. We Bluebirds huddled tight together as we ran, Bowden leading us by just a few feet.

Our tightness as a pack had something instinctive about it. There was something primal going on, something that had to do with survival. It seemed Slade's treatment of me and Coach's apparent lack of concern about it had affected all of us Bluebirds. We were officially scared.

About three miles out of town, the continuous walls of flickering green corn at our sides were interrupted by a sad little crumbling bridge which squeezed the already narrow road to one lane. The bridge spanned an anemic trickle of a creek. Small gnarled trees arched above the creek in a canopy. Bowden stopped on the far side and we abruptly came to a stuttering halt, all of us nearly running into him we were packed so tightly together.

"This is where it happened," he said. Then he inexplicably turned and stepped off the road, down towards the creek.

I followed him, thinking that was what Bluebirds were supposed to do—follow their designated senior leader—when Bowden pulled down the front of his shorts and began pissing onto some bright green poison ivy. After almost running into his backside, I quickly shielded my eyes, did an about-face, and headed back to the road where I found my fellow freshmen dripping sweat, nervously waiting for Bowden to come back from peeing. "Dumbass," muttered my brother in embarrassment.

"Just over there," said Bowden as he returned from re-lieving himself, still adjusting his shorts unconsciously, "up this road about a hundred meters or so. That's where it went down ..."

Now, I don't know if Bowden knew what he was doing, if he was a superb storyteller and a bit of a tease, or if he was just so laid back he didn't realize he was building suspense, but he left us hanging like that, not telling us *what* had gone down. He just stared up the road, watching the scene he was imagining play out in his head, until, that was, Adam Keane asked the obvious question.

"That's where *what* went down?" said Keane.

Bowden smiled a smile that makes me think he must've known what he was doing all along and said, "That's where Jeff Slade nearly beat a man to death with the man's own gun." Then he crouched down, retied a shoelace, stood back up and said, "Well, we better keep going. You Bluebirds are supposed to get in at least six today." But we didn't return to our planned workout. We just walked up the country road, all seven of us.

He continued his silence, requiring us to speak up and ask questions. My brother spoke up this time. "Well, what happened? What went down?"

Then Bowden got into true storyteller mode, and we didn't have to ask anymore. "It was a warm night, just a month or so ago," he said as we all walked. "Slade's been freaking out about you guys. He's been training like a fiend all summer long. He's been getting in seventy and eighty miles a week, doing two-a-days on his own."

We arrived at a spot on the bone-colored road where a pair of long black skid marks stretched out before us. "This is where it happened," said Bowden, his eyes down on the tire tracks. He stopped and we all stopped behind him.

"One thing you guys ought to know about Slade," Bowden said conspiratorially. "He's nervous as hell. He gets all wound up and he can't shake a thought. You guys need to remember that about him. And," he raised a finger in the air to make the point extra clear, "when he's that way you guys just need to stay the hell away." He chuckled a little. He glanced at all of us in turn. "Well, even more than normal." His face grew serious again. "That's the way he was on that night. He was all worked up. Probably thinking about you guys."

My earlier longing to join the football team and sit the bench became more than a simple whim at this point. Now it seemed less like a good idea and more like a necessity for survival.

"So, Slade goes out for a long run. A nine or ten miler, even though he's already got twelve in for the day. It's nearly midnight, but he just takes off and heads out here. He said there was a full moon, it was easy to see, but I wonder if the guy in the truck really meant to hit him or not." He looked around, up into the sky. "See how there're no street lamps out here or anything? And who'd be looking for a runner or a walker way out here at midnight?"

An oafish, good-natured kid we came to call Popeye because one of his eyes was nearly squinted shut all the time said, "Nobody," and we all stared at our fellow Bluebird, embarrassed for him at his misunderstanding of the rhetorical question and our own association with him, however recent and tenuous. But Bowden didn't care. He was a cool guy.

"So, Slade's out here running, and this guy in a jacked-up pickup truck comes haulin' ass up the road. Slade says he can hear him coming, you know how those big off-road tires buzz, but he's got just as much right to the road as anyone, right? So, he stays out of the high grass and keeps to the side of the road like normal. Then the guy gets right up on him. He's not slowing down one bit. Slade even says he sped up. Slade says the guy *tried* to hit him."

I don't know what it was, but a little switch somewhere in me flicked at about this time, and I knew I wasn't going to quit the cross country team. Maybe it wasn't Slade. Maybe it was Bowden, the kind, and cool way he had with us freshmen. Maybe it was Coach and his cursing. In any case, by the time we all got back from our run into the country I'd changed and wanted nothing to do with football.

One thing I was sure of was that the freshmen on the football team, most of them standing around watching practice while wearing their hot helmets and pads, standing there silently while other guys ran one minutely dissected play after another, weren't hearing a story like the one we were getting. And they never would. Bowden went on.

"The guy's rearview mirror flicks up against Slade's shirt. And he always wears these shirts that he rips the sides out of, and it catches and it tears his shirt off. Clean the hell off. Slade's shirt is now hanging on the guy's review mirror."

"No way," murmured Popeye.

"Way," said Bowden, his eyes wide. "Anyway, Slade screams at him. *Get back here you dirty mother!* he yells. And the guy jams on his breaks and stops and opens his door, and Slade says he sees a gun rack. And then the guy pulls a shotgun off the rack in his truck, clacks it, gets out of the truck, and starts walking toward Slade."

"Dude," said Squid, the only non-freshman on the team unworthy of being a Hawk or an Eagle. "These tracks are where he slammed on his breaks!"

"No, man," Bowden said with a knowing smile, "just let me tell it. These aren't his tracks from where he slammed on his breaks." He pointed back towards where we'd come from at a short pair of black skid marks. "*Those* are the tracks from where he slammed on his brakes. *These,*" he said pointing down at pair of much longer black marks, "are from where he *took off.*"

Squid looked like he didn't quite get all of that, but I did. My fear and my admiration for Slade were both growing exponentially.

"The guy is coming at Slade, right? He's got his gun in both his hands across his chest, and he's moving towards him, saying, *Did you just yell at me you lunatic?* But ..." Bowden grinned here. "What he doesn't know is who he's dealing with."

Bowden pointed up the road and we followed him up to where the tracks finally faded and the road was again unmarked. We stood there, all seven of us including Bowden, and stared down at the last faint remnants of rubber on the road. "This is where the guy's tires stopped spinning when he peeled out. Trying to get away from Slade."

We then made a small circle around the end of the marks, staring down at them like a bunch of junior detectives.

"The dude," said Bowden, "should've noticed something was wrong when Slade didn't back up or hold up his hands or something when the dude was walking toward him with the gun. I mean, from how Slade tells it, he was *running* at the guy the whole time. And he never *stopped* running. By the time Slade was on him, I guess the guy had some sense that he'd messed with the wrong man. But by then," Bowden smiled, showing us his teeth, "it was too late."

Slade, according to legend, had snatched the gun out of the man's hands and had begun beating him with it before the man knew what was happening. He had beaten him, slapping and whacking him on his shoulders and back, all the way back to his truck, and, after the guy crawled into the cab and shifted it into gear to get away, Slade had chased and battered the sides and tailgate of the truck with the stock of the gun until he couldn't keep up with it anymore.

According to Bowden, he then threw the gun into the cornfield, turned around, ran home, drank a half-gallon of Gatorade, and slept like a baby.

"*You can keep the shirt!*" Bowden smiled. "That's what Slade yelled as the guy drove off into the night."

As we made our way back to town, we were, strangely, a lot less scared than we had been on our way out. We ran in a spread-out line, filling the country road, owning it you might say. We talked loudly and laughed often. Bowden smiled at us and answered our questions. He ran with us, not in front of us. The thing was, somewhere along the way, we had all decided that the craziest, meanest, scariest guy in the school was on our side. He was one of us. Bowden, in his storytelling, had, without saying it, somehow made that clear.

Still, I realized the predicament I was in. Slade still hated me. I had resolved nothing.

I decided, when we went out to get shoes that afternoon, I was going to get the same brand and model that Jeff Slade wore. Whether they felt good or not. In every subtle way I could conceive of, I intended to kiss some serious ass for as long as it took to get Slade to like me.

ONE OUT OF A THOUSAND - DNA - NATURE AND NURTURE - A BEAUTIFUL YOUNG SCHOOL PSYCHOLOGIST - EATEN BY A BEAR - AN EMBARRASSMENT - DEVIL TAKE THE HINDMOST

Of the less than two out of a hundred people who arrive here on Earth with "womb mates," as Leonardo Chavez, my fellow Bluebird, used to like to call my brother and me, less than one in every ten share a single zygote, which is what scientific types call a single fertilized egg.

Let me restate those numbers: one out of a hundred are born twins to begin with, then one out of ten of those ones out of a hundred are identical. My brother and I were those ones. Each of us ended up the one in a thousand so blessed as to have an identical twin. So what does that mean? How does that play into this story?

Monozygotic (more commonly known as identical)

twins share nearly the same DNA, and DNA, if you don't know, stands for deoxyribonucleic acid. Deoxyribonucleic acid is the stuff that contains the blueprints of growth and development for all living organisms, including humans. The fact that identical twins share DNA means that they have the same blueprints as another person. So, what it means is that I was born with a virtual clone.

Now, I knew all of this going into my freshman year of high school. After all, I'd been an identical twin my whole life. Maybe I wouldn't have used the fancy scientific words, but I knew that my brother, Hyter, and I were "the same." Looking back, the surprising thing about my brother proving himself a talented runner was that I was surprised by it at all. I mean, I should've seen it coming, right?

We were the same height, same weight, same IQ, same hair color, same shoe size, same lazy left eye. So maybe I'm not as smart as I think, because when he beat both Keane and me at Devil Take the Hindmost, I was first shocked, then devastated.

DNA, as everyone knows, isn't all that makes a person what they are. The DNA is the "nature" side of the equation. It's the part a person's born with. The other side, commonly referred to as the "nurture" side, also called a person's "environment," is the other side. That being said, it would be logical to assume that identical twins really are, in most cases, nearly truly identical in both nature and nurture.

After all, most twins aren't separated at birth. They grow up together. They share the same parents, the same hometown, the same schools, the same brothers and sisters or lack of brothers and sisters, and all the other things that make up a person's environment. This was certainly the case with my brother and me. The problem is, that analysis leaves out one important element of a twin's environment—the other twin. The other twin is the wildcard. And my brother was a true wildcard.

By my freshman year in high school, I can honestly say that I wished he had never been born. I will go so far as to say that, when I was fourteen, I wished he would die. Even a painful and tragic death would've been acceptable, although not necessary. I just wanted him to vanish, after all. I just wanted to be able to be myself without people thinking I was him. I wouldn't have gone so far as to say I wished someone would kidnap him and torture him. I drew the line there. But I often daydreamed of a day I gained freedom from him. Here's one way I envisioned it:

A beautiful young school psychologist stands at the closed door of a classroom. She's distraught at the news she must deliver and a little curious about the young man she must deliver it to. Inside, the teacher, a cute young blonde herself, a twenty-something with a sweet heart-shaped behind, but not nearly as hot as the psychologist standing outside the room, is happily teaching. The children in the class are happily learning. Yet, this beautiful psychologist standing at the door must deliver news of the worst sort to some poor, poor child. Of course, I am the child in question.

She looks in through the tiny rectangle of glass above the doorknob and spots me: a surprisingly handsome and mature eighth grader, small but well-proportioned, and well beyond my years in sophistication and sensitivity. She's noticed me around the school. This makes her job even harder.

Not only does she have to inform me about the tragic death of my identical twin brother, but she knows by overhearing the talk of junior high girls how sophisticated and sensitive I am. And even though she's heard of me via the adoring gossip of my female peers, my striking physical presence (small but strong—lithe, perhaps one might say) she hasn't counted on.

She is unsettled by the strange attraction she feels toward me as she stares through the rectangle of glass, watching as I draw a nearly perfect depiction of a stage of Donkey Kong I've been struggling with recently. And the news she must deliver ... it's so dire, so awful ... this is the hardest thing she's ever had to do in all her twenty-three years.

She bites her lower lip and runs her hands through her blond hair, hoping for and achieving that really sexy tousled look. She tucks her white, whispery blouse firmly into her form-fitting black skirt. This accentuates her lovely breasts. She knocks on the door of my classroom. Her smoldering brown eyes are focused on me.

After that, I'll summarize: she ends up telling me my brother was eaten by a bear while on a field trip to the zoo, I cry on her perfect bosom, smell her wonderful female scent, and then I'm required to see her every day for three hours of counseling. We end up having wonderful and instructive pity sex, which continues throughout my high school years. This eventually turns into real love on her part when she realizes she's losing me because I'm going to college on an athletic scholarship, and she freaks out and begs me not to leave her. We do it one more time and I get a restraining order on her when I'm in college where I meet my lovely future wife to whom I never mention the beautiful school psychologist.

This was only one of many of my brother's imaginary deaths. I'd say there were about seven or eight scenarios like that one that I played out in my head pretty regularly.

But let me be clear, it wasn't really about his death. I didn't really want to hurt him. I just didn't want him around.

I wanted, most accurately speaking, for him to have *never been here to begin with*. It had a lot to do with the fact that he was a spastic, overly talkative freak.

My brother, whom I love now for all his eccentricities, his quirks I wouldn't change for anything, was a big embarrassment from age ten to age twenty. He was the know-it-all even the teacher gets tired of. He was the guy with his hand in the air all the time, the one they finally have to ignore. He was the kid who falls asleep first at slumber parties. He was the guy who got you caught when you were sneaking out at night, and he was the guy that messed up the lie you told to cover yourself and got you into even more trouble. He was the guy who wore the same T-shirt every day because it was "comfortable." He was the reason some girls thought I was a nerd when I really wasn't. They thought I was, because they thought I was my brother.

To me, at age fourteen, he was beyond embarrassing. And running, I dreamed, was going to distinguish me from him forever. I would be the runner and he would be the honors kid in the yellow, pit-stained T-shirt with his hand in the air all the time.

You see, with that one race against Willie Davis, I had somehow, in my own mind, laid claim to running as *mine*. Even during those days when I was still playing the ball sports, I knew I'd eventually be a runner, and my visions of myself as a runner never included my twin.

However, my brother would have been right there with me and Willie Davis as we rounded the bend for the finish had he only been in that race. Remember, same DNA equals same blueprint, which means same VO2 max, which means same ability to get oxygen to your muscles, which is the core of distance running talent. Same DNA equals same everything. The only difference between us in terms of running was that he simply had not yet had a chance to show his talent, because he hadn't yet run a race.

The staggering truth of my situation came to light during the first hard workout of the year—the infamous Devil Take the Hindmost workout, also known as Angel/Devil.

A GOOD DAY FOR THE DEVIL - NEW RUNNING SHOES - THE CEMETERY - INSTRUCTIONS - POPEYE'S DUMB COMMENT - LEONARDO'S PRAYER - BETS - BALLSIEST AND BRAINIEST - MISERY LOVES COMPANY

It was early August, three in the afternoon. It was hot—a good day for the Devil. In fact, it was Hell hot, like when you open the front door of your house to go outside and it feels instead like you've opened your oven door after it's been baking something at 450 degrees for an hour or so—a hint of what souls doomed to slave away in the Bad Place of joke, cartoon, and Old Testament lore must experience. Even in the shade, the day was stifling. Coach deemed it perfect weather for the infamous Angel/Devil, a workout also known as Devil Take the Hindmost.

    I was wearing my new Tiger X-Calibur GTs. They

were blue with silver stripes, just like Jeff Slade's. He didn't seem to notice.

My brother had gotten the same shoes, which bothered me deeply, but I knew better than to whine to my dad when he was shelling out sixty bucks for each of us for shoes we would only be running in. We would purchase new shoes for school a few days later, and Dad would wonder out loud why he was spending so much money on footwear. Back in the fifties, he said, a kid had one pair of Chuck Taylors for the whole year.

"You're only going to run in them?" he'd asked, puzzled, after we both came down to dinner with our old shoes on. We'd already explained once at the shoe store. Hyter explained again there at the dinner table that Coach said we should only use our running shoes for running until we were done with cross country.

Dad, an ex-nose guard and the son of a Depression-era grocer, looked like he wanted to spit out something that tasted bad. But he kept his peace and allowed us to be led by a man he would later refer to as "a complete lunatic."

No, Slade didn't notice my shoes on that day. It was the kind of day that was so hot nobody noticed anything but the heat. It was so hot the trees were wilting like stalks of broccoli left out overnight. It was so hot the ants stayed underground—the kind of heat that makes you want to see whether you can *actually* fry an egg on your driveway. I was sure Coach was going to tell us all to go home, that it was far too dangerous to run in such blistering weather. Instead, he whipped out one of the hardest workouts of the year.

"Alrighty, boys!" said Coach. "Today we're gonna find out what you're made of! Devil Take the Hindmost is the name of the game. Bluebirds, you're last so's you can see how to do it. Eagles, you're up first. Hawks, you're in the middle. First, show them Bluebirds the course so's they don't screw it up. Jog over there, and I'll meet you at the pump."

I should've known something bad was going to happen when Bowden, always on even keel, rolled his eyes and groaned.

The workout took place, appropriately, in a cemetery. The cemetery was only a mile or so from the school, so we got our warm up in on the jog over, although why anyone would need to warm up on a day that had to have been ninety-five degrees is beyond me. As we shuffled through the massive wrought-iron gates, kicking up gray dust and avoiding the brown hump of burned-up grass that ran down the middle of the main cemetery road, I felt like we were never coming out.

Coach's Subaru was there next to an ancient hand pump when we arrived. He'd marked a start-finish line in the gravel road with his foot. "Take 'em around once," he said. "Damn it's hot," he muttered as he fanned his face with a copy of *Track and Field News*. "Even in the damn shade."

The course was approximately 300 meters and was a winding loop. As we made our way on the dusty gravel road through the marble and limestone monuments, the game, if something as excruciating as Angel/Devil can be called that, was explained to us Bluebirds. A somber senior named Devin Swart, a short guy with thick glasses, a bowl haircut of the yellowest hair you've ever seen, and a nearly perfect SAT score, broke it down for us in his surprisingly deep voice.

"The game works like this: there are two rounds, the first round is called Devil Take the Hindmost. All six of you Bluebirds are going to start together."

The six of us were me, Adam Keane, the odds-on favorite in my book, my brother, Popeye, Squid, and Leonardo

Chavez, who then looked to be eleven or twelve and was nearly certain to be the loser.

Swart went on. "In Devil, you guys all start together by the pump. You run this course we're running now. Whoever gets to the start line last, loses. The deal is, you don't have to race right away. You can run as fast or slow as you like. But, like I said, the last guy across the line after the lap is done gets taken by the Devil. That means he loses. Angel," he added as an afterthought, "is the opposite. You cross the line first, an angel grabs you and you're done. We run that second. It doesn't really matter as much."

"What does he have to do then?" asked Popeye. "I mean in Devil, the guy who gets taken?"

"Nothing. That guy's the loser and he's in the hands of Satan."

"Well that doesn't sound so bad," said Popeye, a big smile on his face.

This was when all the Hawks and Eagles stopped running and we Bluebirds nearly ran into them. I thought, in the silence of the next few seconds, that Popeye might prefer digging himself a hole next to one of the graves and burying himself. The uncharitable attention his attitude towards being taken by the Devil had produced in the Hawks and Eagles was hard to witness. I was just glad it wasn't me who spoke up, because I'd been thinking the same thing as Popeye.

Slade stepped forward. He stood right before Popeye, he was kind of looming over Popeye as a matter of fact. To the point that a drop of Slade's sweat dripped from the tip of his nose onto the bridge of Popeye's nose. The kid was smart enough not to move or wipe Slade's sweat off his face. Barely.

"If you lose, the Devil gets you," said Slade quietly in a voice that was nearly a hiss. "The Devil may not get you today. And he may not get you tomorrow. But he'll get you ..."

It was an anxious moment. I couldn't figure out if Slade was talking about the actual Devil—Satan himself, Lucifer, all that ... I thought, after five or six silent seconds, that that *was* what he meant and that he was done with his lecture. I was surprised to see such religiosity in my team captain. But he went on then. He asked Popeye a question. He asked, "Do you know who the Devil is, little Bluebird?"

"No," said Popeye.

Slade leaned down into his face. "I am," he said in a whisper.

I'm pretty sure I saw Leonardo Chavez cross himself right after that.

Devin Swart then went on describing the rules as if he hadn't been interrupted. "Okay," he said, almost sounding bored. "So you can't be last in Devil, that's the main rule. If you're last at the finish line, the Devil gets you. Since there are six of you guys, that means the winner and the second place finisher will run five laps each. That's a little less than a mile. But it's all about the kicking before the line and the strategy you use not to be last."

"It's all about strategy," advised Bowden as we began jogging again. "Usually the best runner wins, but sometimes, if a guy's got some balls and he's smart, he can sneak out a win. Balls and brains, that's what it takes to win Angel/Devil."

The Eagles went first. Slade took the lead and looked like he was daring anyone to try something funny. Bully that he was, he controlled the race by the threat of what he might do if anyone tried anything.

Bowden finally gave him a run after three laps, pushing from the very start of the fourth lap, not slowing from his kick from the third lap. He stretched a lead out to about twenty meters before the pack, only three runners by that point in the race, saw his strategy. Slade took off and there was too much distance left for Bowden to cover for him to hold on. But I do think Bowden proved his balls and brains comment. He probably should've been fourth or fifth instead of second.

After the Eagles were done, while the Hawks were duking it out, I was getting nervous. I was sure Keane was going to charge hard from the start and leave the rest of us in the dust, proving without a doubt that he was the best runner among us. And then I was sure that I would suffer in the lead while Keane pranced along behind me, using little effort to cross the line second to last with each lap, only to hammer me and leave me for dead like all the other corpses in the graveyard on the ultimate go-round. I didn't think at all about my brother.

When we got to the line, the Hawks were bent over, gobbling air for oxygen, wet with perspiration like they'd just climbed out of a pool. But the Eagles had had ten minutes at least to rest and were standing by the start line. Bowden was taking bets.

"I got gas money for a week on Kindle One," he said. And that was me. He smiled at me and I probably smiled back, I don't really remember. I do remember wanting to tell him that he was going to lose money on me. Thankfully, I wasn't quite that big a weenie.

Slade said, "I got Keane," then spit on the ground. "And if you lose Keane, I'm your Devil, too. Even if you don't come in last." Suddenly I was thankful not to be the favorite. In fact, later that night, I thought about Keane, how it must be tough to be so clearly physically talented.

I was five-eight and a hundred thirty pounds. I might be able to bust out a sub-five mile, but put me in a lineup and I didn't seem like anything special. Keane *looked* like a thoroughbred—six-two and a lean one-seventy. He looked like he ought to be a state champ someday. My brother on the other hand, who always seemed to have his fingers up his nose or on his penis, just unconsciously pushing that thing around in his shorts, was nobody's choice. All bets were on me or Keane.

But when the coach yelled "Go!" my brother let go of the tip of his yang and took off like he was shot from a cannon. It was the ballsiest, and, it turned out, brainiest, move of the day.

Restraining ourselves, Keane and I led the pack around the graveyard twists and turns in what felt like a 5:30 mile pace. Neither of us wanting to hurt too much, we simply stayed put until we turned a bend in the road up a small hill and saw Coach's car next to the pump where we knew the finish line was. Then we took off sprinting.

It took about five hard strides to see that poor Leonardo Chavez was right to say his prayers, because it would've taken an act of God to keep him from the Devil on that day. Relaxing, Keane and I stayed shoulder-to-shoulder, Squid and Popeye pounded the ground not far behind us. Coach yelled, "And the Devil takes young Chavez!" as we crossed the line and began our second loop.

The Hawks, I noticed, had pulled themselves together to watch the race. They stood with the Eagles and cheered.

I expected to be admired for my patience, my racing savvy, as I calmly began my second lap, but Bowden, as excited as I'd ever seen him, ran alongside me. "Your brother's gonna run away with this!" he yelled. And after we'd lost sight of him on the first lap, I realized that I, and I believe Keane too, had forgotten about him. "He's not slowing down!" yelled Bowden, his big Adam's apple bobbing in his throat. "I got money on you!"

The course had been well-designed to teach strategy. As we rounded the first turn, we came to the only straightaway of any length on the course. After that first left turn, the straight was about seventy-five meters, then you weaved into the cemetery, making lots of rights and lefts that kept you focused only on the next twenty-five meters or so.

Hyter had taken full advantage of our lack of awareness and our slight regard. He was seventy-five meters ahead of us. As we started down the straight to begin our second loop, he disappeared back into the cemetery. He was completely out of range. He had stolen the race.

"You better get your ass in gear Keane!" shouted Slade. And, at that, Keane found the stride that had taken him to a 4:42 mile as an eighth grader. It seemed a dead sprint as I chased along at his heels. Squid and Popeye didn't have a chance anymore. The tactics were over. My goofy brother had totally outsmarted us.

Keane and I put on a good show for the Hawks and Eagles. We both desperately tried to catch up, but we'd given up far too much on that first lap. By the time Keane edged me for the right to run the last lap behind my brother, there was absolutely no hope of him catching Hyter.

I stood there huffing and puffing, my shorts soaked in sweat, avoiding eye contact with anyone who'd put gas money on me. The older guys all cheered and clapped, even Slade, when Hyter came grinding up the last turn for the win. Keane lurched in ten seconds after him, utterly spent.

It was the first time he'd looked mortal to me.

I was proud of my brother. Deep down, I know I was. But mostly I was aghast that my vision of myself as the best runner on the team, the best freshman at least, was quickly gurgling down the toilet. My response to this setback was not what I wish it had been.

Instead of cranking up my training, gunning for my brother and Keane and anyone else who might stand between me and that gray Champion sweatshirt with coach's number one scrawled on it in black marker, I did what people most often do when they realize things are going to be tough. I found someone to tell me that it was okay to give up. Misery loves company, they say, and nobody was as miserable as Squid.

FRUIT SALAD - THE PROBLEM WITH BEING A RICH KID - PORSCHE, LAND ROVER, FERRARI - FAKING IT - 20 MINUTES - THE BARN

As Squid and I high-stepped out of the barn through the yellow grass leading to the road, Coach's red Subaru pulled up right in front of us, the tires crackling on the black tarry streaks on the pavement.

He opened his car door, leaving the Subaru running. He slammed the door shut.

"You guys didn't make it to the turn-around point," he said, his hands on his waist, his eyes, red-rimmed and tired looking. "You been hidin' in that barn?"

I didn't know how to respond. I suddenly felt as if Squid had betrayed me, lured me into his evil ways somehow. I felt duped.

"Coach," said Squid matter-of-factly, "I hide in that barn

every time we run out here. I hide in the kiddy playground when we run through the park. And when I can't find a decent place to hide, I walk. I almost never do the actual workout."

I was surprised and confused by this tactic. I had been formulating a lie, something to do with a fear of sunstroke or an injured foot. Anything but the truth. I didn't get it.

"I'm not cutting you, Sydney," said Coach in a tired voice.

"I'll give you my lifetime free card at Pollo Loco," Squid whined. "I'll pay you."

"I'm done with this conversation, Porter. Now, you run back to the school. It oughta take you no more than twenty minutes if you just jog slowly." Then he turned his attention to me. "K1," he said, "get in the car."

I looked at Squid. He shrugged his soft shoulders. "Lucky you," he said. "Looks like you're getting a ride back."

"You know Porter, I need to make another group for you," shouted Coach as I walked around the back of his car to the passenger's side door, wondering what I'd done to deserve a ride while Squid had to hoof it back. "You don't do the proud bluebird justice."

Squid shocked me by giving coach the finger as he began lumbering back towards the school.

"Fruit salad, Sydney," shouted Coach happily, in spite of being flipped off by his worst runner. "Eagles, Hawks, Blue-birds, and Fruit Salad. I'll post it. You are now a group of one."

Coach got in behind the driver's wheel and turned his small, dark eyes on me. He just stared at me for five or six seconds before shaking his head disappointedly.

"Does that mean I'm Fruit Salad, too?" I asked.

"Nope," he said. "You're still just a little Bluebird. You've lost your way, but you're still a Bluebird."

That was Squid, ruining my existence.

Why is it that extreme wealth is such an unhealthy backdrop for a kid's life? Perhaps it's that boys or girls from wealthy families always believe, deep down, that they're taken care of, that they've got a vast safety net stretching out from cradle to grave beneath them and that sense of security creates a deep apathy in them. Maybe it's that our culture values and admires wealth so much that someone from a moneyed background feels deeply superior to those around him and doesn't harbor the deep compulsion, the need, you might even say, to prove oneself. Maybe rich kids don't feel that anxiety that often leads to greatness. Or even competence.

Whatever the reason rich kids are so often a mess, Squid was a case in point. He was Exhibit A for how being rich with someone else's money, his father's I mean, he never earned a dime of it, is mentally and emotionally unhealthy.

Squid's father dropped him off every morning for practice. He arrived in a Porsche 911 convertible if it was hot. A blustery rainstorm coming, weather providing a chance for some rugged outdoorsmanship, and he rolled up in a British racing green Land Rover Defender. Perfect days were the days we waited for. If the day was deemed "a perfect day" by Squid's dad, no chance of rain, light or no wind, high of seventy-five degrees, he and his son would growl into the school parking lot in a bright red Ferrari Testarossa.

Squid's dad had made a fortune with a franchise of Mexican fast food restaurants called Pollo Loco. That means "crazy chicken." It seemed a slightly undignified way to make piles of cash, serving hundreds of thousands of greasy fifty-nine cent tacos to the lard-covered folks of the American Middle West, but the majesty of those cars made up for that.

Squid said there were more than three-hundred Pollo Locos in Indiana, Ohio, Kentucky, and Illinois, and he had a card that got him as much free food as he wanted at any of those fine establishments. At the time, he seemed one of the luckiest guys in the world to me. His family was rich. His dad kept a loose rein on him and bought him everything, almost, that he wanted. I didn't envy his gelatinous body or his incredibly slow mile time.

I came to learn that his mild obesity was a key element in the running story of Sydney Porter. His dad, while he didn't have much time for Squid, wasn't going to tolerate having a fat son, at least without attempting to do something about it. So, the question is, how did Squid, the slowest guy on the team—the only non-freshman Bluebird (until he became Fruit Salad)—and I become training partners and eventually partners in crime?

Well, after my nerd brother destroyed me in Angel/Devil, I hit a bit of a rough stretch. My confidence dropped through the floor. It was also true that the miles were starting to add up and my body was being worn down. Having never trained before, having never run even Bluebird mileage, less than thirty miles a week, the training we were doing was taxing on my virgin muscles. They weren't used to being used every day, and they were rebelling.

I remember struggling down the stairs in the morning, hobbling like an octogenarian, feeling like my legs would never loosen up again. It felt as if someone had been working my thighs and calves over with the peen side of a ball-peen hammer. I came to suspect that gnomes lived under my bed—gnomes that liked to work over my legs with their cruel little tools as I slept.

Nearly every night during those first weeks of training, I woke up to excruciating cramps in the arches of my feet. It was as if vice grips had been clamped on the muscles, then cranked tight until I woke in spastic agony, nearly flopping out of my bed due to the pain. Combine the physical torments with the mental anguish of having my future identity stripped from me by my goofy twin brother, and I was ripe for the pickings of a guy like Squid who was, like me, miserable and looking for company.

Always a strong liar, I sulked around and faked a few days' worth of injuries after Angel/Devil. During practice, while Keane and my brother were out getting better, I sat with a cute girl from the soccer team who was also faking an injury in the dark cool high school training room.

We both iced imaginary strains and massaged make believe pulls. We listened to the radio and chatted about what high school was going to be like. We gossiped about teachers and other freshmen. We talked about movies we'd seen. It was all very pleasant. But then her coach required her to get back at it, and I didn't like sitting there in the training room by myself.

When I got back on the roads, I lagged far behind the lead Bluebirds. I was a dog with his tail between his legs. I even let tiny Leonardo Chavez and oafish Popeye pull away after the first mile of our workouts. That left me with Squid.

"I hate this crap," he told me one surprisingly fresh and pleasant August morning, the corn on either side of us rippled like a vast green inland ocean as we lagged further and further behind the pack. "The only reason I'm here is because my dad's making me."

"I hate it too," I surprised myself by saying. "Why do we do a sport that's so hard?"

"This is the only sport that doesn't have cuts," Squid replied, looking at me as if I was stupid. "If I don't do a sport, I've gotta work at Pollo Loco. No way that's happening.

Besides," he added, "I kind of like Coach. He's really crazy."

Squid's breathing, even though we were slogging through a nine or ten-minute mile that felt like a shuffle to me, was loud and raspy. He slapped the soles of his hundred dollar trainers—gray New Balance 999s, total old man shoes that no real runner would wear—on the pavement with each step. We were heading out to The Hinterlands and the slapping of his shoes competed with the morning whir of the bugs and chirps of the birds. "And," he huffed, "if I break twenty minutes my dad said I can have one of his cars."

I immediately thought of the Testarossa. "Even the Ferrari?" I asked.

"Not that one …" He rolled his eyes at my presumption. "But any of the others." He passed a long, high-pitched fart without seeming to notice. "It doesn't matter. There's no way I can break twenty."

What Squid would have had to accomplish in order to earn himself a $50,000 Land Rover Defender or Porsche Carrera Convertible was run six minutes and twenty-five seconds per mile for three miles and about 200 meters. While that's not a bad effort, it's true that most guys who stick with cross country through their senior years break twenty. In fact, most do it in their first year. Breaking twenty is probably doable if you just decide you want it bad enough. And there was, to the naked eye at least, nothing physically wrong with Squid.

These were my thoughts after Squid told me his dad's bargain. What I said to Squid was a less analytical and slightly more emotional response. "You've gotta be shitting me!" I shouted. His comment that he couldn't do it hadn't even registered. I was already envisioning the two of us behind the windshield of that awesome Land Rover, nonchalantly pulling into the DQ parking lot like a couple of studs.

"I'm not shitting you," he said, huffing and puffing. "Let's stop for a while. I'm really tired."

"Man," I said, excited for both me and my new best friend, "that's cake! You can do it this year!"

Squid eyed me. He looked at that moment *exactly* like the stereotypical spoiled rich kid. He had a mop of dirty blond hair, no distinct triceps or biceps, just soft tubes for arms. He had baby arms. He also had a pair of flabby breasts that would've embarrassed a fifth-grade girl they were so big. He definitely could've used a training bra. He looked like the kind of kid whose mom gave him chocolate when he got tired. And who got tired a lot.

"Didn't you hear me?" he said. "I'm not breaking twenty. There's no goddamn way." He nodded up the road a little way. "Let's go hide in the shade in there," Squid pointed at a ruined, gray barn that looked like it had fallen in on itself sometime during the Depression. "We can hide out until everyone passes us on their way back to the school."

Now, I didn't mind blowing off workouts, I didn't even mind the dishonesty of faking an injury. Every time I faked an injury, I somehow got myself to half-believe that I might actually be a little bit injured. It didn't seem like a complete deception. However, hiding from my coach and teammates seemed a little much.

"Don't you think it might be dangerous in there? It's probably private property," I said. "There could be dogs. Boards with rusty nails in them."

Squid waved his hand dismissively. "I hide in there all the time," he said.

It was *kind of* a hot day. At least it would be in a few hours. Keane and my brother were now clearly out of my reach, seeing as they'd had a good week of practice while I had wallowed in self-pity and deceit. If you're gonna be a bear, be a grizzly, I thought. Or, in my case, if you're gonna half-ass it at all, why not be a complete and utter weenie like Squid? I decided it was fine to join him in the barn. Just this once.

I have to admit, there was a real feeling of pleasure, even a strange superiority of a sort, as we sat in the cool of the barn and watched first the Eagles struggle past, Slade leading the grim-faced pack, Bowden and Swart bringing up the rear, talking about colleges. Then came the Hawks. There was something exciting about hearing their soles slapping on the pavement and sitting silently in that barn, knowing they didn't know we were there. Then Keane and my brother, leading the Bluebirds by a quarter mile, all streaming with sweat. Then Popeye bumbling past looking like he was about to fall on his face, his head staring down at the pavement like he'd been hypnotized by the faded yellow dashes on the road. Lastly, Leonardo Chavez, seemingly near death, crept past us, his eyes nearly shut, his face tilted slightly upward toward the sky in an attitude of prolonged agony.

"Now we jump right back in where we were," said Squid, a big rich kid grin on his face. "I get away with this every time!"

Right after those karmic words was when Coach rolled up and caught us, sending Squid on his way and inviting me into his Subaru for what would prove a most interesting ride.

DECISIONS/METAPHORS - IN THE CORNFIELD - SCREW-UP - THE WRESTLING ROOM - GOOD COACHING OR SIMPLE INSANITY?

As I rode in Coach's car, it didn't take long to see that we were headed in the wrong direction. We were rapidly driving away from the school. I didn't want to open my mouth, as it's an instinct of mine to keep my mouth shut when I'm in trouble. Eventually though, Coach forced me to speak. He was driving out into the real hinterlands, true farm roads I'd rarely or never been on. He was driving fast, over seventy. We were quickly approaching a T in the road when he shouted at me, his eyes staring straight ahead, "Left or right?"

I pushed myself back in my seat, pressing an imaginary brake on my side of the car to no avail. I was sure we were going straight into the wall of corn we were quickly approaching.

"Left or right," Coach said again, this time with more urgency.

He didn't let up on the gas until I shouted, "Left!" for no good reason. Then he slammed on the brakes and we skidded into a left turn. I felt the right rear wheel drop off the side of the road and grab for traction in the dirt edging the field. We spun out slightly, then the all-wheel drive kicked in and we lurched back onto the safety of the pavement. "You're not very good at making decisions," said Coach.

I didn't know what he was talking about. Should we have gone right? Why?

Quickly, the Subaru was cruising along again at seventy. "We're heading in the wrong direction," said Coach. "What do you do when you're heading in the wrong direction?"

I had no idea what he was talking about.

"I said," he turned his attention from the road and stared across the front seat at me, "What do you do when you're heading in the wrong direction?"

"You turn around?" I stuttered.

Coach slammed on the brakes, bringing the car to a screeching halt. We sat in the middle of the road for just a moment before, without a word, he put the car into reverse and we were halfway off the road, into the corn. He slapped the shifter back into drive and peeled out, sending dirt flying behind us. We were heading back the way we'd come.

"This is all a big metaphor," said Coach, his eyes hard on the road ahead. "You know what a metaphor is, Kindle?"

I thought hard. But I couldn't remember if a metaphor was the one that used "like" or "as" or the one that didn't and I didn't want to screw it up. "I think so," I said.

"A metaphor," Coach said as the engine whined and we drove faster even than before, up to eighty, "is a comparison between unlike things. Like when you say a girl is a walrus because she's fat and ugly. That's a metaphor. Which way should I go?"

We were hurtling back to the T we'd taken left earlier. "Which way!" Coach shouted as we were almost past it.

"Right!" I yelled.

But I was too late and when Coach slammed on the brakes and skidded into the turn we were carrying too much speed. We slid into the cornfield, throwing up steaming rich black soil, the car slamming into and mowing down the first row of corn, the thick stalks and heavy ears pounding on the roof and hood of the car. I nearly wet myself.

"Dammit!" shouted Coach. He pushed open his door, having to put his shoulder into it due to the stalks pressing in against him. "You make bad decisions and you make them too slowly!" he yelled. "Where the hell are we now?"

"We're in a cornfield," I said quietly, stupidly stating the obvious.

"Damn straight! We're in a cornfield! Do we want to be in a cornfield Kindle?"

"No," I felt my lip quivering. I was on the verge of tears.

The smell of freshly turned soil and humidity washed into the car where I sat buckled. The engine of the Subaru ticked away, idling. Coach stood in front of the car, staring in at me through the windshield. He must have seen that I was near tears, because his attitude changed as abruptly as the direction of the car had moments before. His face went from angry to sorry. "Aww," he said. "I didn't mean to scare you."

He walked around the front of the car, opened the driver's side door, and slouched back into his seat. We sat there in silence for a few seconds, both of us considering our situation.

Coach's eyes, I saw when I glanced across at him, really were red-rimmed. He looked like he'd been up all night. He took his glasses off and rubbed them as if to corroborate my inference. "You know, Kindle, if I'm a bad coach, it ain't because I don't care enough ..." He stared down into his lap.

I wasn't sure where this self-criticism was coming from or what it required of me in response. After all, it was plain that I'd screwed up. I'd been hiding in a barn minutes before. I wasn't thinking he was a bad coach. I was thinking I was a pretty bad athlete. Coach then proceeded to cry. For the first time. It would be a month before I would see him cry again in the silence of the wrestling room on that fateful October morning.

I must have asked him something stupid then, like, "Are you okay?" You know, the kind of question you ask when someone breaks down in front of you and they're *clearly not* okay but you have to say something so you say something stupid and, denying the obviousness of the situation, you say something like, "Are you okay?"

"You could be so good," said Coach quietly as he rubbed his eyes and forehead. "Do you know how good you could be? You could be awesome ..."

"You're crying about me?" I asked, shocked that he cared so much.

"You guys, you, your brother, Keane ... hell, Kleiny and Chambers ... some of the sophomores we got are pretty good ..." Coach put his glasses back on and sighed. He stared off into the cornfield. "I'm gonna wreck it. I'm gonna screw it all up. You know, my life is a complete goddamn crash 'em up derby." At this thought, his shoulders began hitching, and he stared back down into his lap. I saw a tear drip from the tip of his nose onto his steering wheel.

"It's okay," I said stupidly. I was so shocked that this adult—my coach—had broken down in front of me that my own imminent tears had dried up completely and been forgotten.

"I ruin everything I touch," said Coach. "I'm not a good father to my kids. I'm an awful husband. I just wish I was good at something."

A light bulb went on in my head. I had something useful to say. "You're a good coach," I said, eager to help.

"Ahh," Coach said, waving my praise away. "I been coach for three years now and we never even been out of Sectionals. I'm no good."

"Sure you are," I said. I tried to think of some evidence to prove this claim. Nothing came to mind.

"I can't even get guys to run their workouts right," Coach sighed.

"You can't stop guys from cheating like we were. You can't watch us all the time. We've gotta be responsible for ourselves. There're too many guys to watch." Whatever I could think of to prove he wasn't a bad coach, I said.

Coach thought this over. His attitude seemed to shift. "Do you really think so? I mean, other coaches, you think their athletes go hide in barns and stuff like that?"

"Oh, sure!" I said, happy to be of consolation. "Kids cheat all the time. You can't stop it. Everyone does it."

"Well," he said sniffling a little, "I guess that makes me feel a little better."

"Sure," I said, "it's not your fault."

"I'm a screw-up," he said. "Sometimes we gotta just face the facts and go on as best we can from there." He looked hopeful suddenly. "You know what though … if we could just make it out of Sectionals … I might feel a lot better then. A lot better."

"Mr. Viddstein," I said, "I swear we will."

"You think so?"

"I swear to God we will." And I felt it, too. Whatever it took, we were going to move on to Regionals. "I'll never cheat on a workout again," I said, my voice husky with emotion. "I'll do my best."

"Well," said Coach gently, "that's a start." He turned the ignition in his Subaru and the engine squealed and buzzed, as it had never been turned off. "Ouch. Thought I'd turned the car off. Now, let's see if we can get out of here."

He shifted into drive and we crawled out of the loam and back onto the road. We drove in silence back to the school. To this day, I have no idea how much of Coach's coaching on that day was calculated and how much of it was simple, honest madness. All I know is that it worked. For a while. About a week.

GNOMES UNDER MY BED - WHAT HIGH SCHOOL MEANS TO ME - MY OUTFIT - SMELLING TROUBLE - SENIORS IN CHARGE - DUCT TAPE - KEANE AND ME - MY FIRST DAY OUTFIT - BONER ISSUES - SQUID IN THE HINTERLANDS - TELLING - A HINT OF BACKBONE

Before we knew it, our first meet, the Washington Central Hokum Karem, was a week away. My legs still felt like gnomes were crawling out from under my bed and pounding on them with picks and hammers every night while I slept, but I was getting used to it. I half-believed in them, they did such a thorough job every night. In spite of the pain I felt at the start of every run, I'd left Squid, Popeye, and Chavez behind and hung with Hyter and Keane every day, even when it got tough. Coach's breakdown had done its job.

Sticking with those guys every day, I felt my self-esteem begin to creep back up to where it ought to have been—somewhere about halfway between feeling I was a pile of dog shit and, on the other end of the spectrum, feeling that I ought to be crowned King of Cross Country For All Eternity before I'd even finished a 5K race, a shoo-in for the next Olympic 5000 meters.

My self-esteem would soon come crashing down again, although this time it was different. This time my fellow Bluebirds experienced it with me, which, in the end, somehow made all the difference. The bottom fell out again on the first day of high school.

School started in September and the very word made me think certain exciting thoughts. When I heard *September* I thought of eraser dust, foxy, dressed-up girls glowing with summer tans, the sound of lockers slamming, and the overcooked, overheated smell of school food. I dreamed of cool nights with my window open and the melancholy charms of autumn just around the corner. I really didn't spend a lot of my adolescence in the concrete world most people would call reality.

A case in point was my first-day-of-high-school outfit. I dreamed that it had huge significance. It was the keystone in an entire architecture I had planned out for my high school years. Therefore, a misstep in appearance on my first day of school was unthinkable.

I'm a little ashamed to admit that I'd laid out my clothes and played mix and match with my ensemble from the middle of August all the way up until I went to bed that momentous Sunday night—my last night, in my mind, as a child. This was probably when my dad began to fear that I was gay. He acknowledged this fear to me years later, a crooked grin on his face, as we sat on two barstools drinking cold ones and talking about my impending marriage to a beautiful woman. It was, at last, the moment when he knew he was surely out of those particularly troubling woods for a father.

My first-day attire consisted of a nice thin sweater, pale yellow, over a white Lacoste golf shirt. I admit it, I was a preppy, which for an old school guy like my father was clearly on the gay spectrum. I had a slick-looking pair of khakis laid out that I'd never worn before, and my brand-new blue-and-white checkerboard Vans slip-ons gave the whole look a little bad boy/stoner/surfer twist that was the icing on the cake. The shoes make the outfit, they say. So I was set.

I was set, that was, until Coach ruined it for me and I ended up sitting through the first day of high school in my embarrassingly high cut Adidas running shorts, a completely stinky pit-stained T-shirt, and my blue and silver Tigers—the same clothes and shoes I'd worn to morning practice that day. That was the fate of all the freshmen on the cross country team. And Squid.

The day began well, actually. I had my ensemble nicely folded in my gym bag. Hyter had his. I'd made sure he wasn't going to wear his favorite yellow-brownish, once-upon-a-time-white T-shirt on the first day of school so I'd have at least one day when I couldn't be mistaken for a complete dirtball. Mom dropped us off outside the locker room just after dawn, around 6 a.m. It was early, but I was wide-awake and excited, it being the first day of my life as a high-schooler and all.

Hyter and I walked down the steps to the locker room and went in to find we were among the last to arrive. All the other guys sat in a U around the chalkboard where Coach normally posted the workouts by group. On that day, however, the chalkboard was blank.

I have always had a bit of a sixth sense for trouble. Some people have it, some don't. Some guys always leave the party right before the cops show. Some guys don't go through with the stupid physical dare that ends up with a broken collarbone. Some guys have a knack for smelling when things are going to go badly and I, luckily, am one of those guys. On that morning, I smelled trouble immediately.

It had something to do with the fact that there was nothing on the board, but it had more to do with the looks on the seniors' faces. They weren't grinning madly, nothing obvious like that. They didn't glare at us like we were about to be tortured like gerbils in the hands of a sadistic ten-year old. It was subtler than that. In fact, it was a conspicuous effort on their part to look as if nothing unusual was about to happen that let me know something was dangerously amiss.

I stared at Bowden. No eye contact. Normally, I'd have gotten a head nod at least, but, on this particular morning? Nothing.

Slade, I noticed, was whistling an upbeat song. He never did that. Slade either complained about something or he sat with his Walkman on full blast, drowning out the world with Black Sabbath, Metallica, Anthrax, or, if he was feeling lighthearted, Van Halen. Today he was neither complaining nor was he escaping into his music.

I suddenly felt like a cow must feel as it heads for the slaughter room to be turned into steaks—definitely uneasy, bordering on alarmed, but entirely unsure why and totally clueless as to what to do about it.

Then Coach came in, eyes down. That was no good either. No braying East Coast chit-chat, no small talk. On that first day of school, instead of his typical banter, Coach simply walked in, picked up the chalk from the little ledge on the chalkboard and wrote "Have a great day!" Then he looked at what he'd written and underlined it, apparently deciding the exclamation point wasn't quite enough *umph*. Then he turned and faced us. The Eagles were especially eager and ready to listen.

"Seniors are in charge today," he said curtly, a fishy little smile on his face. "I'll see all of you this afternoon." And then he turned and went back to his office. I can't remember if Leonardo Chavez crossed himself at this point, but he should have.

Bowden, the senior we'd all come to trust, the senior who cared for us and let us in on the inside secrets we needed to know, stood and took center stage in front of the chalkboard. I saw that he had a roll of duct tape in his hand. This was beyond alarming.

"Bluebirds," he said in his soft calm voice, "you have thirty seconds." And an evil smirk I didn't think him capable of took over his kind face. His big Adam's apple bobbed in his neck twice.

"Awww, man," whined Squid. "You mean I have to go through this again! I'm a sophomore!"

"You're a Bluebird," said Swart accusingly, aggressively even. He was pointing at him from across the way. "That's your fault! You didn't have to be a Bluebird again. It was a choice!"

"He's not even a Bluebird. He's Fruit Salad," said a senior with a face full of acne and a mop of greasy hair—a kid named Chad Yost who never seemed quite fast enough to break through to the varsity seven but who trained as hard as anyone and was therefore resentful of those who didn't try as hard as he did. This included just about everyone on the team. Yost's beady eyes were barely visible through his dingy hair. "Bluebirds and Fruit Salad," he went on in a cruel croak of a voice, "you better run."

"That's not fair!" Squid said.

"The fair was in August," said Bowden coolly. "It's now September." He tossed his roll of tape from one hand to the other. "You're all down to fifteen seconds."

And with that, Squid decided the time for arguing was over and took off as fast as I'd ever seen him run up the steps and out of the locker room.

"Ten, nine, eight," counted Bowden. The other seniors had duct tape as well, I saw. The juniors and sophomores were all smiling grimly. Although they didn't hold rolls of tape, they were clearly on the right side of this particular equation. "Let's get the hell outta here," said Chavez. And we all bolted up the steps after Squid.

A beautiful sunrise spread across Pennsgap that day. The birds were chirping and a nice cool breeze cut through the air, hinting at fall. Had it not been for the screaming of six teenagers as they ran through the streets and the maniacal shouting of their horde of pursuers, the people of our town probably would've woken gently and pleasantly, rising from their beds in that comfortable and unhurried fashion perfect mornings facilitate. Actually, make that five screaming teenagers. Squid took off for The Hinterlands. It was a choice he would regret.

What I didn't realize then but do now is that we were unknowingly reenacting a cross country ritual stretching back to the ivied traditions of Exeter and Oxford, the finest prep schools in England where cross country originated.

The term "harriers" is often used for cross country runners. Most people don't know why. It has to do with the hounds and the hares and the hunts involving them that took place over the Victorian era English countryside. The first cross country races often involved a group of "hares" who were sent out first, then were chased by a group of "hounds." The hares left a paper trail behind them, in good ole sporting England, and they were certainly not in danger of being duct-taped to trees or telephone poles, although the idea was generally the same.

Whatever the history, none of us cared about it on that day. We were all fully in the present, trying to avoid the humiliation of being taped to a tree or a pole and the later physical pain of losing large amounts of body hair when the tape eventually was ripped from our bodies.

Popeye, Leonardo, Keane, my brother, and I flew down the tree-lined streets and ducked into the alleyways around the town square, hiding behind dumpsters and jumping backyard fences in hopes of escape.

Hyter vanished down an alley while Keane and I stuck together. We spent a solid three or four minutes on the courthouse lawn, dodging and weaving like tailbacks as the Hawks and Eagles laid a hand on us here and there but couldn't quite latch on well enough to tackle us and then tape us to a bench or sign post. Eventually, we realized there were too many of them and that we were doomed to be caught if we stayed where we were. So we sprinted across the bridge, over the river that ran through town and into the park where there were many restrooms and shelters to hide in.

Strangely, that morning built my confidence in a way no other workout would have. That morning I realized that Keane and I were truly faster than everyone else on the team, even Slade. They couldn't catch us.

But we couldn't run all morning. We had to get back to the school in time for the bell. The trick was to find a place to hide so they might give up the chase and we could slink back to the school and shower and change.

Time passed too quickly. Soon I knew my first impression as a high-schooler, a grown-up, was going to be woefully inadequate and nothing like the fine-tuned image of myself I'd worked so hard to create.

"It's nearly seven," I remember Keane telling me as we walked alongside the fairway of the town's nine-hole public golf course, still at least a mile from school. "Maybe we can sneak back in now." I think we both knew then that we'd be wearing our smelly running clothes all day. School began at 7:35. Even if we ran hard straight back to the locker room and miraculously avoided any upperclassmen, we'd barely have time to rinse the sweat off and change before the bell.

"We've gotta try it," I said. "We'll see if someone's guarding the locker room."

Right after I heard those words come out of my mouth, I was sure someone was guarding the locker room. I sighed. It was a grown-up's sigh, a sigh of resignation, so maybe in some small way on that first day of high school I truly wasn't a child anymore. Resignation, it seems to me now, is the natural state of the adult human being.

"We'll probably just have to go to class like this," I finally admitted to both Keane and myself. "It'll be better just to be on time than to be showered and dressed and thirty minutes late to school on the first day."

We ran in silence, taking alleys and side streets. When we got outside the locker room door, there were two seniors standing there like a pair of gargoyles. They both had rolls of duct tape in their hands. As we walked in through the main doors, dripping in sweat, stinking of B.O., we attempted to blend in. It didn't work. An older girl with spiky black hair and seven or eight earrings in one ear laughed out loud at us. My running shorts never felt so tiny. I became hyper-aware of my penis. Paradoxically, just thinking of how embarrassing it would be to tent-out my shorts in front of the whole school made the satiny smoothness of my shorts suddenly very apparent to me. As I wove my way through my hundreds of classmates as they milled about, I tucked myself into my waistband and hoped for the best.

By midday, it seemed the entire school had had our "senior-led" workout described to them. Instead of blending in, making a good impression, listening to my teachers, and looking for some quality female prospects in each of my classes, I spent my entire first day of high school focusing on not getting an erection. This effort backfired completely. Never had I been more aware of my own genitals than on that day. I carried my new books at waist level and did not, under any circumstances, set them down if I was not safely seated in a chair under a desk. It was a transparent gesture, but it was the best I could do.

I arrived at biology to discover Squid was in my class. It turned out he had flunked freshman biology the year before and had to take it again. His first-day-of-school attire also consisted of his running shorts, shoes, and a stinky T-shirt. His arms and legs, I saw, were streaked with broad red lines about the thickness of duct tape. Before class began, I pulled a chair up next to him.

"What happened to you?" I whispered.

"A farmer set me free around nine o'clock," he said. He was gazing off into thin air.

"Nine?"

"Man," sighed Squid, his eyes unfocused as if still in shock, "I ran farther than I've ever run. I was *way* out there.

Like, maybe two miles past that barn we hid in." His face remained blank as he told his tale. "There were four of them that followed me." He finally made eye contact with me. "And they just kept following me. It was like, they could've caught me way before they did, but they just kept following me, like twenty feet behind me. Just pushing me farther and farther out." He shook his head. "And I just kept running. I didn't know what else to do. They said I needed to get more miles in so I could get that Porsche. And I just kept running."

"What happened when they caught you?" I asked.

"I just fell on the ground, right in the middle of the road. I was, like, totally exhausted. So I just dropped. I refused to move. They stood around me for a few seconds then they lifted me up and took me over to this telephone pole and taped me to it. It was surreal. I didn't fight at all."

I could tell this last part confounded him.

"Man," I said. "I didn't think they'd really do it."

I'm not sure why I said that. I was certain from the moment I'd seen them with that tape in their hands that they'd use it if they got the chance.

"They did it," said Squid. "Dude, about twenty people drove past me before that farmer stopped." He looked at me, his eyes wide. There was hurt and confusion in those eyes. "At least twenty people live in this town who would let a kid stay taped to a telephone pole. I'm having a hard time with that right now."

"Are you gonna tell your dad?" I asked.

And this question, I see now, was a telling one. I believed that people with money had power, even then as a naïve fourteen-year old. I'm still pretty sure that's accurate. When someone who has money has a problem, things get done.

I was certain that Squid's dad, once told of his being taped to a telephone pole and missing nearly half of his first day of school, would raise hell. I envisioned suspensions from school, guys getting thrown off the team, maybe even Coach getting fired. And when you've got that kind of power at your disposal, you use it. Right? So I was pretty sure Squid would tell his dad what had happened.

But he surprised me. Yes, he was rich. And yes, he was a whiner, and yes, he was lazy. But the kid did have a backbone.

"No way am I gonna tell my dad," he said incredulously. "What kind of weenie do you think he'd think I am if I did that?"

I know, it wasn't much. The kid didn't say he was going to get revenge on the guys who taped him. He didn't say he was going to slit their necks and shit down their throats. He didn't say he was going to show everyone by breaking twenty minutes and driving that Porsche or Land Rover over their dogs. He didn't even say *he* felt he'd be a weenie if he told—he said *his dad* would see him that way. But he wasn't going to let his dad do that. He wasn't going to tell his dad that he was the only sophomore who got chased and that he was only one of us who actually got caught and taped. It was more than I expected, and it created in me a hint of pride by association.

I'd been debating whether or not to tell my own father. During the first period at school, I'd envisioned my dad raging into the school, his face set in a scowl that would send the secretaries in the principal's office scurrying. I'd envisioned him making Coach cry and Coach getting fired. I had wanted that badly while sitting in my first class, my bare legs cold, feeling naked. But now I wasn't so sure.

At dinner that night when Mom asked Hyter and me how our first day of school went, I decided to keep what had happened to myself. Hyter did, too. It was a rare tacit agreement on our parts. If someone else spoke out, so be it, but it wasn't going to be me or my brother who blew the whistle on our hazing. It turned out, nobody else on the team mentioned it either.

We had a secret now, our whole team. Nothing creates bonds in people liked shared secrets. Shared secrets and mutual suffering: the two greatest bonding experiences in life. This truth would be brought home to me that October morning in the wrestling room. But that first day of school I'd lost what little faith I'd had in Coach. And it would get worse before it got better.

THE VARSITY PAIRS - WHAT'S A HOKUM KAREM? - A GENIUS AND INSANE BOTH - K1 AND SLADE - HAY'S IN THE BARN - QUITTING - HATE

Thursday afternoon on that first week of school, Coach stood before us with the list of varsity runners for our first meet written out on a sheet of paper in his hand. We sat anxiously in the U of wooden benches down in the locker room, waiting to hear who Coach thought his ten best athletes were.

"Fifth team," he said in his high nasally voice, "is gonna be Bowden and Yost. A coupla seniors that really went out and pounded the pavement this summer." I wasn't surprised by this. I'd have had them at nine and ten on the team myself. "You earned the honor, boys," concluded Coach.

Bowden put his hand out to the senior next to him—the hardworking, greasy-faced, and frustrated kid named Chad Yost who had aggressively voiced the opinion that Squid deserved no mercy due to his being a sophomore on hounds and hares day just four days previous. Yost grimly and quietly gave Bowden five.

"Bowden," Coach squawked, "you're leading off." He nodded at Bowden and got the thumbs up back. "Yost, that means you're gonna bring it home. Think you can handle being anchor?" Yost nodded solemnly. "You ain't gonna be a pussy when it hurts, are you?" Yost shook his head back and forth vigorously, almost maniacally, I thought. Yost was quickly becoming the senior I was second-most worried about on the team.

"Fourth team," Coach went on, "is gonna be Chambers and Kleinhelter."

Chambers and Kleinhelter were two sophomores. They were Hawks—a couple of pretty solid runners. Chambers was a tall, athletic-looking guy, over six feet tall, who seemed only to be held back by his large and heavy feet, and Kleinhelter looked to be one-hundred percent a runner. He had broad shoulders for his size, was skinny, and weighed in at about a hundred and fifteen pounds. His only issue was that he lacked the muscle even to carry his small frame over an entire effort. He regularly faded at the end of tough workouts. They had both fluttered around the seventeen-and-a-half minute mark as Bluebirds and had put in some good miles over the summer. I was certain of their place on the varsity in the years to come.

"Chambers first, then Kleiny," said Coach. "You guys oughta press for a scoring time. Kleiny, don't go out like an idiot and fuck up your last mile split. Save something." Kleinhelter nodded. "Chambers," Coach poked his chin out at Chambers, "be sure you tell him again before the race, so's he don't forget." Chambers nodded.

"Third team," Coach went on. "Kitty-Cat and Victor."

Kitty-Cat was Todd Mankato's nickname. Kitty-Cat was silent and showed little emotion. He was moody like a feline. A talented runner, he would go on to run on a scholarship in college. However, at this time, back when he was still just a sophomore, he hadn't yet discovered his ability.

Victor Jones, Kitty-Cat's partner, was Slade's toady. He, like Slade, looked to be a runner during practices and meets and a small town punk the rest of his waking life. He wore a Levi's blue-jean vest with a bunch of sewn-on patches over a small plain white T-shirt nearly every day. His hair was kinky and orange, his skin almost a weird bluish-white, as if he couldn't stand the sun. About a foot shorter than Slade, he was a nearly perfect sidekick. He was the only runner I've ever known who smoked more than the occasional cigarette. The ashtray of his '82 Cutlass overflowed with butts.

Victor cursed quietly when he heard he was paired with Kitty-Cat. He glanced at Slade. The two of them, it was obvious, had hoped to run together. "You guys are set to count," said Coach, oblivious of Victor's disapproval of his partner.

"Victor," he said, his eyes locking on the little hooligan's, "that means no drinking Friday night. And no messing around with your slutty little girlfriend, either. You know how I feel about sex and athletic performance. Don't go wasting it."

Victor snorted in response. I couldn't decide whether the snort meant it was silly for Coach to think he'd drink booze the night before a race, or if he thought it was silly for Coach to ask him to abstain from drinking booze on a Friday night, Saturday race or not. Or, perhaps, he thought it was funny that Coach called his girlfriend slutty. Whichever was the case, Victor snorted.

"And remember, boys, it's not the places that matter … it's the times that count. This is the only event this year places don't matter and time does."

The Hokum Karem was originated at Wabash College, a small, all-men's liberal arts school in Crawfordsville, Indiana, by the late J. Owen Huntsman, the head cross-country coach at the University of Chicago at the time. It was designed as an early season training event. In a Hokum Karem, five teams of two runners each run alternating miles for a total of six miles. Each runner runs a total of three miles, tagging after each one-mile leg. Think of it as an intense repeat workout. You run your three one-mile repeats as hard as you can and get a four-and-a-half minute (if your partner is awesome) to a six-and-a-half minute (if your partner sucks) rest between miles. A pair running under thirty minutes is averaging under five minutes for each of their six miles, which is really good. The overall winning team is the team with the lowest overall time with three pairs out of five counting. To win a high quality Hokum Karem a team almost always has to run sub-ninety minutes overall.

What I, along with everyone else sitting around the blackboard, was wondering was who the number one team would be. The second team, which he announced next, made sense. "The freshman duet of K2 and Keane," said Coach with a smile on his face, "will be our second team. Keane, you're anchor. K2, you just do it like you did it during Angel/Devil. Get Keane up there where he feels like he's in the race."

And then a strange tension filled the locker room. Even the mouth breathers, the handful of guys who never seemed to know what was going on, realized something was amiss. Of potential candidates for the honor of being named onto the first team, only Slade seemed to be left. But he had to have a partner.

There was Johnny Feeney with his big goofy black glasses and stumpy, hairy legs who always took off like a bat out of hell on easy runs. But Coach was crazy, not stupid. He knew Feeney wasn't really that good, that he just loved to win workouts on easy days like a moron. Surely it wasn't him. There was Tim Traung, a glass-eater of a senior, a first generation Vietnamese-American with an accent so profound I understood him about half the time, but whom Coach seemed to love due to his kamikaze attitude and his show-no-pain demeanor. But he had a mile PR somewhere around 5:15—way too slow to be paired on the number one team with Slade. Nobody else seemed even close.

As the guys glanced around, trying to figure out who the other guy on the first team was, I started to panic. There was only one guy, in my mind, who made any sense at all. Then I noticed Yost glancing at me, a nasty look on his greasy, pimply face. It seemed he had the same thought at the same time that I did.

Was Coach a mad genius or just mad? I can't settle on one or the other. I'm beginning to believe maybe I don't have to. Without having done anything to earn my position on the number one team and a pairing with our senior team captain, I was to be Slade's partner.

"Kindle 1 and Slade are the first team," Coach said. "K1 will lead it off and Slade'll bring it home." He closed the notebook he'd been reading from as if that settled that and asked cheerily, "Any questions?"

There were none. I think everyone was too shocked at my being on the first team after my week of dragging ass with Squid to speak. Looking around the room for some support,

I found nothing but shocked faces and a few ugly stink-eyes aimed right at me. The worst from Slade himself.

"Okay," Coach said. "Easy run today boys. 'The hay,' as the people of this backward, hayseed state like to say in reference to their farming heritage, 'is in the barn.'"

As we quietly went up the steps out into the afternoon sun for our easy run, I hated Coach. Hate's a strong word. But I was at the point of hate.

As the guys talked quietly about Coach's decisions, I heard my name whispered a few times. I didn't want to hear what they were saying. On the run, I considered my options.

I doubted if the football coach would still have me. Also, after using my running shoes for a couple of weeks, I knew Dad wouldn't let me quit. He'd made an investment and I'd made a promise without saying a word when I begged for and he bought those expensive Tigers for me. And I knew it was probably about something deeper than the shoes anyway, that there was something I was going to have to face head on.

I had tried to avoid confrontation with Slade by faking hurt and by joining Squid at the end of the pack. I had dismissed the possibility that I'd be on the varsity, probably until Slade graduated. I'd come to terms with that and was content to toil away on the jayvee team with the other admirable slobs, and Squid, of course.

However, Coach had shanghaied all my plans. He'd put me in a bad place I hadn't even considered on those sleepless nights when I thought too much about everything. For that, I give him everlasting credit.

COACH LOGIC - THE BIG YELLOW - YODA AND LUKE SKYWALKER - "YOU CAN'T WIN A RACE IN THE FIRST MILE, BUT YOU CAN LOSE IT" - FLOYDS AND THE SUBJECTIVITY OF ARGYLE SOCKS - TENT ERECTION

"Dude," said Bowden, "he cries to everyone."

"So," I said angrily, "he was lying?"

"Oh no," said Bowden calmly as he prepared for the day's race by twisting a sharp new metal spike into the bottom of one of his Nikes, "he wasn't lying. He meant every word he said. You can be sure of that." He tested the rest of the spikes for tightness with his spike wrench then shoved his shoes back into the bag on his lap.

As I watched him do this, I was silently alarmed. I had no spikes. I didn't know I was supposed to have spikes. It seemed extravagant to me to spend all the cash Dad had coughed up for my X-Calibers. Now I needed another pair of shoes?

I decided maybe Bowden was an equipment freak—that he would be one of only a handful of guys at the race wearing spikes. I decided also not to ask him if I was going to look like a fool in my trainers, my theory being that a state of ignorance, however short-lived, was more pleasant than the outright certainty that I'd look like a foolish cross country virgin at the starting line.

"Coach is one of the few people I've ever met who truly means everything he says," Bowden continued. "It's just that what he says, when you take it all together, doesn't end up making a lot of sense." He rubbed the dark stubble on his unshaven chin thoughtfully. "Actually, that's not quite right. It does kind of make sense, but it's not logical." He looked at me to see if I got it. My face must have indicated I didn't. "Look," he said, "Coach is Coach. He's nuts. But he's totally honest. Everything he says, he means it and believes it one hundred percent …" He considered that, then added as an afterthought, "When he says it."

We were on the Big Yellow, riding to the park where the Hokum Karem was set to happen. As we waited on the bus to arrive on that misty morning, our bags full of gear sitting on the sidewalk, Coach had said that the varsity pairs should sit together. Slade, however, refused to ride with me, saying no pussy who trained at the ass end of the pack deserved to sit next to him. Bowden, always the mediator, said he'd trade Chad Yost for me. I was actually grateful that Slade refused to sit next to me. The forty-minute ride would've been excruciating had I actually been within strangling distance of him.

The ride gave me the chance to talk to Bowden, who had clearly taken on the role of Yoda for all us young Luke

Skywalkers who still didn't know which way was up. I'd told him of Coach's breakdown out in The Hinterlands, expecting his sleepy eyes to grow wide at the image of coach bawling in the seat next to me, his Subaru sitting halfway into the first rows of a cornfield. But instead of widening his eyes, Bowden rolled them and told me Coach had broken down in tears in front of most of the seniors and juniors at some point.

"It's like the guy," he said, "doesn't have any filter between what he feels and what he says and does, you know? It's like he's got to say *exactly* what he's thinking and act out *exactly* what he's feeling all the time."

"So I'm not the only one he's done that to?" I asked.

"He broke down to me when I was a sophomore," said Bowden, chuckling at the memory. "He told me he didn't deserve to live."

The bus was warm that morning. Several of the guys had fallen asleep, pillows pressed up against the sliding windows of the bus. Others had headphones on. A few were eating breakfast out of greasy bags of fast food. The mood was sleepy, the drone of the bus tires on the interstate beneath us filled the bus.

"What did you do?" I asked.

"What? You mean to make him say that to me and cry?"

"Yeah, you know … did you cheat on a workout or something?"

"Like you did?" Bowden asked.

"How did you know about that?" I asked, my heart leaping in my chest. As far as I knew, neither Coach nor Squid had ever mentioned that day to anyone else.

"Look, one thing you've gotta understand is that this team is like a really messed-up family. Everybody, eventually, knows everything. We just don't talk about it at team meetings down in the locker room. We talk about it like this. One-on-one. Quietly."

"So," I said after a silent moment, "did you cheat on a workout or something?"

"Nope, I was just the last guy out of the locker room. The last guy left to listen."

Someone coughed behind us, and someone else told him to shut up.

"Well ... any advice for the race?" I asked, changing the subject.

"You're leading off, right?"

"I think so."

"You are," said Bowden, a little frustrated that I didn't know if I was lead or anchor. "And my advice is this—don't kill yourself on the first mile. You've got three miles to run. Remember that." Bowden took a drink from his bottle of Gatorade; it was going to be a hot day. "Coach always says, 'You can't win a race in the first mile, but you can lose it.'"

"Okay," I said. I shut up then, but there was something on my mind. Bowden sensed it.

"What else do you want to know?" he asked.

"Are you in pain all the time? I think I may be injured. My legs hurt. Like, all the time."

"Both legs the same?"

"Yeah."

Bowden smiled. "That's just you turning into a runner. Your muscles are shredded. That's how you get stronger though. When your body repairs itself, it makes you better than you were before."

"You have to hurt yourself to get stronger," I said, testing the idea out.

"That's life, little Bluebird. That's running."

Bowden shut his eyes and seemed, after a while, to fall asleep. I tried to do the same with no luck. I kept thinking about Coach and how to feel about him. Then the bus slowed, the engine roaring at the driver's downshift, and guys began moving in their seats. We exited off the interstate onto the narrow country road leading to the park. Then a line of trees ended and the course was right there outside my bus window. My heart thumped hard in my chest at the realization that I was a step closer to the time to prove myself.

We clambered off the bus to find a field full of activity. There's a festive atmosphere at any large gathering of people, even a bunch of sadists like distance runners. Maybe even especially among a group of sadists like distance runners. As Saint Augustine supposedly said, only saints and madmen are not, by nature, gregarious. All he meant was that being around a lot of other people is a good thing for most of us.

Neither saint nor madman, I felt the communal buzz of the place, and it excited me. It was a thrill to be there. Yet the nervous ninny in me wished to be home in bed under the childish protection of my sheets and blankets.

Fifty or more tents in a variety of colors sat on the grass under the blue morning sky. The heat of the day was becoming apparent, yet the morning insects were still at their orchestrations. For some reason the whole spread made me think of the Civil War—heat, tents, and bugs in a field.

Packs of runners, guys and girls both, shuffled along the course marked with white paint on the green grass. Strings of multi-colored plastic pennants indicated tight corners as well as the finish chute. The chute narrowed from an opening of about ten feet to a single man/woman wide exit where runners would line up in finishing order, leaning on each other, staggering for breath, relieved to be done finally with the task they set for themselves.

As soon as I saw that finishing chute, I wished I could leapfrog in time to the moment I would exit it, tired and done, whatever the result. But then I realized it was Slade, as our team anchor, who'd be in the chute, not me.

"Who are those guys?" I asked Bowden as we stood outside the bus. I pointed at a group of ten or so lean and lanky runners, many of whom had spotty beards, and all of whom wore green and gold-striped running shorts and mid-calf-high argyle socks, funky dress socks, in the strangest color combinations imaginable.

"That's Floyds," said Bowden. "I know ... they look like idiots, but they got fourth at State last year so they can do whatever the hell they want."

"It's actually kind of cool," I said.

Bowden stared at me for a moment. "You're a little weird, did you know that?"

"I've been considering it a lot lately," I said. "My weirdness."

"Well, as long as you kick ass out there," he pointed at the course, "nobody's going to give a shit if you're weird or not." He nodded at the Floyds team who were running away from us now. "Like those guys. They suck, everybody thinks they're complete tools. They get on the podium in November, everybody wishes they could wear argyle socks like them, but they can't, because Floyds did it first. It's that simple."

"Bluebirds!" shouted Coach as he threw his bag down on the dew-covered grass. "Your first job is to put up the tent. This first time, Swart's going to direct you. Next time, you do it on your own. Listen up and learn. I'm gonna go take a stinker."

Squid raised his hand like a goofy third grader. I don't know why, but he looked really funny with his hand stuck up in the air while standing in an open field. When Coach ignored him, he began jumping up and down until Coach couldn't ignore him anymore.

"What Sydney?" groaned Coach.

"Do I—"

Coach cut him off, anticipating his question. "No, you're Fruit Salad. Fruit Salad is excused from tent erection." I thought Popeye and Leonardo, who'd become something of a tandem, were going to fall on the ground laughing when he said tent erection.

I laughed too, but not very hard. I was preoccupied with my task for the day—not screwing up.

SPIKES? - A FAT KID IN A SINGLET =
SILLINESS - AN IMAGINARY BUS WRECK -
RUN OUT? - "DON'T MAKE ME LOOK BAD"
- THE COACH AT THE HALF-MILE MARK I
SHOULD'VE LISTENED TO BUT WOULD'VE
BEEN TOO IGNORANT TO KNOW WHAT
HE WAS SAYING ANYWAY - ANAEROBIC,
AEROBIC, AND THE INVISIBLE CHIMP - IDIOT
- 200 BEATS PER MINUTE - SLADE GIVES UP

"Where are your spikes?" Slade asked. I barely heard. I was focusing most of my attention on not puking from nerves.

The gun was fifteen minutes away. We were all pinning our numbers on, running to the nearby woods to urinate for the last time and yawning like crazy, which is the body's response when it knows it will soon lack or is beginning to run short on oxygen. Yawning is a survival tactic. Also an interesting side note: yawning is contagious. Even to cats and dogs. Next time you're bored stiff in class or at home, start yawning and see how long it takes for others to start yawning as well.

In any case, yawning was the mildest of my body's responses to the stress I felt just fifteen minutes before the race. It felt like someone was stirring my guts with a stick and I deeply wished there was a sport that didn't require you to do *anything*, a sport whose purpose was sitting on your butt on Saturday mornings and watching cartoons and eating doughnuts like when you were a little kid.

"I asked you where your goddamn spikes were. Answer me," said Slade, his brow furrowed in consternation. I heard him this time. Loud and clear.

"I don't have any," I admitted. I looked around, hopeful that at least some of the varsity guys wouldn't be wearing spikes. They all were. All except for me and my brother. At this point, this observation wasn't entirely unexpected.

As they day wore on, I saw that Bowden was indeed not simply an equipment freak. Squid, Traung, Swart, even Chavez and Popeye, my fellow freshmen, all had spikes. I had missed the boat somewhere.

It had a lot to do with the fact that neither Hyter nor I had run cross country in junior high school. This was our first meet and nobody ever wore spikes at practice. In any case, it had become apparent that the two of us would stand out as a couple of greenhorn rubes when the varsity race came around.

Spikes are the epitome of elegant minimalism. Stripped bare for the elemental purpose they serve, racing spikes are nearly weightless, have next to no stability, and function exclusively to create an optimal grip on the Earth when the balls of the feet press hardest during a race. The best runners are humans as stripped bare as spikes because constant running pares away the excess of the human body, both muscle and fat.

The uniforms of other sports allow an athlete to not be much of an athlete yet still appear to be one. Put a fat kid in a football uniform and he looks like a lineman. Put him in a cross country uniform and he looks ridiculous. Nearly anyone looks like a baseball player if he wears a baseball uniform. This is decidedly not the case with running. And for a cross country runner, the icing on the cake as far as appearance goes is definitely the spikes.

Training shoes are designed specifically for their purpose. Trainers are for cushioning and protection over hundreds of relatively slow miles. They are designed to be durable and stabilizing in order to prevent injuries. A spike and a trainer are as different as an airliner and a jet or a school bus and an Indy Car. Looking down at my feet, my Tigers, which once seemed so sleek, now seemed as clunky as clown shoes.

"Idiot," said Slade as he checked the laces on his spikes, a pair of Day-Glo yellow Adidas Adi-Stars with orange stripes. They were the shoes all the Kenyans and Ethiopians wore when running away with the World Cross Country Championships every year.

Up to that point, it had been a good day for the team, and for me. I'd had fun and been oblivious of my impending doom while cheering on my fellow Bluebirds in the fresh-man two-mile race in which Leonardo showed a hint of his potential by breaking twelve minutes. Popeye was happy simply to have finished his first high school race, and I was happy for him. Squid completed his two-mile jog, the jayvee race, in fourteen minutes and a few seconds, causing him to entertain the possibility of actually training in hopes of earning that Land Rover or Porsche. In the girls' race, a pair of our girls had placed in the top ten. Everyone around our tents was smiling, happy to be done, and looking forward to watching us in the day's final event.

It had grown truly hot by the time the varsity boys' race rolled around. The morning dew had evaporated and the ground was hard and dry. The course was worn bare. Tan arcs of dry, hard-packed ground curved around the tight corners leading up to the exchange zone. A few high lonely clouds scudded across the sky, promising a sunny, hot run.

As we walked up to the line, the other teams came into clear focus for the first time. Twenty teams, a hundred pairs altogether, would be in our race, among them some of the best in the state.

The runners from Floyds in their argyle socks all looked like they ought to be in college. They seemed too mature, too powerful, and seasoned to be lining up with the likes of a couple hundred-and-thirty-pound scrawnies like me and my brother. They all looked like Keane would with three years of hard training under his belt. And they weren't even the best team there.

Both Bloomington schools would be in contention for the state title in November. Anderson High School, which later seemed very cool to me because their scoring five was three black guys and two white guys, was ranked among the best in the state that year. However, the team everyone glanced at, tried hard not to stare at, was the Ridgeline Salukis.

The perennial state champs, eleven years in a row at the start of that season, the Salukis were the team we all wanted to be. Simultaneously, they were the team whose bus we wished would crash into a ditch on the way to the meet, whose bus windows and doors we envisioned jamming shut, and whose coaches and athletes we dreamed would slowly and painfully burn to death.

Well, actually, I didn't hate them that much as a naïve freshmen, but I'd be indoctrinated into the legions of Saluki haters soon enough. I would learn to hate. The Salukis themselves would teach me.

On that morning, however, my head was spinning so hard as we approached the start, I couldn't have told you which team was which, and I didn't really care. I was mostly focused on not blowing my pre-race granola bars and nearly half a gallon of Gatorade (I overdid it in my anxiety) on my big, fat, ugly trainers which twenty-four hours prior had seemed the height of running tech.

"Gentlemen, take a run out if you want it," said the starter through a bullhorn. The starter wore a red sports coat and black pants even though it was hot. I found this to be intimidating somehow. There was something nearly policeman-like about him in his formal attire. Also, he had a gun.

My heart leapt in my chest in fear when everyone took off for run-outs. I thought they were starting the race. I had expected a gunshot, but I took off after them like a moron thinking I'd screwed up yet again and then almost ran up Chad Yost's pimply back when he abruptly stopped in front of me. Thankfully, he was focusing too hard on himself to notice me.

After returning back to the starting line, the pairs all seemed to be giving each other five and patting each other on the shoulder. I even saw a couple of teams shake hands like grownups. I didn't expect any such treatment from Slade and I didn't receive it. Instead, he stared me hard in the face. "Don't make me look bad," he whispered through clenched teeth. I didn't speak a word back, I merely nodded that I understood my mission.

I would endure any amount of pain, I pledged to myself as I stood at that white line, in order not to make Jeff Slade look bad. I would risk death by exploding my own heart if such a thing were possible, because at least then I would die with dignity and by my own actions and not at the hands of my team captain.

The second runners had stepped back, leaving a long line of us standing there at the start. The starter waited for us all to look his way. The crowd hushed. "Runners set," the starter said abruptly into his bullhorn. And then, before I had a chance to think another thought, the gun went off and we were charging down the course.

I hadn't run a race in two and half years, and I'd *never* run a race against high school runners, people who spent a lot of their time training hard and thinking hard about running. The pace for the first two hundred meters shocked me. Had we run any faster at all, it would have been a sprint in my book.

I knew two things: I couldn't keep up that pace for a full mile, and Slade would kill me if I made him look bad.

The thing was, the wide swath of cut grass in front of the starting line narrowed after about a hundred and fifty meters to a slim corridor, three-foot tall wild grass on either side. The mown swath was only wide enough to comfortably allow for three or four runners across. When we hit that spot, we would be forced into a something of a line.

While nobody particularly wanted to be first after a hundred and fifty meters, nobody wanted to be last either. So we probably got through that first 150 in about twenty seconds. In other words, way too fast. A little under four-minute-mile pace.

I was having an out-of-body experience, overwhelmed by what I was a part of, until someone, I have no idea who, caught me on the chin with a sharp elbow. My teeth clicked together with such force I was surprised not to taste blood or feel the grittiness of a chipped tooth in my mouth. I doubt if that blow to my jaw was intentional, but it actually helped pull me back inside myself. Football players often say they need sometimes to take a hit before they feel like they're really playing. Well, that was the way it worked for me. I hit the small opening in the first half of the pounding herd I was a part of.

By the half-mile mark, I'd worked myself into the first third of the pack, believing this was about the place I needed to be so Slade didn't get embarrassed and kill me. At the top of a small hill, a coach stood yelling splits from his watch on his wrist. I couldn't hear what that coach said as we flew by, but even if I had, I wouldn't have been able to make sense of a split.

I could tell, however, by the tone of his voice and the look on his face that we were out either really fast or really slow. He was yelling numbers at us as if warning us against something bad that was going to happen if we kept up what we were doing.

I should've responded when most of the guys around me suddenly relaxed and dropped back. They took heed of the warning, leaving me with only two runners from Ridgeline, two from Floyds, and one guy from Bloomington North in a lead pack that the field allowed to quickly pull away.

Perhaps my brain wasn't getting enough oxygen to function properly or maybe the depths to which Slade scared me made me lose awareness, or maybe it was both. Whatever the case, just after that half-mile mark, it somehow slipped my mind that I had three miles to run, not just one.

There are two main types of exercise—aerobic and anaerobic. Aerobic exercise is what you do when you're out on an easy seven miler with your buddies. You can talk while doing aerobic exercise. Aerobic exercise isn't particularly painful. You can, if you're well trained, work at an aerobic level for a very long time.

One hundred and sixty and one-quarter miles is the world record for running on a treadmill for twenty-four hours straight. In setting that record, Arulanantham Suresh Joachim never went anaerobic. (By the way, as of the writing of this book, he also holds world records for endurance ironing and balancing on one foot, among others.) He never went anaerobic so, while his thighs and calves must've felt like roadkill at the end of his run, he never had that frantic I-can't-breathe, I'm-going-to-die feeling. Anaerobic exercise is the kind that takes you to that place—a place where you can't exist for too long. Anaerobic is the place you go when you're racing.

What happens at this level of effort is that your body begins to produce a nasty substance, at least as far as your muscles are concerned, called lactic acid. When lactate levels get high, you see runners slow way down, tilt backward or hunch forward, and generally look like there's an invisible fifty pound chimpanzee hanging around their necks, hopping up and down between their shoulder blades, trying to cause them to collapse. The invisible chimp climbed on me in earnest somewhere around the 1200-meter mark.

At this point in the race, one of the Ridgeline guys had faded and one of the Floyds guys had faded, as had the Bloomington runner. Now it was just me and two others— one from Ridgeline and one from Floyds—both of whom had been in the top ten at State the previous year. In my foggy brain, however, the only thing that mattered was not embarrassing Slade.

Well, it wasn't like when I miraculously beat Willie Davis back at the Kiwanis Sunrisers Pancake Two-Miler. I didn't win the first leg of my first high school meet, but I did fight my way to the finish within ten meters of two studs that I should've let go somewhere around the quarter-mile mark. The starter, who was now serving as an announcer, shouted out splits as we came to the exchange zone. I remember being shocked that he was still in the 4:30s as the two runners ahead of me tagged. And that I was not far behind them.

As I nearly fell on my face, my hand stretched out to tag Slade's, I saw a look of terror on his face. "Idiot," I saw his mouth say, but I did not hear it. The only sound I could hear at that point was a very high-pitched whistle. I think it was a message from God telling me to stop running or I would die.

I tagged his hand and he was off. Then I was lying on the grass, subconsciously aware that I needed to get out of the exchange zone before I got spiked. I dragged myself to the side under some marker flags and then Coach was leaning down to me, handing me a paper cup of water.

"Drink," he said. And my mind was coming back to me. I could hear again. Then he said, "I don't know whether to laugh or cry."

He crouched down and put his hand on my throat. I thought for a moment he was strangling me so Slade wouldn't have to do it after the race was over. I grabbed at his hand, confused. "I'm checking your heart rate," he said. "Stay quiet."

He stared at the watch on his left wrist and counted in his head. After fifteen seconds he removed his hand. "You're at nearly 200 beats per minute," he said. He rubbed the top of his head anxiously. "Get your breathing under control. Just survive the next mile." Then he finally smiled. "Just survive the next two, okay? Just get through 'em." He rubbed the top of my head. "You done good. You were stupid as hell out there, but you just don't know any better, so you done good."

"What was my time?"

His smile broadened. "Time to get a watch," he tapped at his own running watch.

Just when I thought he wasn't going to tell me, although I was too exhausted to care much, he said, "4:39."

It was a PR by nearly half a minute. Then he ran over to the other first-leg runners who stood beside the exchange zone pouring water on their heads, stretching, getting ready for their next two miles.

I decided I had better do the same and stretch a little, shake all that acid out, although when I tried to stand up the sky went black. I sat back down clumsily. I was in trouble.

I was still sitting there when I heard the starter say into his bullhorn that the lead teams were approaching the exchange zone. It seemed to have been mere seconds since I'd tagged Slade.

In front was a runner from Ridgeline, a tall strong guy with a shaved head and a long stride. His name was Ron Moats and although I couldn't know it then he was to become a big part of my Bluebird season. Right behind him was a short, powerfully built runner from Floyds, his purple, brown, and red argyle socks flashing beneath him.

There was a large gap then. Nearly ten seconds passed before two Bloomington runners came in, then a runner from Anderson, and then two more from Ridgeline and then another from Floyds.

Where was Slade?

After the first fifteen runners or so came in, Keane, not Slade, came charging up and over the hill and around the tight corner near the exchange. He tagged my brother who took off. Hyter had again demonstrated his racing savvy by running a conservative and intelligent 5:05 first mile, and Keane, who'd logged an impressive yet not suicidal 4:58 for his first mile, said between exhalations that Slade had quit running somewhere around the half-mile mark.

"Quit runnin'?" Coach yelled. "What the—" He went off on one of the stronger cursing performances I've ever heard in my life.

And it was true. Slade had quit running at the half-mile mark. After sticking with the lead Ridgeline and the Floyds runners for just over eight-hundred meters, Slade had given up. And, I was sure, it was all my fault.

As thankful as I was not to have to run those next two miles, I would have happily slogged through them. I would have run to the point of passing out rather than do what I was now going to have to do—face Slade, whom I had just caused, in spite of my being told not to, great and awful embarrassment. And, in my mind, it was all Coach's fault.

SLADE'S RADIO - UNDER THE MAPLE TREE - METALLICA UNDER A HOODED SWEATSHIRT - A SLIGHT EXPLOSION - NINE OR TEN THROWS - "FINISH" - THE RITUAL OF THE BUS RIDE - EATING IT - CHEERING FROM THE BACK OF THE BUS

Slade ate his radio on the bus ride home. That's not some kind of weird, confusing figure of speech, either. He actually ate his radio. I sat and cheered him on as he did it along with most of the rest of my teammates. I know: weird turn of events. I'll explain.

After the race, Coach called us all together. We sat in our racing gear under a big maple tree, some of us on a rickety picnic table, others on the dry yellow grass. We drank Gatorade and water. We ate bananas and granola bars and quietly discussed our efforts while we waited on him. All the while we avoided the obvious plotline of the day—the fact that Slade had simply stopped running his race when it got tough.

Hyter and Keane had finished in a very respectable thirteenth place and had the two best freshman times of the day, both averaging 5:07 a mile. Victor and Kitty-Kat had run solidly, placing in the low twenties, and Yost and Bowden put in a smart, workmanlike effort that got them in the top thirty. Overall, we'd placed a respectable ninth out of twenty decent teams. While this was all well and good, there was clearly a cancer, a malignant tumor, on our day in the form of the team of Jeff Slade and me. Slade sat apart from the rest of us, his Walkman turned up so loud we could all hear the furious thumping of Metallica.

Coach arrived with a clipboard and began calmly dissecting our day's performances. Less than half a minute passed before he stopped talking and tilted his head like a dog hearing a high pitched whistle. "What the hell is that noise?" he asked.

Nobody spoke. We glanced at each other and then at Slade. Coach followed our eyes and noticed Slade, his hooded number one sweatshirt on in spite of the nearly ninety-degree heat, the hood pulled up and his eyes down, his music blaring.

Coach stared at Slade then. He stared and stared, seemingly counting on that sixth sense we have that lets us know when we're being looked at. Slade, however, wasn't going to acknowledge him.

"Slade," Coach said. "Slade!" Then he put down his clipboard and walked over to Slade, pulled down his hood, and tore the headphones off his head, pulling the little plug-in out of the side of the Walkman.

Coach stood there, Slade's headphones in his hand, the cord dangling, and there was a moment when you could see

Slade deciding what to do. Should he punch Coach? Should he grab for his headphones? Should he simply tuck his Walkman into the pouch on his sweatshirt and stare while Coach continued on? Well, he did none of those things. What he did was this:

He stood up slowly and breathed deeply, glaring at Coach. An ugly, angry, mean look crossed his face as he reared back and threw his little tape player at the big maple we sat under as hard as he could. When it hit the tree, it didn't explode as I might have thought it would. The cover flew off, the batteries flew out, but otherwise it stayed together.

"That all you got?" said Coach. And then he walked over and picked up the Walkman and threw it just as hard at the tree as Slade had. This time the impact did cause a slight explosion. Some shrapnel hit Swart in the head. "Hey!" he said as he slinked away, arms protecting the back of his skull. The runners who were spread out on the ground near the tree hopped up and moved away.

Slade stared as Coach picked up the Walkman again. "Look," he said quietly, "I'm not done. I ain't completed the job I set out to do. I'd better finish." He threw it again at the tree, causing more bits and pieces to fly off. By this time, everyone had cleared out of the area entirely, trying to avoid flying bits of metal and plastic. Coach went and picked it up yet again.

"If you're gonna start something," he said calmly, "you better damn well finish it." And he threw it one more time against the tree.

We stood there and watched in silence as Coach repeatedly threw Slade's tape player against that tree, time and time again, until it didn't resemble a Walkman at all anymore. There were so many pieces after about the ninth or tenth throw, it might have once been a flashlight, a kid's toy, or a camera. It was when it achieved this state that Coach collected all the pieces he could find, picking them out of the grass and from off the picnic table where we'd been sitting, and took them to Slade.

Slade held out his hands automatically and Coach dumped what was once his Walkman into them. "Learn to finish, Slade. Learn to finish …"

Slade looked down at the pile of trash that had been his tape player. He then looked up and locked eyes with Coach. Neither said a word.

Slade was nearly a foot taller than Coach. His angry blue eyes peered down into Coach's dark brown eyes. The two stood face to face, only inches apart. It was a showdown, a competition of wills if I've ever seen one. Then Slade, without unlocking his eyes from Coach's, shifted the remnants of his radio to his left palm, took up a small shard of metal with his right hand, and placed it in his mouth. Then he began to chew with an awful cracking sound.

Coach jammed his finger into Slade's chest. "Now finish it," he growled.

The bus ride home after every meet, as I was soon to learn, was a ritual heavy with meaning. It was a ritual in that there were rules and procedures, all, of course, unspoken.

One of the rules was that the girls sat in the front of the bus and boys the back. That was true going to and coming home from meets. Another rule was that the best seats were the back seats and those seats belonged to seniors. Generally, age dictated how near the front of the bus you had to sit.

However, if you were a freshman or a sophomore and were *called* to sit in the back of the bus by a senior, then a junior or even a senior lacking in prestige would move forward and you'd get to sit in back.

Slade, by virtue of being team captain and, it should be said, by virtue of being the meanest guy on the team, the guy most prone to actually kicking someone's ass if they didn't do what he wanted, always sat in the back seat. This was where Slade sat on this day, the day that would always be remembered as the day he ate his Walkman. Keane, my brother, and I were called back only minutes into the ride home to serve witness.

"Does it hurt?" Yost asked, a look of disgust and horror on his face.

"Not yet," said Slade. He popped a bit of wire into his mouth and swallowed.

"When he takes a dump," said Bowden, a grin on his face, "that's when it's gonna hurt."

As the city turned to stretches of country and we approached home, Slade showed a side of himself we three privileged Bluebirds hadn't seen before. He was funny. He talked about how it tasted. "Like chicken," he said. He told Swart he was going to keep his crap, the one he would soon have with the undigested portions of the radio in it, in a Tupperware container and bring it in to practice on Monday morning to show him.

"And you can have it!" he told Swart.

"Good mile," he said to me as he prepared to swallow a pill-sized piece that seemed to have once been the volume control. The back of the bus grew quiet when he addressed me.

"Thanks," I said. "Sorry I went out so fast." My eyes dropped.

"You'll learn," he said. "Bet you're happy I pussied out."

I wasn't sure what to say to that, so I just shrugged.

"You know," he said, now talking to all three of us freshmen lucky enough to have been invited to the back of the bus, "you guys could be pretty good."

He didn't eat the batteries. He thought there was acid in batteries or something else that might really hurt him. But he finished the radio about the time our bus rolled back onto the familiar streets of home. When he swallowed the last bit, a metal spring of some sort, the back of the bus erupted in a cheer.

"What the hell's going on back there?" Coach shouted upon hearing our cheer.

"Finished it," said Slade.

"What the hell're you talking about?" Coach said.

"My radio, I finished it!" said Slade.

Coach shook his head. "You gotta be kidding me," he muttered. "How come the only time you idiots listen to me is when I'm totally messing with you." He grabbed his head as if he had a terrific headache. "Oh my God … you're gonna be in the hospital in five hours!"

The bus driver stared, wide-eyed, at Coach. Coach stared right back.

"Well," he said defensively to the gray-haired man behind the wheel of the bus, "how the hell long do *you* think it's gonna take him to shit that sonuvabitch out?"

MY NAMESAKE - THE MOST HEROIC THING YOU EVER SAW - THE CONNECTION BETWEEN FOOTBALL PRACTICE AND TYPING CLASS - CAVE IN - ARMFULS OF DIRT - GRACE UNDER PRESSURE - A BID FOR ATTENTION - "WHAT ARE YOU TRYING TO DO?"

My dad had a favorite coach. His name was Sherman McCord. Sometimes he says I was named after him, other times he says I was named after a guy he was friends with in college who's now a painter in Soho, New York City. Other times he says I'm not named after anybody in particular.

My namesake seems to depend on his mood—what he is valuing at the particular time the origin of my name comes up. When he references Sherman McCord, his mood turns nostalgic and reverential.

"What's the most heroic thing you ever saw?" Hyter asked once at dinner.

It was a family tradition to ask questions around our meal and keep asking them until we happened across a line of stories that would lead somewhere satisfying. Sometimes we went through ten or fifteen questions. "If you were an animal, what would you be?" or "If you could interview any dead person from history, who would it be?" were typical ones. I remember once we even got onto the subject of murder, much to my mother's discomfort. "If you could kill someone at any point in history and get away with it, who would it be?" Hyter asked.

I took the obvious and acceptable way out and killed Hitler. Hyter took the honest and, to my mother, spooky route and killed his fourth grade teacher. Dad killed John Wilkes Booth. Mom wouldn't even think about honoring such a dark question with an answer.

Sometimes it took most of dinner to get to a good question, but that day Hyter asked about the most heroic thing we'd ever seen, Dad responded immediately.

"One September day," he started, "the whole football team was in typing class together."

"Typing?" I asked. "That doesn't seem like something football players would be into."

"They weren't," Dad admitted, poking a baked potato off the serving plate in the middle of the table and putting it on his own. "We all were really bad typists, if I remember correctly."

"How's typing heroic in any way?" asked Hyter. "It's, like, secretarial work."

"It's not heroic," said Dad as he split his spud open with his knife, "but if you let me tell the story, I'll get there."

For a few seconds the only sound was the clinking of plates and silverware.

"So," Dad said when we seemed ready to listen, "we were all in typing." He nodded towards the salt and pepper shakers beside Hyter, who passed them across the table. "We were all in typing because Sherman McCord had insisted on it. You see, the rule was that the teacher who had you for your last class could excuse you at the end of the day when your work was done. And he knew the typing teacher—this old guy named Donovan Smith who had yellow fingers he smoked so much. And he knew ole Donovan didn't take teaching typing all that seriously. So we football players would all get in there, get Donovan's little typing exercise finished in ten minutes, then we'd head out to the football field."

"Seems like they'd have rules against that," said Hyter through a mouthful of green beans.

"Don't talk with food in your mouth," Mom said.

Hyter made a face, and I thought Dad would give him a little lecture, but he was too deeply into his reverie.

"They did have rules against it, but the rule was that practice couldn't officially start until after school. So McCord didn't do any coaching. He just left the balls and the other equipment we used out there so we could use them *if we were so inclined.* And he gave our seniors a plan to follow, *if they were so inclined.* He ended up getting in an extra hour of practice every day."

"What's heroic about that?" I asked.

"I'm still getting there," said Dad. He began shaking pepper onto his potato. "One day, we were all in typing. There was a crew outside digging a ditch to run a water pipe out from the school to the fields. This was back in the fifties, and they weren't using any heavy equipment. It was just a bunch of men with shovels sweating it out, digging that six-foot deep trench out from the school."

"Sounds miserable," Hyter said.

"Another pork chop?" asked Mom.

"We're in there tapping away on our typewriters when we hear shouting coming from where those men are working. 'Cave in!' they're yelling. 'There's a man under there!' someone said. And there was. One of those workmen. He'd been absolutely buried alive—six feet of dirt on top of him."

Dad sat back in his seat to tell the story better. "And," he broke into a big smile, "it was just like Sherman McCord, *just like him*, to be walking out with those bags full of footballs right then and there."

"What'd he do?" I asked.

"McCord was one of those men, you know how strong they are just by the way they look. He'd never gotten in on our drills so we didn't really know how strong he was, but he was over six feet tall and at least two-hundred pounds. We were all scared to death of him and, even though he was kind of old—nearly into his sixties, we all believed he'd be able to toss us around like rag dolls.

"He was that kind of strong you don't see much anymore. He was that strong you get from working on a farm all your life from when you're just a boy. You couldn't see every little muscle on him the way you can sometimes with athletes today, but he was every bit as strong as any of them."

Dad took a drink of his milk.

"Don't stop eating!" said Mom to Hyter and me. "Don't let it get cold."

"Yeah, but what'd he do?" asked Hyter as he picked up his fork.

"Well, we all jumped out of our seats and ran outside. Some of us to see a disaster happen, some of us to help, and some of us just because everyone else was running out of the room. And we got there about the same time McCord did. It couldn't have been twenty seconds after the trench caved in. And those workmen were just staring … they were just staring down where their six-foot-deep hole had been less than a minute before. Only now, it was only a foot deep. There was five feet of dirt on that poor man. And then McCord shouted, 'Dig!' at all of us—us kids and the workmen, too. And that broke the spell. In just a second, dirt was flying everywhere."

"Obviously he didn't die," said Hyter. "The story wouldn't be very heroic if he did."

"No, he didn't die. Sherman McCord saved his life. It couldn't have been much longer than two minutes before we hit his chest then dug out the rest of him as fast as we could until we uncovered his face."

"I'll never forget," said Dad, and there was a glint in his eye when he said it, "the way that man's breathing sounded when we got that dirt off his face. It was almost a howling noise he made, getting the oxygen out of the air. He was howling in reverse."

Dad picked up his fork again.

"Sherman McCord dug most of that hole himself. He was throwing it out of that ditch in armfuls. The rest of us were just scraping away at it." Dad stabbed a bite of potato. "If it hadn't have been for Coach McCord, that guy would've been dead, I guarantee that."

"That's pretty good," said Hyter. And Hyter was tough to please. "You know," he said, always the bore, "In English we learned Hemingway's definition of courage."

"What's that?" asked Dad.

"Grace under pressure," said Hyter.

Dad stuck his bit of potato in his mouth. "That's not bad! Sounds like they're teaching you something worthwhile in that brick-walled monstrosity after all!"

"Sometimes," said Hyter.

"Sherman McCord doesn't sound much like Viddstein," I said.

"Coach is a good coach," said Hyter.

"He's good if getting your runners to eat their radios is good. He's good if letting the seniors try to tape us to trees at morning practice is good."

"What's all this?" asked Mom as she leaned over and stuck a pork chop and dropped it, unsolicited, on my plate.

"Eating a radio!" said Dad. He laughed. "Someone on your team ate a radio?"

"And he cries a lot," I added.

"How come he cries?" asked mom. She hated to hear about people being sad. She sounded sad herself when she asked.

"Doesn't sound much like Sherman McCord to me," said Dad. "Not much grace under pressure in crying in most cases. Crying's usually about surrender. No other options."

"Viddstein's broken down in front of most of the guys," I said, pretending to be disinterested, as if Martin Viddstein was barely worth the breath required to talk about him. But I had Dad's full attention. I could tell. His brow was knit. He put his silverware down. "He told one guy he was going to kill himself," I said, remembering Bowden's comment on the ride to the Hokum Karem.

The room was still. Hyter's eyes were wide, the food in his mouth went unchewed as if he'd forgotten he'd just put some in there.

"This sounds serious," Mom said quietly. "He sounds like he's got some real issues."

"He sure does," said Dad. He picked up his napkin and wiped his mouth. "Does Dr. Billings know about this?"

"I dunno," I said.

"I'd probably better talk to him about that," said Dad.

Later, as my brother and I were getting ready for bed, he whispered to me as we brushed our teeth side by side in the bathroom. "What're you trying to do? Get Coach fired?"

"Yes," I said.

THE SCIENCE OF RUNNING - COACH'S THEORIES - TUESDAY LECTURES - THE LOINS - GENESIS AND ADAM AND EVE - A VERY SHORT STACK OF UNDERWEAR - QUESTION AND ANSWER - NOTHING ABOUT THE HUMAN BODY IS EMBARRASSING - FIVE OR SIX

The science of the human body when pushed to its limits is beyond complex. I used the term "oxygen debt" before. In checking myself, I discovered in the literature on the science of such things that the term is actually incorrect. The answer to why a runner's muscles seize up like an old car engine sans oil when he or she pushes too hard may seem simple: the muscles aren't getting enough oxygen to function. Yet the truth is not so simple. There's *something* to that explanation, but, at least as far as the scientists say, that ain't all of it. The rest of it I couldn't understand, and, I have a sneaking suspicion, neither could most of the scientists.

Go into any running store and you'll discover shelves somewhere burdened with training manuals and guides and they all, to some degree, feel the need to explain what the training they suggest will do to the runner's body. Many of these explanations, you'll discover if you dig in and read and compare one to the others, are ultimately contradictory. The basics are pretty clear, but get into the finer points about the best way to train a human being to run a certain distance as fast as possible and you'll find a lot of different answers.

Well, Coach ignored all those different answers and bought into almost none of those scientific explanations. I've never met a coach, in fact, who cared less about what the authorities said. But he did have many theories of his own.

Coach didn't believe in stretching, before or after a run. He always said, "The cat don't stretch before it chases the mouse." As if that settled it.

He didn't believe in hard and easy days. He said that was only for swimmers. He never explained why swimmers would need hard and easy days when runners wouldn't, as I once asked him. It seemed to me that the two sports were pretty similar.

Also, he didn't believe in treating injuries. He felt that any injury, if the runner simply gimped through it, would ultimately clear itself up. He believed in the human body's mysterious healing powers almost without exception.

And he believed that having sex during periods of competition was disastrous to performance. Judging from the way he talked to us, a bunch of nerdy, greasy, stinky teenaged boys, many of whom wouldn't even kiss a girl until we were old enough to register for the draft, he believed we all had the option of having sex nearly all the time.

During the season, Coach lectured on Tuesdays. On Mondays he gave us Xeroxed copies of his obsessively scribbled notes concerning our Saturday races, which he wrote on Sundays. They were so detailed with each runners splits and so many thoughts jotted down on race strategy that I imagined it took him most of the day to write them. He expected us to read them on our own and pointed out only one or two things he'd found particularly interesting and useful before our Monday workout.

On Tuesdays, however, we learned to expect to settle in on those old wooden benches down in our moldy locker room for at least half an hour while Coach expounded on whatever running-connected theme he decided upon.

"This," whispered Bowden into my ear when we sat down that second Tuesday in September after the Hokum Karem, "is the one we all wait for." He nodded at the freestanding chalkboard at the head of the U. A poorly drawn yet still recognizable outline of the human body filled the middle of the chalkboard. An arrow was drawn to the groin area and the word LOINS was written beside it in all capitals.

It was pretty clear that Coach was fired up and on point as soon as he walked into the room, a piece of white chalk in his hand.

"I am in charge of several aspects," he started, using language, I noted, that was slightly elevated compared to his normal slang-laden chatter, "of your training." He was wearing his owlish glasses too. "Yet, there are many aspects of your lives that I cannot control. As much as I would like.

"You're in my hands only for a short time before school each day when you get your run in and then from three 'til five afternoons on school days. Saturday mornings are for racing. The rest of the time is your own. Now," he began pacing back and forth, head down, pushing his glasses up on the bridge of his nose when they slid down, "whatcha do in all that time I'm not looking over your shoulder is your own business. But there's some things you gotta do if you want to be a great athlete. And," he paused for effect and made meaningful eye contact with us, "there's some things you ought'n do."

"Here it comes," whispered Bowden. He was grinning.

"The male loins," said Coach, pointing at his drawing, which looked like the body outline of a murder victim at a crime scene, "are the source of much power."

Yost, that sour senior, was sitting next to Squid. He must have arrived late and found no other seats available. He nudged Squid in the ribs, and, when he did, Squid had to cover his hand with his mouth to keep from laughing. It was one of the few times Chad Yost acted like a genuine friend to anyone on the team. The fact that it was Squid made it all the more surprising.

"The loins of a man," Coach went on, "some believe, constitute the physical beginnings, the Genesis one might say, of the entire universe." He stopped talking for a moment and tapped the chalk-drawn arrow on the blackboard. "Look, if you'd like, at the Bible when you go home today. You'll find, in the book of Genesis," and he raised a finger to emphasize the use of the word Genesis, how uncanny it was that he'd only moments before used the word himself, "the story of Adam and Eve. Which is the story from which we learn how the human race began."

Popeye looked at Leonardo Chavez next to him. His squinty eye always made him look skeptical anyway. "What's he talking about?" he whispered loudly.

Leonardo, his brown face the blank slate it always was during Coach's lectures, shrugged.

"The power of the human race," continued Coach. Then he pounded once with his fist on the groin area of his drawing, "is in the loins." His face lit up as if he'd made a great connection, a brilliant flash of insight right then and there as he spoke. "The power of *your race* is in your loins," he said, very satisfied with the poetry he'd spun out for us.

This was when my brother raised his hand.

He had been so good those first weeks of school. He smoked it on Angel/Devil, he wore the clothes I'd asked him to, he didn't get caught on that first day of school morning practice when we'd been chased across town, and he'd run a strong Hokum Karem. I was beginning to think high school had changed him. I soon found out it hadn't.

Coach was surprised to see a hand in the air but welcomed any questions. "K2," he said. "What's on your mind?"

"Well," Hyter began, "you say the power of the human race comes from the loins." Hearing him use the word loins caused my head to drop. I stared at my own loins, waiting for him to shut up. "And then you talk about how the human race came from Adam and Eve. But wasn't Eve made with a rib? According to the Bible?"

Coach thought about that. Then he simply tapped on the blackboard in the area of the groin. "The loins," he said with an air of finality. And, thankfully, that shut Hyter up for a little while. But not for good.

"Now, the same power that creates human beings and makes the world go round is the power you use when you run a race." Coach raised his hands as if expecting contradiction, "Now, I know that it's the legs and heart that we train every day. It's the legs and heart that matter most when it comes to distance running. But," and he tapped the blackboard again right where his outline drawing's balls would've been and Victor groaned causing Slade to chortle, "the next most important aspect of racing is the loins."

Coach paused then. It must have been an overly long pause, because I thought, for some stupid reason, that we were done. I thought the lecture was over. And I was glad.

It had been embarrassing to sit there and edge around the subject of sex when I'd not come within shouting distance of any act with a girl that might be categorized as even remotely related. I'm sure Popeye and Leonardo were in silent agreement with me on that. What was worse was that I'd only recently been having issues at home. Very secret issues which had to do with my loins, a part of my body I couldn't seem to control at that particular time in my young life.

"Where are all your underwear?" my mother had innocently, but a little too loudly, asked just the week before as our entire family sat in front of the television. She was folding my brother's and my clothes and putting them on the living room table in front of her, making a stack for my brother and a stack for me.

Hyter's pile of tighty-whities was about seven or eight pairs deep. My stack of boxers (I insisted on this difference. It grossed me out to think I might be wearing his underwear so I chose to wear a style that would ensure my undergarments were not confused with his) wasn't a stack at all. It was one pair. All the others I'd clandestinely thrown down the sewer grate in front of our house in the darkness of early morning.

Nocturnal emissions were what my junior-high health teacher had called them. Nearly every night I was having a wet dream. While my teacher had assured us that these were natural occurrences and nothing to be ashamed of, I couldn't help but look at my soiled underwear as a sign of depravity on my part. Each pair reminded me of the filthy, sometimes bizarre, dreams that ended in a pair of soiled jockeys. So, every morning I woke to find my boxers wet, I'd slip them off and stuff them under my bed. Then, on some predawn morning during the week, I'd get up and sneak outside and throw all that condemning evidence down the sewer grate in front of our house and into the sewer below. The guys at the water treatment plant must've wondered what was going on after about a year of this.

To my mother's question about the location of all my underwear I stuck with that tried and true lie, the best of all lies in its utter vagueness and impossibility to prove false. I said, "I don't know."

My mother, the best mother on Earth I believe, didn't ever confront me about my underwear again. She must've bought me about fifty pairs that fall and winter.

But back to Coach ... the lecture was not over. The lecture had just begun.

"Now," Coach said, erasing with his open palm his drawing, arrow, and the word "LOINS," "the power is in the loins, but one can be more specific. Can anyone tell me," Coach put his now white-and-dusty hand behind his back, "where, in particular, the power that resides in the loins is?"

Victor raised his hand. Coach nodded at him. "The dick," said Victor.

"No, not the dick. Anyone else?"

Slade raised his hand. Coach nodded at him. "Jeff."

"The nuts," said Slade.

"Exactly," said Coach, smiling at his prize student.

Traung leaned over and offered Slade a congratulatory handshake, which Slade graciously accepted.

"The power of the loins resides, more specifically, in the nuts," said Coach. "And what do we call that power in its most elemental form?"

Nobody raised his hand for a moment. Swart's shoulders were hitching up and down he was trying so hard not to laugh out loud. Victor raised his hand again, willing to give it another shot for the team.

"Victor again," said Coach.

"Coach," said Victor, a confident look on his face, "I think you're referring to cum."

"Cum," said Coach. He smiled. "That's right, cum. Also known in the scientific community as semen."

At this, Swart, who was sitting next to Bowden, let loose a loud bark. He then tucked his chin down hard against his chest. His entire body vibrated subtly on his bench seat in his effort not to explode with laughter. His trapped laughter was contagious, however, and Bowden, too, soon had his face covered with his arm.

"Semen is a magical substance that can both produce babies and win races," said Coach, seemingly oblivious to the silent laughter that had taken over the room. "The evidence is clear. The greatest warriors and athletes have always known it. For example, the Spartans of ancient Greece were not allowed to be around women leading up to battle. Boxers, including The Greatest himself, Muhammad Ali, would not and do not have sex before fights. This is because the semen contains the substance that makes us men hungry. It's the stuff that brings out the competitor and conqueror in us." Coach glanced around the room. Swart and Bowden had pulled themselves back together during this explanation. "So, here's the deal. No sex for any of you during the season."

I glanced at Popeye and Leonardo Chavez. Popeye, I was pretty sure, would still enjoy playing with his G.I. Joes more than being confronted with a girl. Leonardo looked like he was about eleven. I didn't think the no sex rule was going to be too tough on them. Or on me either, for that matter.

"Okay, everyone raise your hand now. We're making a team pledge."

We all raised our hands.

"Repeat after me," said Coach. He scowled, "Get your hand up Victor."

When he was sure everyone's hands were in the air, Coach began, "I promise."

"I promise," we replied.

"Not to have sex," Coach said.

"Not to have sex," we all chanted.

"Until after the season," he finished.

"Until after the season," we all said.

Coach clapped his hands together. "Alrighty then! That was good!"

I thought we were done for real then, and we would have been had it not been for my brother. The whole team was standing, shaking hands on their bargains made, Coach was pushing the blackboard out of the way. We were done. Then I heard Hyter's voice. I knew I ought to make a run for it right then.

"Coach," he said. "Coach ..."

At the sound of his insistent voice, everyone stopped what they were doing. The noise stopped. All eyes were on Hyter.

"Yeah K2, what is it?"

"What about masturbation?"

I remembered our health teacher again—a hippy-dippy lady named Miss Teague. She always had a smile on her face, wore a pair of half glasses, and loved to talk about sex. Everything, she said about sex, was natural and good. The human body, she said, was perfect. What it did was simply what nature intended it to do and it was only the strictures of human culture, the stultifying shame-creating rules that human beings made up arbitrarily, that made us so embarrassed by what our bodies did, were, and looked like. Nothing was cause for embarrassment but the prudish way people went about being ashamed of themselves for doing things that were natural.

Well, Hyter took her at her word. I guess he assumed everyone in the room had had Miss Teague for health and felt the same way she did, because when he brought up the subject of masturbation in that room full of high school guys, he didn't seem to have a clue that he might be setting himself up for some serious mockery.

"What'd you say?" said Coach. Although I'm pretty sure he'd heard Hyter. I think he just couldn't believe what he'd heard had been what Hyter had actually said.

"I said, 'What about masturbation?' Can we masturbate?"

At this Swart, who had been on the edge since he'd seen that word LOINS written up on the board, began laughing so hard he couldn't stand. He simply sat down cross-legged on the concrete floor of the locker room and shook.

Coach, ignoring Swart, thought about it. "How much are we talking about, K2? Like, once or twice a week?"

Hyter considered for a moment his answer. My heart stopped.

I thought about it and realized that recently, when we were at home, Hyter was often nowhere to be found. Some-times, in the middle of dinner, he would ask to be excused and return after a few minutes. And this was normal, it seemed, except for the fact that he always used the upstairs bathroom near our bedrooms and not the one right next to the dinner table. And just that Sunday, I'd needed to go to the bathroom myself two or three times over the course of the day and had been surprised, the third time in a row, to find that Hyter was always in there. But I hadn't made any suspicious leaps. Not, anyway, until I saw the look on Hyter's face as he computed his answer to Coach's question. A steam whistle in my head was silently screaming while everyone on the team anxiously awaited his response.

"Five or six," he finally said.

"Five or six times a week?" Coach replied. I could tell he was amazed that Hyter was running as well as he was with all that energy lost.

"Five or six times *a day*," said Hyter without a hint of embarrassment.

I was pretty sure we were going to have to call the paramedics to come and get Swart from off the floor. He was howling so hard I was certain he must've hurt himself.

Coach took his glasses off and stared at Hyter in amazement. "Son," he said, "I'm amazed you even have the energy to stand."

And for this incredible embarrassment, I did not blame my brother. I blamed my coach.

RIDGELINE - BEATING THE HOT DOGS - COACH MAJOR TURNBOW - ELEVEN-TIME REPEATING STATE CHAMPS - EIGHT MILE WARM-UP - FIFTEEN POINTS

"Where are all their varsity guys?" said Swart as the Ridgeline buses unloaded onto the parking lot of our course.

Bowden stared as well. "Widener, Moats, Biddle, Slazenger, Christy ..." he said, rattling off the names of Ridgeline's ridiculously good regular scoring five. "None of them are on there."

"Neither are Russo or Thompson," said Slade. "None of 'em."

"Maybe they were all sick," said Squid. Nobody dignified his remark with a comment. Even Victor allowed it to slide. They were too confused by the absence of our competition to waste their energy on Squid.

It was the middle of September. The weather had turned glorious. Seventy-five degrees every day and long afternoons of the clearest daylight, the deepest blue skies, and cool nights with almost no humidity that allowed you to open the bedroom windows wide and not wake up in a moist bed. Our first dual meet of the year was under our belts. It had been a success primarily because we ran the Frankfort Hot Dogs.

Frankfort's best runner couldn't break eighteen minutes, and he was the only one on their team who stuck with us as we packed it up in the first mile, going through in 5:20. Slade then went on to regain his dignity after the Hokum Karem debacle. The last two thirds of the race, his summer miles were in evidence as he powered through to run a 16:47 and claimed the number one gray hoody for his own. Keane and my brother, known now as "The Champ" or just "Champ" due to his supreme auto-stimulatory feats, followed him in just over seventeen minutes, Keane outkicking Hyter for second. My lack of training throughout August showed itself and I struggled in nearly a minute behind my Bluebird brothers. At that point in the season, my legs were aching. While the cramps in my feet had ceased, going down steps was a challenge. Also, one of my toenails was black. I showed Bowden, but he was unimpressed. "That one's a goner," he said. "Cut your toenails or you'll lose more." Victor was our fourth, fifty meters in front of me. We'd gone one through five for a perfect cross country score of fifteen points. Even though Coach told us on the bus ride home that Frankfort sucked and we shouldn't let our perfect score go to our heads, we'd felt pretty good about ourselves. That was, until we grasped the fact that our next meet was a showdown with the bullies next door, the Ridgeline Salukis.

I mentioned that many people hated the Salukis. It was mostly sour grapes, as they were the best team in the state and the rest of us, at least on some level, wished we were them. But there was more to it as well. The Salukis didn't just beat you; they beat you down. This had everything to do with their coach, a legend by the name of Major Turnbow.

Turnbow came to our county in Indiana in the mid-seventies at the start of the first running boom in America, the one driven by Jim Fixx's famous book *The Complete Book of Running*, which sold over a million copies.

Turnbow was in his twenties then, and he immediately turned Ridgeline into a cross country power. It helped that the little town of Ridgeline grew by leaps and bounds just before and during his era and became known as the suburb of Indy you moved to if you wanted to be a success. Rumor was most of the Ridgeline runners drove BMWs or Mercedes Benzes to morning practice. This was just one of many reasons to hate them.

Turnbow ran with his runners every day, and the intensity of their workouts became the stuff of legend. A former college runner who couldn't give up the Spartan lifestyle or the intense competition, Turnbow was a coach who actually ran with his team, and, in his early days, he could beat all of them, even the state champs. He was among the first of what is now common: he was an actual running coach. Before him, cross country and track coaches were most often simply gym teachers told by their principals that they had to watch over a bunch of skinnies from September until November. These were coaches whose idea of a cross country workout was running around the high school's cinder track ten times. Turnbow was an entirely different species from those guys. A graduate of the prestigious and famously freethinking

Oberlin College, he could've been nearly anything, a lawyer, a doctor, a CEO, but he loved running and had the kind of independent mind that allowed him to ignore the conventions of his time which dictated that smart, ambitious people didn't become high school cross country coaches.

He coached because it was what he most wanted to do, and, as hard as he pressed his athletes and as intense and harsh as he could be with them, his runners loved him for taking them as seriously as he did. They responded by winning eleven state championships in a row and seemed a lock to win my freshman year as well and make it twelve.

The legends about Ridgeline extended beyond Coach Turnbow to his runners and their workouts. Some of Turnbow's early athletes, it was said, had run marathons regularly, during season. They logged the mileage necessary, sometimes nearly a hundred miles a week, so why not? It was often said that the second best team in the state was Ridgeline's jayvee. What we didn't know on that beautiful early fall day as we scanned the buses for Ridgeline's varsity seven was that we were about to become the stuff of Ridgeline Cross Country lore ourselves. And not in a good way.

"Coach," shouted Slade after he and Bowden and Swart had affirmed that Ridgeline's varsity seven weren't on the bus, "what's going on? Where's their varsity?"

Coach shrugged. "How do I know? We run against whoever they put on the line. We run against ourselves. What do I care where they are?"

This wasn't good enough for Bowden. "I'm gonna find out," he said. And he marched over towards the Ridgeline buses to see what he could see.

The Ridgeline athletes all wore maroon and silver Adidas warm-ups. There must have been nearly eighty of them, enough to require two buses, and each of them, I saw to my envy, carried a dark red Adidas bag with Ridgeline written on the side in impressive block letters. Also on their bags were their last names stitched in silver thread under the sleek silhouette of a saluki stretched out in full stride, the saluki being an ancient and regal Persian greyhound. Outfitted like a nation marching in the Olympic Opening Ceremonies, they looked rich and confident. And they didn't just look it, they were.

I was suddenly not amused by Squid's laziness and I was suddenly very conscious of Victor's beat up Cutlass with its ashtray full of cigarette butts sitting next to the Ridgeline buses. I was ashamed of my baggy oversized gray sweats with the number five written under the chin in Coach's hand. Everything about us seemed tawdry and insufficient in the face of the mighty cross country machine that Major Turnbow had built.

Bowden stopped several Ridgeline runners as they walked to set up camp. I couldn't hear, but his gestures indicated the questions that he was asking. The answer he got first seemed to confuse him. A puzzled look crossed his face. Then his eyes grew wide in surprise.

Following one last question, his thick black eyebrows furrowed in anger. He shook his head in what looked like disgust at whatever he'd just heard. The Saluki to whom he was talking gave him an apologetic look, then shrugged and carried on with his business.

"What's up?" asked Victor when Bowden returned to us.

Bowden began to speak, but then laughed and rolled his eyes. He took a deep breath. It seemed he was delaying bad news of some sort.

"What's going on?" said Slade. He was already getting hot, even though he didn't know why.

Bowden laughed again, but it was clear that what he was laughing about wasn't really funny. It was a laugh to keep from yelling, cursing, and throwing a tantrum. "Their varsity's not here yet," he said finally. "They're on their way."

"What do you mean," asked Swart. "They're on another bus?"

By this time our entire varsity had formed a circle around Bowden. All in our gray sweats, we looked like a bunch of bums compared to the Ridgeline runners in their expensive customized sweat suits.

"They're not on another bus," said Bowden. His smile faded completely. He just looked worried.

"Damn," shouted Slade. "Just tell us!"

"They're running here," said Bowden quickly, as if making a confession.

"What?" said Swart, his eyes wide.

"The guy I talked to said they're running here."

"It's ten goddamn miles to Ridgeline," said Victor.

"More like eight," said Swart thoughtfully. "Shit," he whispered. "They could do that . . ." He looked up at the rest of us, a deep frown on his face. "I can't believe they are, but they could ... it's just about the right distance ... not *too* far."

While Keane and I had learned to live by the rule of keeping our mouths shut and seeing what happened next, it seemed my brother never would learn that strategy. "We'll kill 'em," said Hyter happily. "They'll be totally worn out after running that far!"

But the grim looks on the more experienced Hawks and Eagles faces showed they agreed with Swart and believed otherwise. "They run that far most mornings," said Swart. "They train like animals. They're used to it."

Nobody seemed to have anything to say until finally Bowden spoke up. "One of two things will happen here today," he said, his voice quiet and tight. "Either their real varsity is going to run here, and they're going to beat us after an eight mile warm up, or they're going to run their junior varsity and they're going to beat us. Either way, we look like a bunch of complete losers."

"But we can beat them!" said Hyter.

Keane and I disappeared a little then, stepping slightly back and out of the tight circle we'd formed.

"Look, Champ," said Swart, always the logical realist. "Their jayvee runners are better than most team's varsity." He ran his hand through his blond hair and it immediately fell back into a bowl shape around his head. "They'll all be under seventeen. Their jayvee scorers."

"Maybe they'll run their real varsity," said Hyter, looking for some hope in the situation.

"That'll be worse," whined Victor. "They'll kick our asses then turn around and run back home."

It was about then that a quiet cheer and a smattering of clapping arose from the Ridgeline camp. The Ridgeline varsity seven, led by Coach Major Turnbow, the legend himself, came running into the parking lot, finishing the easy eight miles along country roads they'd just logged. They ran in a tight pack and seemed fresh and ready to race.

It turned out that we did run against their actual varsity who had just run from their town to ours before the race. And it turned out they would post a perfect score of fifteen on us. And it turned out that they would run back to their school following our race, logging nineteen or twenty for the day with a mildly hard effort sandwiched in the middle. It also turned out that I came to understand why some people wished the Ridgeline buses would crash and burn, their coaches and athletes roast in their expensive Adidas warm-ups.

I learned that day that there are few better fuels to drive an athlete than pure, unadulterated hatred of an opponent.

LEGIT OR HORSESHIT? - LEONARDO SPEAKS UP - CONTROL WHAT YOU CAN AND IGNORE THE REST - STUPID - RUSSO THE RABBIT - A CONVERSATION BETWEEN SLADE AND MOATS - THE FIRST MILE - TOTAL DISREGARD - RUSSO'S REWARD

"Look," said Swart. "All I'm saying is that they're just preparing to be state champs again! I'm not saying I liked it."

Victor leaned in towards Swart, his finger pointed aggressively at him. "That was horseshit! To do that to another team is classless!"

"I've never heard you worry about the having or not having of class before, Victor," said Bowden from across the U.

"So you agree with Swart?" Victor nearly shouted. "You think what they did wasn't horseshit?"

"I didn't say that either," said Bowden. He let it rest at that.

I agreed with Swart, I thought. But I also was glad that Victor was pissed at him. I thought Swart was going too far by saying it out loud, saying their eight-mile warm-up and cool down was justified, when *we* were the team that looked bad because of their pragmatic indifference to the ideals of sportsmanship.

We were down in the locker room, waiting for Coach and attacking each other. Everyone but us Bluebirds was gnawing away at someone else, bickering, and disagreeing. We knew, should we open our mouths and state an opinion, that we'd get pile-driven or swirlied. Even Hyter seemed to realize how tenuous voicing a thought would be and kept his trap shut.

"Those tools shouldn't have done that," muttered Victor. "And Turnbow's leading them for crying out loud! What kind of asshole coach encourages his team pull that crap? What kind of coach *leads* his team in that kind of stuck-up bullshit against another team? He *required* them to make us look like a bunch of puds!"

"Maybe we shouldn't have let them," said Leonardo.

It was a bold move to speak up on the part of my tiny Central American friend. I believe the only thing that saved him from being jammed into a locker just then was Coach's timely entrance.

Coach whistled happily as he passed out his Xeroxed sheets. Crammed with cramped handwritten notes, arrows shooting across the page linking one idea to another, Coach's handout looked like a crib sheet for a test when the teacher says you can use any information you can fit on one piece of paper. It was jammed with comments and splits for every runner, varsity and jayvee. Coach clearly put hours and hours of work into his notes, but I was sure the Ridgeline runners received feedback in a form that didn't hint at mental illness. I wasn't sure whether to show it to Dad or not as evidence in my case against Martin Viddstein.

Over the previous weeks, since I'd conceived my goal of getting coach fired, I had been collecting evidence. It was not in my father's nature to interfere with a teacher or coach, but I believed I was getting close to making a strong case. If Hyter hadn't stepped in during the loins lecture, I could have used that. Talking about the power of semen with a bunch of teenagers seemed like bad policy to me, but I had to throw it out because I couldn't bear the thought of listening to my brother talk about masturbation with my mom and dad.

"Why didn't you just save some time and write 'pathetic' on a piece of paper and copy that and hand it out to us?" asked Victor.

"That wouldn't have been specific enough," said Coach happily. "I wanted you to know in *exactly* what way each and every one of you is *particularly* pathetic."

"Thanks for caring," groaned Yost.

"Look," Coach said, hands on hips, "You guys wanna bitch and moan, I'll leave for one minute and then, when I come back, you're done."

He waited for someone to say we wanted to bitch and moan. Nobody did.

"Okay then. Let's figure out something we can learn here. Make goddamned lemonade from these lemons."

"Ridgeline's ten times better than us, can we deduce that?" said Yost.

"Yost," said Coach, "You shut the hell up. If you don't have anything constructive or hopeful to say, don't say anything at all."

Yost pantomimed turning a key next to his mouth. He then threw the invisible key over his shoulder.

"That should be the last any of us ever hear from Yost," said Bowden under his breath.

"Okay then," said Coach with a sigh. "Forget them and what they did. Focus on what you can control and ignore what you can't. What you couldn't control yesterday was this—you couldn't tell 'em not to make you look stupid by running to our course, beating you like a drum, and then running back home without giving the courtesy of even looking in your face and acknowledging you."

"That's not true," said Victor, rising up off his bench seat in agitation. "Moats, that big bald bastard, acknowledged Slade at the starting line. Slade made him acknowledge him." Victor slipped his hand out and Slade tapped it. "Called him a piece of shit," Victor said proudly as he sat back down. "To his face."

"You called Moats a piece of shit?" asked Coach looking at Slade.

"I might have," said Slade, a hint of a smile edging up the corners of his mouth.

"Why didn't you just beat him?" said Coach. "You could've, y'know ..."

Slade's smile disappeared.

"He only ran 16:50." Coach's brown eyes were intent on Slade. "You've run faster than that with no competition. Just last week at Frankfort. You at least coulda made him kick to beat you."

Slade looked at the floor.

"I'll tell you why you should be upset," he said to the room in general. "And it's not because you lost. We're all gonna end up losing some time or another. It's because you were stupid and you let your pride get the best of you." He was pacing now. "The fact that they ran here and showed us up, we couldn't control that. That was their choice. But what we could control, we didn't. And that's stupid." Coach pointed at Keane. "What was your first mile split?"

Keane looked at his sheet. "4:56," he read.

"What was yours?" he asked Hyter.

"4:56," Hyter replied.

"Yours?" he asked Slade.

"4:53," said Slade.

"You know what that big bald piece of shit Moats' first mile was, Slade?"

Slade fidgeted on his bench. "No," he said.

"Of course you don't. He was too far behind you at the mile mark for you to have any clue what he ran." Coach picked up a piece of chalk from the blackboard tray. 5:18, he wrote on the board. "And that's still faster than his average mile had to be to run a 16:50. With a 5:18 he had seven seconds in the bank. 16:50 breaks down to three miles at 5:25."

As we stood at the line the previous day, the Ridgeline runners, it was true, hadn't even looked at us. Well, except for Moats when Slade called him a piece of shit. We might not have been there for all they cared. When Slade cursed Moats, the tall lanky runner with the shaved head, Moats had grinned at him.

"Just hang on as long as you can," Moats had said as if he were talking to a child. "We'll pull you through to a PR Of course," he added pleasantly, "we can't let you break up our pack." His smile disappeared. "That's not happening today. Or ever."

At the sound of the gun, one maroon-and-silver-clad Saluki broke to the front of the pack in a near flat-out sprint.

It was Dennis Russo, I was later to learn, a sophomore not usually in the Ridgeline scoring five.

Slade and Victor's blood was boiling, and they took off hard on Russo's heels through a blistering first half-mile just over two minutes and twenty seconds. The rest of our team, whatever our separate and unspoken feelings about Ridgeline's decision to run to their race against us, had joined Slade and Victor in the suicidal chase.

"You all," said Coach pointing to the 5:18 on the board, "got suckered. What did Russo end up running? Anyone know?"

Hyter raised his hand. "Champ," said Coach.

"He ran a 17:34," said Hyter. "He was the only one of them that any of us beat."

Coach put his index finger to his lips, his brown eyes sparkled. "Hmmmm, I wonder if Russo thought he was gonna win that race? Kitty-Cat?"

Todd Mankato's head jerked back slightly at the sound of his own name.

"What did you think? You think Russo thought he was gonna win that race? You think that sophomore figured he'd run away from John Biddle, third in the state last year?"

"No?" It came out more of a guess than an answer.

"That's right," said Coach. "Russo *didn't* think he was gonna win that race. Ever. Russo was a rabbit, and you were a bunch of stupid hounds that went out too fast chasing him."

Coach sat down on the bench next to Leonardo. "Leonardo's right," he said quietly. "You shouldn't have let them go for a perfect fifteen against you." He scratched at the thin black beard he'd started. "It musta hurt when that pack of six guys ran by you." He glanced across the U at Victor. "Did that hurt, Victor, when all six of those guys went by in a pack?"

Victor didn't say anything. He stared at the floor.

"Did that hurt, Slade? When that big bald piece of shit Moats went by with his five teammates?" Coach stood and took center stage again. "They was talking, wasn't they?" he said with a big grin on his face. "It looked like they was talking from where I stood. Tell me the truth. They was chatting like a buncha girls at a lunch table."

Slade didn't answer, but I could testify that they had been. They'd been talking about the run home, how they might be able to get Turnbow to let them take a shorter route. That was how slight their regard for us had been. They hadn't even been thinking of us *during* the race.

"Here's exactly what happened, if you didn't get it by now," said Coach. "On the jog over, Turnbow tells Russo that he's gonna have to fall on the grenade and hurt for the team by running a kamikaze first mile. He knows you guys're gonna be so mad after seeing his guys run to the meet that your emotions'll get the best of you and you'll do something stupid. He tells the other guys to let you go and run even splits, knowing that they're gonna run away with the meet because you guys'll all be trashed after chasing their rabbit for the first mile." Coach clapped his hands together with a loud pop. "And that's just what happened."

As I sat there, I saw that coach was right. His notes might look like a letter from an insane asylum, but they were, I had to acknowledge, on the mark. He might bawl in his car, permit hazing, and encourage his runners to eat their radios, but he obviously knew something about racing. This didn't change my feelings for the man.

As we put our notes in our lockers and prepared to go run, Coach added one last thing. It was a detail that showed just how observant he could be.

"Anyone but me notice, when those guys took off after the race, running back to Ridgeline, how many of 'em was running?"

Nobody had.

"There was seven of 'em, including Turnbow," he said. "One less than they came to our place with." He flashed a knowing smile. "Russo got a reward for falling on the grenade. He got to ride home."

KOALA-SIZED HAIR - TRASHY/HOT - STRINGS ATTACHED - MATCHMAKER - CHEMISTRY - SENIOR GUYS AND FRESHMAN GIRLS: WHY IT SHOULDN'T HAPPEN - SCARE TACTICS - MY CAT - HAIRSPRAY - THE INVISIBLE FLAME - PROBLEM SOLVED

A girl in my class had the most amazing hair. Her name was Danielle Jameson and her hair was the size of a koala. A good-sized koala. A thirty pounder. Imagine a thirty-pound koala clinging to a girl's scalp and you'll get an idea of how big her hair was. If koala doesn't work as a visual, then it was the size of a huge Thanksgiving turkey. It was kind of that shape, too. Except for the claw in front.

The claw was a fixture of adolescent and post-adolescent girls' hairstyles that reached its apex just before grunge hit and overnight suburban white kids' hair went oily, flat, and dingy.

I remember one girl squealing to another when they first saw each other at prom. "Your hair's *so big!*" she said. "Yours is *even bigger!*" her friend squealed back. These were compliments.

It would be a push to say that Danielle and I were friends, but we had a couple of classes together, and I talked to her when our teachers allowed us to talk. She was pretty in a trashy way. I'd thought about what it would be like to make out with her quite a lot by the second or third week of school, but I wasn't terribly interested in her and she certainly wasn't interested in me.

While Danielle wasn't exactly an illustration of what I would've chosen in a mate, her towering hairspray-spun confection which extended nearly half a foot from her forehead in a wave-shaped coiffure attracted a certain type of guy like gaudy flowers draw honeybees.

Her face was sharply angled and a little cruel-looking, a look she accentuated by wearing blood-red lipstick and heavy, dark eyeliner. Also, she was somewhat tall, had a tiny waist, a minimal behind, and huge breasts for a girl as thin as she was. She was only fourteen, just like me, but she looked like she longed for the bar scene of some cheesy Florida spring break town—Fort Myers or Daytona.

Once he'd laid eyes on her, Jeff Slade believed he'd discovered the perfect woman.

Since we'd watched Slade eat the radio on the back of the bus, there had been a change in his attitude toward all us Bluebirds and towards me in particular. Just as I'd hoped on that day Bowden told us the story of how Slade stole a man's own shotgun one summer night out on Promise Road and beat him with it, Slade had gone from being a violent lunatic opposed to my existence to a violent lunatic advocating my existence.

Overall, the change felt pretty good. But there were strings attached. The first was that I had to introduce Jeff Slade to Danielle Jameson. Complicating matters was the fact that I'd heard during our runs what Jeff Slade did with the girls he dated.

While it was great listening material, and, I'm sure in the case of my brother the pornographic basis of many minutes of solitary pleasure, I didn't want any part of any matchmaking Slade might have in mind. It seemed immoral to me to hook up anyone I might even consider a friend in the most remote way with Jeff Slade. He was, after all, legally an adult, being over eighteen years old. And also, of course, he was crazy.

"K1," said Slade as we jogged through the park one early morning in late September, the leaves just beginning to turn from green to yellow, "you gotta hook me up with that girl."

"Which one?" I asked, although I knew he meant Danielle. I'd been avoiding his hints for nearly a week when he cut to the chase, no longer able to contain himself.

"You know, the one with those sweet-ass chest puppies that sit up and bark at me when you come out of chemistry. The slutty looking one ... with the hair."

Even if statutory rape laws didn't exist, freshman girls shouldn't date senior guys. It's a bad situation, mostly because the two parties don't want the same things. At all.

Freshman girls who date senior guys, in many cases, want prestige. They want other freshman girls to know they're dating a senior. The most important audience for girls, almost all the time, is other girls. Guys barely notice anything, which makes them a terrible audience. But it's not just that vain desire that causes some fourteen-year old girls to go out with eighteen and nineteen-year-old guys.

At a deeper level, they want a real relationship and not just some childish pantomime of one. They want a real man and freshman guys don't fit that category. Freshman guys are not real men—nowhere near. Anyone who'd rather light a fart or see if he can drink a gallon of milk without puking instead of taking a girl out to dinner is not yet a real man. So, some girls skip past playtime and move up to seniors.

Senior guys who choose to date freshman girls? I think we all know what they want.

"Can you hook me up?" Slade asked on that morning's run.

Of course, I couldn't say no.

In chemistry class that day, our task was to melt something in a test tube. I can't remember what it was, but we had on the lab coats, the gloves, and the goggles. We looked like a bunch of mad scientists.

Danielle was on one side of our table and I stood on the other. It was pretty mindless work, actually. The teacher had gone through exactly what would happen during each step of the experiment, explaining the point of each lab note we were to take. That didn't mean there wouldn't be any surprises that day in chemistry.

"Danielle," I said as I poured some yellowish granular substance into a test tube. "Do you think you'd ever date a senior?"

"Why?" said Danielle. She was a no-nonsense kind of woman when it came to dating.

"Well," I said, pouring a couple of ounces of water into the test tube from a beaker, "I know this guy ..."

"*You* know a guy?" she said dubiously.

"Well," I said, "maybe."

Danielle rolled her eyes.

"What?" I asked.

She sighed. "You're a runner. You're a freshman runner."

"What's that got to do with anything? And you're a freshman, too," I said. "Don't forget that."

She pulled an end of her gum from her mouth and twirled it around her index finger. "No offense," she said, "but you guys, runners, aren't exactly my type. And I'm sure the only senior guys you know are runners."

"Well," I said, suddenly a little offended, although she was right—I didn't know any seniors except the guys on our team and ninety-nine percent of cross country runners would not have appealed to a girl like Danielle. "This guy isn't your typical cross country runner." I pointed at the little flint scratcher we used to light the Bunsen burners. "Hand me that, please."

She leaned across the table, which was a pretty good stretch, and it made me wish she wasn't wearing that bulky lab coat. It hid her best features. She handed me the lighter. "Who is it?" she asked sounding bored.

"His name's Jeff Slade. He's about—"

But before I could continue describing him, Danielle's eyes lit up and she gasped. "Jeff Slade! Oh my God."

"You know of him?" I said.

"Know of him!" she gushed. "I dream of him! He could be in a band!"

"Well, he knows of you, too."

I lit the burner in a couple of tries, although it was hard to tell that I'd succeeded. The flame switched from blue to purple to yellow and then, when I turned the gas up as high as it would go, it became nearly invisible. Confused by its invisibility, I stupidly put my finger where the flame should've been and quickly discovered it was, indeed, burning.

"That was stupid," said Danielle, distracted from the thought of Jeff Slade for a moment by my quiet cursing over my new blister.

"Thanks," I said as I sucked my finger.

Danielle looked at me funny.

"That was sarcasm," I explained.

When she looked even funnier at me I took my finger out of my mouth and said, "Never mind."

"But what about Jeff Slade?" she whined as soon as she remembered what we'd been discussing.

At this point, I was of two minds. I was thinking Danielle was kind of a jerk for not caring more about my burnt finger, and that she was obviously stupid to have a crush on Jeff Slade, who, it was clear to me, would use her like a Kleenex and throw her away when she got boring, which, based on my limited experience with her, wouldn't take all that long. I was thinking maybe I ought to just hand her over and let Slade chew her up and spit her out. But the good angel on my shoulder was looking out for my fellow freshman. I couldn't allow even a nincompoop like Danielle to get worked by the likes of Slade.

What I had to do, I realized, was tell her Slade was hot for her, while at the same time persuading her not to go out with him. And I had to do it in a way that wouldn't allow her to realize that I was against her dating Slade. If it got back to him that I'd warned her off him instead of talking him up, I'd be back on Slade's hit list for sure.

I decided to tell her exactly what Slade had been saying, my theory being that she'd get scared.

"Well," I said as I held the test tube over the burner using a little wire grip, "Slade is crazy about you."

"Really!" she said. Her black ringed eyes opened wide.

"Yeah. He says he'd love to get you in the back of his van."

Stupidly, I believed this would be shocking enough, that Danielle would shy away at the word "van" and all its sordid connotations, end of story. I was very wrong.

"What does he say he wants to do to me in the back of his van?" she said slyly.

Suddenly, I was on my heels. "Well, I can't remember … let me think …" I scrambled to find my rhetorical feet.

Danielle tapped the eraser of the pencil she was using to take our lab notes with on the table. She was feeling her teeth with her tongue in anticipation.

"He said he wants you to …" I began, but it was suddenly hard for me to speak. I clammed up. For the next minute or more I just kept saying, "You know! He wants to …" and I'd spin my hands around in the air as if that meant something.

I had to actually say something if I was going to scare Danielle, so I went beyond what I ever thought would sound legit to her. I went for a shocker right away, hoping to end with one disgusting sexual reference what had become a surprisingly difficult discussion.

"He wants you to suck his …" I said. I raised my eyebrows twice and did the hand thing again because I couldn't go through with it and say what I thought I was going to say. But I didn't have to. Danielle got it.

Instead of a look of horror crossing her face as I had expected, Danielle smiled a little knowing smile. "What else?" she asked, not even blinking. I noticed she was leaning in closer to me across the table, her rear end swaying back and forth. She reminded me of our horny cat.

"Well," I said, trying to come up with something else that might scare her. "He said he wants to get rough with you, you know? Like he wants to spank you or something. He says he likes it that way."

She smiled a dreamy smile and nodded. "So," she said, "he's one of those."

This wasn't working at all. Instead of deterring her from going out with Slade, I was clearly stoking the fires of her passion.

Meanwhile, our chemistry experiment was continuing smoothly, much more smoothly than my effort to keep Danielle from dating Slade. The next step, according to my directions, was to remove the solution made from the yellowish solid and the H_2O from the heat of the burner. I placed the test tube, now containing a boiling yellow liquid, into the test tube holder we'd been given.

"He said," I went on after I read that we were now to allow the solution we'd made to cool for five minutes, and I tried to think of the worst thing a guy could do to a girl. Nothing was coming to mind.

"He said," I repeated, "that he wants to tie you up in the back of his van and have sex with you. And he wants to keep you in there, and he wants to have sex with you anytime he wants. You'll be, like, his hostage?" It came out as a question, and I attempted to make up for my lack of conviction by cringing at how awful it would be.

"Sold," said Danielle in a voice that sounded more like a purr.

Danielle, I saw, was physically aroused by my simple descriptions of what Slade was going to do to her. I dared not go on for fear that she would lose control of herself right then and there in class. Also, I couldn't think of anything nasty enough to deter her. That was obvious. I'd failed.

"He's so bad," she said in a low growl, her eyes sparkling and alive. She stretched her hands out across the table toward me, her lab coat opening slightly. She was rubbing herself against the table. "What else did he say he wanted to do to me?" she whispered, leaning even closer.

Earlier, I mentioned Danielle's hair—how big it was. I also mentioned the flame on the Bunsen burner—how it was invisible. I didn't mention yet what hairspray is made of, but it's important to what happened next.

Hairspray is mostly composed of water and alcohol. Alcohol is flammable. In fact, one of Squid's favorite things to do, when left unsupervised, was to collect all the aerosol cans in his house, many of them different hairsprays his mother had tried, and see which made the biggest fireball when he sprayed their contents into a lit flame. One of the cans of hairspray always won.

Now, Danielle's claw was one of the biggest in our school. She told me once that she got up at five every morning, and that it took her nearly two hours to prep every day. She said much of that time was spent spraying her hair—her claw, although she never would've called it that—into place. It took layer upon layer of hairspray to achieve the volume she insisted upon. She went through nearly a can of Aquanet every morning, she bragged.

Once, when Squid threw a can of his mother's hairspray into a fire pit, the explosion was enough to make the neighbors come running. And that can, Squid kept saying after the fact and in amazement, was only half full.

As she leaned over the table and her hair came within range of the clear flame of the burner, it began to react the way cotton candy reacts to water. It began to crinkle and shrink back towards her forehead. In a matter of seconds it nearly disappeared. She kept smiling her dreamy smile, but all the while, her hair was shrinking, turning into what looked like tiny black worms coming out of her head.

I couldn't find any words. I simply pointed at her forehead, my eyes wide, until she snapped out of her drowsy eroticized state and began screaming and slapping herself on the top of her head like Larry, Curly, and Moe did on *The Three Stooges* when they were really frustrated about something.

By the time she got the fire out, all that was left of her once monumental hairball was a black stinky splotch on her forehead. "I look awful!" she said.

I kept my mouth shut. She did. She was half-bald. She looked like a Barbie some boys with a lighter had gotten hold of.

As we left class that day, Slade was standing just outside our classroom, ready to reap the rewards of my introductory discussions with Danielle. Instead of a worshipful freshman girl, however, he was met by the toxic stink of burnt hair. Danielle slipped quickly away down the hall, her books covering her head, before he could talk to her.

"What the hell's wrong with her?" demanded Slade.

"She burnt her hairball off."

"On purpose? She had a great hairball!"

"No, not on purpose."

Slade, unconsciously I'm sure, felt his own heavily sprayed mullet, making sure all was well up there. "Damn," he said. "She looked like a girl I could get serious with."

"It'll just be a little while," I said helpfully, "before her hair grows back."

"I can't wait that long," said Slade. He shook my hand. He could be oddly formal at times. "Thanks anyway, brother."

I replayed him calling me brother in my mind the rest of the school day. All had, amazingly, turned out well. That harmony and balance would not last long.

In fact, only a few days later, I blew the whole thing up.

ANYONE ELSE - LECTURE TUESDAY - THE INDIAN AND THE STAR: A FABLE - BEARS, LIONS, AND ELK - THE GREATEST WARRIORS - A MACHIAVELLIAN PLAN - THE TRUTH MUST OUT

There is something about brothers. If Coach had suggested I try to be like anyone else, whether Truong, Yost, Keane, even Squid … if he hadn't said my model should've been *Hyter*, things would've been different. That's not to say they would've played out for the best.

I believe what happened *was* for the best ultimately, but that doesn't mean it was easy. In fact, it couldn't have been much harder. But hard is good. Hard is what makes us who we are. All I'm saying is that it wouldn't have happened the way it did if Coach hadn't compared me to Hyter. He meant it as a compliment and a challenge in the best sense of a challenge, I can see that now. But there's just something about brothers …

It was a Tuesday. Coach was in form. His subject: the power of setting goals. He spoke that day in metaphors and fables. He spoke of bows and arrows and stars in the night sky and a young Indian trying to be great. It was hard to follow, actually. I think he made it up on the spot.

"An Indian boy," he said as he sauntered back and forth in front of his blackboard, the word GOALS! written large enough to fill it, "wanted to impress his village. He knew that the greatest warriors showed their greatness by bringing down the greatest prey. Grizzly bears, lions, elk …"

Hyter's hand went up. You'd think Coach would've stopped calling on him after the LOINS! Lecture, but he didn't. "Champ," he said impatiently. "What'cha want now?"

"That sounds really *great* and all," Hyter grinned and glanced around, waiting for approval. Nobody got it so he hurried on. "And I'm very interested in where this is all leading us, but those animals don't live together. Not in the same environments, I mean."

"Goddamit," sighed Yost, his knee bobbing spastically. "You're an idiot. Just let him finish so we can go run."

"They don't," said Hyter, a little offended. "How can the Indians in the village in this particular story kill *those* three animals? There are no bears or elk in Africa and Africa is the only place lions live. Unless he means mountain lions—cougars." His face turned pensive. "Actually, there are some lions in Asia too, not mountain lions but real lions, but there aren't any elk or bears there. At least not Grizzlies. Those only live in North America. Elk too. Actually, it could work if …"

"Shut the hell up," interrupted Victor.

"Fine," said Hyter, his hands palms up in submission as if he recognized, for once, his tendency to ramble. "I'll shut up."

"Okay then," said Coach to Hyter. "And you," he pointed at Victor, "watch your mouth."

"Look who's suddenly all holier than thou," said Victor. "Captain Curse-a-lot. I'll watch my mouth when you start watching yours."

"Shut up," said Coach, "and let me get on with this so we're not here 'til tomorrow. Anyways, this Indian boy, he knew the greatest warriors killed the greatest animals," he glanced at Hyter, "whatever the hell those animals were for where he lived … is that satisfactory K2?" Hyter nodded. "And he wanted to outdo everyone who ever killed an animal before him because he wanted to be the greatest Indian of all time. So, the Indian boy knew he'd have to do something pretty special. One night, he looks up in the sky and sees the stars. He's with his dad or something, and he says, 'Has any Indian ever killed a star?'"

Coach paused, not to see if Hyter wanted to comment, but for dramatic effect. He raised his eyebrows and put his finger up in the air as if to say *this is getting good*. He went on. "'No,' says the dad, 'no Indian has ever killed a star. It's impossible,' says the dad, 'Impossible.'"

And that's where things went weird. There was something about the boy shooting his arrow all night and all day up in the air. "And it would come down," said Coach, making a big deal of looking down on the locker room floor as if staring at the Indian boy's arrow, "and the boy would shoot it back up," making a big deal of pointing up at the ceiling.

In the end, the boy shot himself with his own arrow, I think. Or maybe he just died of old age, but he never stopped shooting that arrow. In any case, it didn't really work out for the boy. Coach seemed pleased, though.

"K1," he said as we restlessly waited down in that dingy locker room for the moral of the story so we could go do our workout, "you'll be a state champ one day if you can focus like that Indian boy." And at this, I was no longer so anxious to get out of there. I was flattered, in fact. As long as Coach kept saying my name and speculating on how great I was going to be, we could stay down there forever as far as I was concerned.

By that point in the season, my hatred for Coach had been eroding as the troubles he had had a hand in creating for me—Slade, my brother, the first day of school—evolved or softened with time. The chronic soreness in my legs was fading. As I approached forty miles a week, subtle changes were happening to my body. The veins in my arms seemed more prominent, and the individual muscles in my thighs more defined. I liked the changes Coach had wrought in me. Had he not gone on and compared me unfavorably to my brother, I believe things would've been different. But he did.

"You and Keane, you'll all three be state champs," he said, *"if you can just focus like your brother."*

He smiled after he said it. He meant no dishonor, but I was back, in the time it took to utter that one benign little sentence, to being his constant victim. At least in my screwed up head.

During the run that day, I formed a Machiavellian plan that scares me now when I realize that I, as a fourteen-year old, was capable of conceiving it.

It was very simple, I realized as I silently jogged next to my brother and Keane, half-hearing them laugh about the Indian boy and his arrow. Coach was too messed up to defend himself. I didn't need evidence. I didn't need the truth. The man was a lunatic. I just needed to get him in the same room with the school principal for five minutes, keep my own mouth shut, and provide him the opportunity to destroy himself. My story wouldn't even matter.

A SACRED PLACE - THIRTY MINUTES - MY CRIMINAL BRAIN - THE RIGHT TOOL - COUNTDOWN - BLOOD - EDGAR ALLAN POE - INCAPABLE OF EVIL

Behind our house stood a small, neatly kept, single-car garage. The smell in there was a complicated bouquet of masculinity. The scents of dirt, paint thinner, grass, rubber, wood, and gasoline were all present. I loved that smell. And it was so quiet in there. Even with the big sliding wooden door open, the murmur of cars passing on the street and neighborhood dogs barking seemed remote. When the door was shut, it was so quiet you noticed it. You listened to it as if silence was a sound itself.

Light slanted in the dust-coated, opaque windows illuminating the dust motes that floated about in a sleepy, magical way. It was a magical place. When I was a kid, I used to go in there when I was in need. If I was lonely or bored, if I was angry or sad, I knew if I just went in there and sat for a while, things would change. I never went back in there in that way after what I did to defile that sacred space that Tuesday afternoon. On that day, I ruined it.

After hurrying home from practice, I had about thirty minutes to execute my plan.

"Mom? Dad?" I shouted up the steps of our house. The cars were gone. Nobody seemed to be home. I had to be sure. "Hello?"

Luckily, Hyter had agreed to help Popeye with some math homework. I'd left the two of them down in the locker room, still in their stinky sweats, a book open between them. Hyter was taken care of, so was Coach. Just after our run that day, I visited him in his office.

"What am I doing?" asked Coach as he wrote a note to himself on his desk. "Got an idea for next week's lecture. I'm just getting it down here." He added about four exclamation points to his note and then threw it in his desk drawer. He looked up, giving me his full attention. "I don't know what I'll do now. Guess I'll drive out to the lake. Get a little run in myself."

"Just you?"

Coach laughed. "What? You worried about me K1? Don't worry. I can take care of myself."

My devious little criminal brain crackled with pleasure. He wouldn't have an alibi.

Twenty minutes later, I pulled open the garage door. The air seemed filled with electricity. The familiar smell of the place filled my nose. Tools hung from the red-brick-colored pegboard on the wall. The garage was empty. I pulled on a chain. A bright 100-watt bulb lit up the space.

I slid the door closed behind me. Nobody could see what I was about to do.

Standing in front of the tools, I considered my options. A hammer? It seemed too hard and focused an instrument, not at all like a fist. I pulled a large pipe wrench from between two pegs. Still not right. The edge on the wrench might resemble knuckles, but the blow would possibly cause a cut. I didn't want to go to a hospital. I didn't want to have to explain my wound to a doctor. Then I saw it.

At first, I wondered what its purpose was. I later asked. Years later, when the whole episode was a distant memory. "It's for pounding on things you don't want to dent or scratch the way a regular hammer would," my father told me. "Like when you pound a piece of wood in place and don't want to mark it up. It's a rubber mallet."

The head of it was about the same size as a man's fist. As I judged its weight, swinging it about in front of me, I felt that it was plenty heavy to do the damage I needed to do.

Hitting yourself in the face is not an easy task. As I stood there in the garage, I began counting backwards from ten. The silence was broken when I heard my own voice say the word, "ten." I knew when I got to zero I would bring the mallet head hard to my eye. Nine and eight panicked me. Seven got me under control. Six, five, and four I said loudly and slowly, my conviction growing. Three and I found myself angry. Two and I was certain I was doing the right thing. One, I was truly committed. I never said zero.

As I sat in the garage on a little wooden stool, blood dripped from my eye onto the dusty concrete. Leaning slightly one way or the other, I directed the drips of red and watched as two dots became one larger dot as a third joined them. For twenty minutes at least, I sat and silently created patterns with my blood on that concrete floor. It was the behavior of a madman, some psycho straight out of Edgar Allan Poe. Nobody saw that madness in me though. Everyone believed me.

"What on Earth!" my mother shouted when I shambled into the kitchen holding the sweaty T-shirt I'd worn to practice that day against my eye. I'd cleaned the blood up off the garage floor with it and arranged it for dramatic effect, bloody side out. "Did you get in a fight? Was it a classmate of yours?"

"I'm not talking about it until Dad's here," I said.

When he and Hyter arrived, I told my tale. We were alone in his office after practice. I asked him not to cuss so much. He became enraged and punched me in the eye. "He called me bad names when he did it," I moaned. My mother was near tears, my father's fists tightly clenched.

Hyter's face expressed utter confusion. "I don't get it," he said. "It just doesn't *seem* like him." He looked at me. "You asked him not to cuss so much? Why'd you ask him that? You love it when he cusses."

"Look at my eye!" I shouted, removing the clean rag my mother had given me, revealing an ugly purple bump. The rubber mallet had been the right choice.

"I see it," said Hyter, "I'm just saying. It doesn't seem like something Coach would do."

"Well, he did! I didn't do this to myself!" I wished, as soon as I said them, that I could take those words back. But nobody heard them the way I feared they would.

The bottom line was that I was a kid and I took advantage of that. Being just a kid, a Bluebird freshman, nobody believed I had it in me to make up such a vile, malicious lie. Kids are innocent, incapable of evil. That was the myth I relied upon.

"You'll have to be there, son," said Dad after hanging up the phone following his conversation with Dr. Billings, the principal. "We're going to meet with your coach and principal tomorrow afternoon. You'll have to be brave about it. Everyone's got to know the truth."

I had no idea how hard it was going to be.

THAT FATEFUL WEDNESDAY MORNING - DEAD ON THE FLOOR - GOD'S GAME - "YOU'RE A GOOD MAN" - THE POSSIBILITY OF BEING KICKED OUT

"Let's just go," groaned Yost. "We know what we're supposed to do."

It was a cold, damp morning, the kind that inspires the notion, the deep longing really, to just go back to bed rather than go for a run. When the weather isn't pleasant, you have to jump into the day like it's a cold swimming pool. We still had our toes in the water.

"I wonder where he is," Bowden said. He pulled back the sleeve of his sweatshirt and looked at his watch. "He's fifteen minutes late." He looked toward me, "Dude, that eye looks awful. How'd you say you did that again?"

"It happened yesterday after practice," said Hyter, eyeing me nervously. Our family had agreed that we should keep the truth of my injury to ourselves until after my meeting with the principal that afternoon. I'd worn my hooded sweatshirt that morning, I was number four then, and pulled my hood up, obscuring my face. I didn't speak much that morning and wasn't challenged on my near silence. Hyter had avoided lying by simply insisting on when it happened and avoiding the question of how.

"It doesn't look that bad," said Slade, yawning. "My dad's given me worse. Let's do this if we're gonna, I'm thinking I'm sleeping in the car unless we hit it right now."

"I've got to pee," I said.

"Not in the locker room bathroom," said Bowden. "Coach didn't unlock it yet. I already tried. Piss down the shower drain like I just did."

"Gross," said Leonardo.

"Remind me to wear flip flops in there," yawned Popeye.

"Go down the hall," growled Yost. "Third door on your left. We're gone in sixty seconds. With or without you."

And that was when I found him, dead, I thought, on the wrestling room floor. That's when he told me the secret. It was such a strange encounter, and I was so shocked by it that I barely thought about my own dark secret—my attack on myself that was also an attack on the good man before me.

He sighed. "My family," he said. "My wife ... I been kicked out."

"You've been kicked out of your family?" I said. It didn't seem possible. Your family was your family. There was no kicking out allowed. The child in me insisted on this. It was too terrifying to even consider.

"My house ... I been kicked outta my house. Ahhh, hell . . . my family too." Coach's face crumbled. He raised his hands and covered his eyes. He wiped his tears away and went on. "I ain't allowed to see my boy or my girl. My babies. My damn wife … she got herself a lawyer …" He looked up and his eyes met mine. He steeled himself against a thought. His face hardened. "You boys're the only family I got now. This team … that's all I got."

I touched my eye and thought of the meeting Coach didn't yet know about.

"What the hell happened to your eye?" Coach asked, touching his right eye in a sympathetic gesture. "That looks like it musta hurt."

I touched my eye again. "I don't know," I said.

"Jesus! It looks like someone hit you with a mallet!"

This jolted me. It seemed uncanny that he should say that. I had a trippy solipsistic moment then in which the world, Coach included, seemed designed only for me. The universe was a game between me and God, but God wasn't against me. He was seeing what I would do, and putting me in really weird tough spots like the one I was in now was how he had fun. The game was all about giving me the opportunity to make choices that would make me who I was and see how I turned out. It felt a little like déjà vu, only a hell of a lot scarier. I feel now, looking back, that this was also a defense mechanism—my solipsistic brain flip. If Coach didn't exist, I wouldn't *actually* be hurting him, no matter what I did.

"Here's the thing," Coach went on. "You're the only person I told about this—about my family. And I ain't got nowheres to stay. Like I said, I been kicked out. So I been sleeping in here."

"How long?" I asked.

He considered the question as if it were somehow confusing. "Last night was it, actually," he finally answered as if surprised. "We had the big blowout last night when she told me about the lawyer and the restraining order and all that. That fleabag joint in town, I couldn't find nobody to give me a room. Man, it's been a long, long night." He rubbed his head. His hair was flat on the side he'd been sleeping on. "I'll try again today. Must be someone in that place … you ain't gonna tell anyone, are you?" His eyes suddenly locked on mine. "I'm already walking the damn tightrope with the administration here. Seems my teaching ain't up to par, K1." He exhaled as if blowing out a bad thought. "I couldn't stand to lose you guys right now."

"I won't tell," I said.

Coach smiled. He reached over and patted my shoulder, then he stuck his hand out to shake. "You're a good man, K1," he said. "You're a friend."

To these comments, I had no response.

It was a long day. Eventually, I went and saw the principal. I told him I had lied. He called my dad, handed me the phone from his office desk, and made me tell my father myself what I had done. When I got home, only Mom would talk to me. Hyter shunned me. He wouldn't even look at me. My father didn't speak to me for days. Once he spoke to me again, it was only when speaking was necessary.

There was a coolness in him toward me that terrified me more than anything I'd yet experienced in my short life. It was worse than outrage, worse than being hit. There was real contempt. It wasn't that he was disappointed in me, it was that he didn't like me. Our relationship had changed near the root. It hinted that, just like Coach, being kicked out of my family was possible.

COMING TOGETHER - AUTUMN IN LAFAYETTE - A COLD RAIN FALLS - A POSER - RACING IN BAD WEATHER - BEING NOTICED - THE WOODS ARE QUIET, DARK, AND SLOPPY - SLADE'S AN AIRPLANE - PROTEST - VICTORY IS OURS

Fall, in its bleak, wet, gray guise, swooped down on us suddenly the first Saturday in October. When we got off the bus after a two-hour ride through steady rain, the low clouds promising a full day's worth of the wet stuff, it wasn't fifty degrees.

Lafayette, Indiana always seemed to me the kind of town where rain and cold and darkness were the rule. Like London except without the history and culture and meat pies. It wasn't logical, but we never ran a race in Lafayette that wasn't cold and wet and dark. On that particular Saturday, less than a week after my lie about Coach and the resulting chill in my house, the environment up there felt like a reflection of the inside of my head.

While my own character seemed to be deteriorating with every choice I made, our team was trending in the opposite direction. After the Ridgeline humiliation, we had responded, after our initial bickering, by working harder. We became realistic about where we stood and how far we needed to go. Two Saturdays in a row, we ran in invitationals at which some of our competition was State meet podium quality and had picked up an overall team third at one. At the other, my brother and Keane finished in the top ten and I was third for our team after a Slade meltdown in the last mile. We were getting better. We three varsity freshmen had, by that time, all cracked the seventeen-minute barrier for five kilometers. According to Coach, seventeens were okay for freshmen and jayvee runners, sixteens were decent for varsity runners, fifteens made you a contender at State, and fourteens made you a legend.

As we came into Lafayette, our bus rolled past vast auto-mobile manufacturing plants, over gravel-strewn train tracks, and past strip malls full of stores I'd never heard of before. Train tracks seemed to criss-cross the town like a two-year old's scribblings, and at the third train we encountered on our way to the meet, Coach shouted back at us, "Nothing comes easy in Lafayette." It sounded right. It would turn out to be wrong.

"You guys look like a couple of queers," said Victor to Popeye and Leonardo. They were hugging under a shared blanket in the corner of a baseball dugout we'd discovered beside the course. It was better shelter than our tent. The hard-packed dirt of the dugout was dry.

Popeye and Leonardo laughed and hugged some more.

Squid was down there with them and wore a ridiculously expensive down jacket that looked like gear appropriate for a summit attempt on Everest. He sat shivering dramatically, rubbing his hands together and chattering his teeth until Bowden told him to stop being such an idiot.

After settling in, Coach gave us a short speech. "I love October," he began. "You're all gonna get faster this month." I assumed this was because the season was wearing on, our training was starting to pay off, the competition was getting more intense. Wrong on all counts. "The air's getting denser," Coach explained. "More oxygen for your muscles." Popeye waved his hand in front of his face, trying to feel the new surplus of oxygen. "I know it's cold and sloppy out there," continued Coach. "But you don't sell yourselves short today. Get out there and get after it. Make something happen."

Coach was upbeat. He was happy. I hadn't heard anything more about his family situation, and it seemed he had no idea about mine. My lie, apparently, hadn't ever made it to his ears. For this, at least, I was thankful. It seemed the one break I'd been given.

As we walked and jogged the course, those of us in the varsity grays had to roll up our pant legs to avoid them becoming water-soaked and pendulous. A steady drizzle dampened us from the top down while the soaked grass grabbed at our ankles, the water somehow wicking up our legs. By the time we were done, our cotton Champion tops and bottoms were worthless against the chill and heavy with water.

The race began at noon. The sun still didn't show any signs of making an appearance. Although the rain had stopped, large brown puddles and wet marshy grass were the rule on the course. The races had begun just after nine and had been non-stop since—several different junior high boys and girls races, the jayvee races, followed by the girls' varsity race. By the time it was our turn, the grounds were beyond well-trodden. There was a section of woods near the finish that was slick with greasy spots of mud and downright treacherous.

After the gun, the heavy footing and slick muddy stretches caused hesitancy among all the runners. An odd poser wearing a pair of Nike Internationalist trainers (I'd gotten spikes after the embarrassment of the Hokum Karem and was now contemptuous of anyone who didn't wear them while racing) took the lead for half a mile before he lost a shoe in a bog and was never heard from again. We passed him sitting in the bright wet grass, trying to untie his mud-caked laces.

When conditions become less than ideal, strange things can happen. Some runners are "mudders" and do well when the ground is mucky and soft. Other runners allow less than perfect conditions to play with their heads. Most become cautious when conditions are abnormal and, when a race gets out slow, the best runners are allowing the rest of the pack to shorten the race, as it were. That was exactly what happened.

By the mile-and-a-half mark, halfway through the race, the field was still tightly bunched, nearly fifty of us packed together like a school of sardines with a long comet's tail of slower fish stretching out behind us. The better racers needed to make a break for it. They had waited, and waited, and now it was certainly time to lose the scrappers like me, my brother, Keane, and Slade. I could sense their growing restlessness, and there was some jostling for eight hundred meters or so, but when we hit the two-mile mark, nearly thirty runners still must've felt they had a shot to be in the top ten.

A tall, dark-haired, knobby elbowed runner from one of the Lafayette schools, an All-State runner, noticed the four of us in that lead pack in our generic white and black jerseys. I doubt if he knew who we were, but he took note of our identical jerseys and decided his guys had waited long enough. He looked at a blond-haired teammate. "Where's Dan?" he huffed. The other guy put his hands up; he didn't know. "Shit!" the All-Stater shouted, then he waved his hand to his teammate. They took off like a shot and we jumped on their move. We were now in the front of the chase pack.

Slade made meaningful eye contact with me. He and I had noticed that the guy had noticed us, and it felt good. It gave us confidence. "We can win this," Slade huffed. And Slade, our senior captain, had never been on a team that had won anything more than a dual meet.

As we entered the woods, the crowd lining the course in their plastic rain jackets and under dripping umbrellas suddenly disappeared. The woods were wet and it was silent and dark under the overarching branches. It felt like running through a cave.

"Kindles!" shouted Slade in the quiet of that tunnel, the only sound the slapping of feet on the wet ground, rainwater splashing underfoot, and the labored breathing of the large pack of runners we were a part of. "Keane!" he shouted. "You're better than me."

It seemed like a strange time to talk about it. We had all three been pulling away from him in our faster workouts, that was true. I couldn't figure out what he was trying to say, though. Was this some kind of Come to Jesus confession? "You go on!" he yelled. "Leave me."

I wondered for a second if I ought to say we wouldn't go on without him—the whole clichéd scenario of one guy telling another in some blazing desert or on some gusty snow-covered mountainside to "just leave me, I'll only slow you down—save yourself, I'm a goner" passed through my mind. I was about to hold up my end of the scene and dramatically insist that we would never leave him when he said what he meant all along. "Goddammit! Go! Now!"

It seemed he wasn't interested in acting out some age-old martyr's ritual after all, so we went. After those murky woods, the finish line was two-hundred meters away. We still had nearly a quarter mile until we exited the woods, but Coach had told us during warm-ups not to wait until we got out onto open ground to make a final move. He said that's what everyone would be doing and that we had to beat 'em to the punch. At first I thought maybe Slade was just echoing coach, but when I heard the first angry shouts from behind us, I knew something else was up.

As we charged through those dark woods along that trail and left Slade and the pack behind, I turned my head to see what the source of the commotion was. What I saw made me believe at first that Slade truly had lost it. He'd clearly become delusional because he was pretending to be an airplane. Like a joyous five-year old, he ran from one side of the course to the other, his arms extended like wings. But he wasn't being an airplane or a joyous five year old. He was being a wall.

"Don't look back!" he yelled. "Go!"

Of course, it was totally illegal. He was completely cheating. It was awful sportsmanship. I must say, it was awesome.

"Slade's holding 'em back!" I huffed. The words gave us Bluebirds a jolt of energy and we found another gear, all three of us, and pulled further away from the rest of the field who were now stuck behind Slade.

By the time we exited the woods, only one guy had gotten past Slade. And not without taking a spike in the shin. By the clearing, Slade had a lineup of twenty pissed-off runners backed up behind him. He had held the pack back for nearly ten seconds. It was plenty of time for us to break away.

After the race's conclusion, there was, of course, a protest by the other teams. The coaches stood in a circle around the starter in his red jacket, a plastic bag over his official hat, apparently to keep it dry. It was pouring again and rainwater ran off the plastic bag protecting his hat in streams.

One coach threw his clipboard down in the mud he was so mad. They all stood with their hands on their hips. In response, Coach just shook his head and said he hadn't seen anything. "Had anyone else seen Slade holding back all those runners?" he asked. But there had been no spectators or coaches back in that murky copse of trees. There had been no witnesses.

When the official came over to our camp in the dugout and questioned Slade, he said those guys were all just mad at having been beaten by three freshmen. He was tired and might have been weaving, he acknowledged, but even if he had been, it hadn't been on purpose.

Keane, my brother, and I took fifth, sixth, and seventh in that meet. Slade was wasted after his performance in the woods, but held on and finished in the twenties. Chambers was right behind him. And we won.

Unfairly, yes, but it was the first time in anyone's memory that our team had won anything big enough to be proud of. The seniors were ecstatic. We Bluebirds were giddy at the fact that we'd played such a vital role in their first invitational win.

At the awards, several teams booed when Slade went up to accept our trophy. He brazenly gave them the finger and was reprimanded by the official who, it was clear, didn't like him or believe his lame excuse about being tired. He didn't shake Slade's hand when he handed over the hardware even when Slade stuck his hand out to him. Victor hooted when he saw this.

I wore the number-two sweatshirt that day, having outkicked my brother, beating him for the first time. Keane wore number one. I had one more month to wear that number one sweatshirt, I was determined I'd pull it over my head at least once.

On the bus ride back home, we all sat in back and laughed and cheered in spite of how cold and wet we were. We thought it had been a great day. Until Coach came back and sat with us.

BUT WE WON! - TEACHING - THE TROPHY - VICTOR'S COMPLAINT - THE PUNISHMENT FOR CHEATING - NO SHORTCUTS - TRASH

"You did cheat then," said Coach as he sat leaning into the aisle. He sat on the seat across from Slade in the back of the bus. He lurched, along with everyone else, as the bus screeched to a halt at yet another set of train tracks. The driver opened the bus door, the breaks went *whoosh*, and the engine roared again as we pulled away.

"Yeah," said Slade, a big grin on his face. "But we won!" He raised the trophy in his hands above his head. The back of the bus cheered. "Viddstein, you idiot! We won a race! I'm a senior, dammit, and I don't care how we did it!"

A sad look crossed Coach's face. "I'm not teaching you right," he said quietly, almost to himself. And then I was sure the waterworks were turning on. But instead of growing weepy, Coach got determined. He seemed almost angry. "I'm not teaching you right, but I'm gonna teach you now." He shook his head once firmly as if making a promise to himself. He pointed at the trophy in Slade's hands. "We're sending that trophy back. We didn't do it right."

Even Leonardo and Popeye, normally off in their own little buddy-world, from seven seats up were leaning over the backs of their seats listening. The girls in the front chattered on as normal, totally oblivious of the drama playing out behind them.

"But Coach," said Bowden, "nobody's gonna care anymore." He laughed and shook his head. "It's over. The day's done … I mean, don't we just give all our team trophies away at the end of the year anyhow?"

He reached over the back of his seat towards Slade. Slade handed him the foot-tall overall team champion trophy. It was gold with a vertical strip of sparkling blue plastic, a runner leaning forward in mid-stride on top. It was just like the ones I used to polish and race against each other back in my uncle's childhood bedroom.

"But it ain't the trophy that counts," said Coach. "It's what it took to get it. It's what it means."

He reached across and Bowden handed him the trophy. "And this one means the wrong things now. It means cheating."

"Awww, screw me," sighed Victor from the seat in front of Coach's. "Of all the goddamned adults that tell me endless bullshit about right and wrong, you're the last one I want to hear it from."

Coach sat the trophy down on the bus floor. "What the hell you mean by that?" he said.

"First of all," said Victor, "you're a complete mess yourself."

"That's right," said Coach. "I'm a mess. What of it?"

I was suddenly very tense. I'd never heard a kid and an adult talk the way Victor and Coach were talking. Especially in the midst of a group of kids listening.

"You got kicked out of your house, didn't you?"

My heart leapt in my chest. I expected Coach to glare at me. I prepared to defend myself. I hadn't told anyone. I had kept my promise. But Coach didn't glare at me. He stared right at Victor. The look on his face, it wasn't angry. It was sad.

"Lay off, Victor," Slade growled.

"Agreed," said Bowden, his eyes narrow slits.

Swart nodded, too. "Lay off Coach," he said.

Everyone was leaning toward the back of the bus, listening in. It was like some weird intervention except I couldn't figure out yet upon whose behalf we were intervening and over what.

"I won't lay off," said Victor angrily. "Because of what I was gonna say next." And it seemed suddenly that Victor was overwrought. His face twisted up a little. He was fighting something inside himself that he didn't want to let out but had to. "The second reason I don't wanna hear from you how we did wrong when we *actually won a race* is because you're the only adult who I *actually care* what you think because you're the only one who actually cares about me. And we never won anything before . . . " Victor glanced down, unable to keep his eyes up. "I wanted to win one for you, Coach."

Coach's face softened. He glanced down himself and seemed to be collecting his thoughts. He looked up. "The thing is," Coach said softly, "I ain't been teaching you right. And I don't mean because Slade did some crazy-ass stunt to try to win the race."

Everyone laughed a little when Coach said "crazy ass." It was a Slade and Victor word. Victor smiled upon hearing Coach appropriate it.

"I ain't been teaching you right because you didn't believe you could win that race without the stunt … understand?"

The faces turned toward coach became thoughtful. Someone coughed.

"Look," said Coach, "going into them woods, we had four guys in the top fifteen. Four guys!" he said. "And that invite ain't half bad. Ridgeline and some of the others ain't there, sure, but it ain't bad. And them woods was *only* half a mile until the finish. Even if Slade don't do his airplane impersonation," Coach held his arms out to his sides in imitation of Slade and everyone chuckled again, "we're still gonna win."

It took a moment to consider what he said, but it was true. We four up front hadn't been dying. In fact, we may have fought to our places without Slade's maneuverings. And Chambers had been held up in the pack behind Slade. Who knew what he would've done without that hindrance? "Slade," Coach continued, "did that airplane thing wear you out? You feel shot when you came out of the woods?"

"I'd blown my wad like Champ does," said Slade. "Five to six times a day."

Hyter, to my disgust, grinned and gave him a thumbs up. Everyone laughed again.

"Well, if Slade gains five spots because he doesn't wear himself out holding everybody back, and if the Bluebirds can outkick some people on their own, which I'm sure," he glanced at us, "they could've. Then we're still holding this trophy on this bus ride, but them other teams on their bus rides home ain't talkin' about how we stole it."

And he was right.

"And even more," he went on, "if we won it straight out, no nonsense, you'd know it yourself … that you got it the right way. That you earned it fair and square." The back of the bus was quiet.

"You go about cheating in life, boys, the punishment's in the cheating itself. Remember that. When it comes to cheating, nobody's gotta catch you. Nobody's gotta know about it, because the punishment for cheating is built in." He nodded emphatically. Hyter glanced at me then. He stared at my black eye, unconsciously touching his own face. Coach went on. "The punishment's the feeling that you couldn't have done whatever it was you did *without* cheating. That's what eats at you. And then, over time, that feeling becomes a belief that you can't do *nothin' good* without cheating, that you ain't up to it. That's the punishment for cheating." Coach handed the trophy back to Slade.

"I may be a mess," he said quietly, pointing over the seat at Victor. Then he smiled and looked directly at me. "Hell, I *am* a mess. In the goddamn race of life I'm at the back of the pack." He turned his attention back to the group. "Ain't no doubt about it. I told K$_1$ the other morning. My wife hates me, my kids worry about me, and they're too little to have to worry about their old man." He covered his mouth for a moment with a shaking hand before he went on. "My car's about ready to blow up. I don't even think my dog likes me much."

We all smiled, though it wasn't happy, what he was saying. And then his face grew tight, and his jaw clenched once. "But I'm earning it every step of the way." His voice was as tight as his jaw. He was looking right into Victor's eyes. "As best I can, I'm earning it fair and square."

Victor nodded, his mouth tight as well.

"I'm earning what comes to me, son. And I know there ain't no shortcuts." He smiled, breaking the tension slightly.

"Lots of trapdoors for a guy as crazy as me but no shortcuts."

Slade rose from his seat, the trophy gripped in his hand. He set it down under the bus window and, in spite of the cold and blustery rain outside, slid down the window with a clack. He picked the trophy back up off the seat with one hand and, before any of us knew what he was doing, he threw it out the window. It was suddenly gone. Disappeared. Then he slid his window back up with a click and sat back down. He didn't say a thing.

"That's littering," said Yost, finally breaking the silence. He didn't say it judgmentally. He was just stating a fact in order to say something.

"It was junk," said Slade.

THE MELANCHOLY BEAUTY OF AUTUMN - PARADES - TOWN & COUNTRY - THE LOCATION OF THE FRESHMAN FLOAT - BECCA LAMBERTH'S GRANDPA'S FARM - TONY THE TIGER - THE NINJA AND THE CHAINSAW - REVENGE

The rain cleared away and was replaced by a last beautiful gasp of summertime. Nothing's prettier than those rare October days that harken back to mid-summer. The edge of the sun's heat is gone and the humidity gone with it, leaving only the most pleasant kind of warmth. The days feel ticklish almost.

Add to those perfect, bright-blue days the realization that they will soon be replaced by winter's cold and dark, and the melancholy, slightly heartbroken yet pleased-to-be-alive feeling you get is, in its own subtle way, the apogee of human experience. Also, October's a great time of year to egg people's houses. Or their floats, as the case may warrant.

Homecoming was taken seriously at my high school. Football wasn't. Our teams were only rarely any good, but the boys in the helmets and pads were under pressure to win at least one game a year. That game was Homecoming.

People who lived in Pennsgap spoke of town and country. You either lived in one or the other. And in town, everybody loved a parade. The brick streets overarched by ancient oaks and maples and the big old limestone courthouse with its surrounding green lawn, perfect for spreading a blanket and having a picnic, seemed built for them. And thanks to the farmers living in the country, there was no shortage of flat-bed trailers covered with kids and floats to drag under those trees and around that square. There was also no shortage of antique tractors to pull those burdened flatbeds at precisely the speed of the high school marching band, which led all the parades as an unwritten rule.

There was the Fourth of July Parade, the Memorial Day Parade, the Christmas Parade with Santa riding in his sleigh at the end. We had parades for holidays I didn't know existed. But there was no parade like the Homecoming Parade.

School slowed down during Homecoming Week. Only the grouchiest and bitterest teachers assigned homework or gave tests. It was understood that we would be busy that week. Aside from the members of the football team, who would grind through practice until dark every night in hopes of avoiding a Homecoming embarrassment, we had our class floats to build. And the other classes' floats to attempt to destroy. But I get ahead of myself.

Coach lectured on peaking and tapering that Tuesday of Homecoming Week. He didn't believe in either.

We were bending into the climax of our season. Our conference meet was Saturday and our sectional, which was the beginning of the state tournament, was just over a week away. Coach was sure some of us were waiting for him to back off on our mileage and effort. It wasn't gonna happen.

"Tapering," he said, and he spat out the word like it tasted bad in his mouth, "is an act of pure superstition. It reeks of a fragile mind."

Now, I loved how overwrought Coach got for his Tuesday sermons. Whereas before I found myself impatient, angry, and doubtful as I sat listening to him on that hard wooden bench down in the musty locker room, I now found myself charmed by his insight and wit. Whereas before I had seen him as less than he was, I now saw him as better than he himself did. It wasn't just that I felt sympathy for him, I actually believed in him. The truth of the body, when you feel yourself getting stronger, is a powerful thing. He had changed me through his workouts in a physical way, a way I could see in the mirror after showering in the morning. My body was now lean and hard. However, I was having trouble focusing on this particular lecture. The Hawks and Eagles kept prodding all us Bluebirds.

Every time Coach turned his back to us to write something on his board, they jabbed and whispered. They were after information, and they all wanted to know the same thing.

"K1," Bowden leaned into my shoulder and whispered. "Where's the freshman float gonna be?"

"Why do you wanna know?" I whispered back.

"No reason," he said, his big Adam's apple bobbing in his throat, "no reason in particular."

For the first time ever, I didn't trust Bowden. Even that morning Squid had been duct-taped, the morning of the hares and the hounds, Bowden's demeanor had been direct and forthright. He was going to tape someone to a tree if he could catch them and that was that. But the smile on his face now suggested deception was at hand. Like most honest people, Bowden was no good at lying.

Swart went right to the weak link among us freshmen. As Coach went on about training through Sectionals, how our bodies were thriving on the work we did each day and the insanity of changing anything, Swart keyed in on Popeye.

Popeye's squinty eye shut completely when he listened hard, and it was shut as he leaned over toward Swart. When Swart leaned away, Popeye smiled and nodded. Sure! He knew where the freshman float was being built! And then he began to draw an invisible map on the palm of his hand with his index finger to show Swart exactly where it was. Thankfully, Coach noticed and cut him off.

"Hey, Popeye," Coach said, abruptly ceasing his lecture. "Whatcha doing?'

Popeye looked around, his hand still flat out in front of him. He glanced at Swart next to him. Swart stared at Popeye as if he had no idea what the goofy dork was doing with his hand stuck out like that. Then Popeye looked around the U of benches at all of us.

"Me?" he said, finally dropping his hand, his eyes wide. He looked terrified.

"No," said Coach, "the other Popeye."

It took him about five seconds, which is a really long time in a room full of silent guys waiting to see what'll happen next, to realize there wasn't another Popeye on our team. That took him right back to his shocked and abandoned look. It was one of his three expressions, the other two being goofy-laughter face and mouth-breather daydreamer. It was clear after about ten seconds passed that he'd forgotten entirely what he'd been doing. Maybe even where he was.

"Popeye," said Coach.

"Yeah?" responded Popeye.

"Just shut the hell up."

After Coach continued, the whispers stopped. Coach's antennae were up. The upperclassmen would have to wait to pry the information about our float from us. Although I didn't know why they wanted to know, I had a powerful intuition that we shouldn't give it to them.

We did six repeat eight-hundreds that day out on the grass of our course. We ran them faster than race pace with a three-minute rest in between. My brother, Keane, and I were supposed to be between 2:30 and 2:40 for each of them.

It was tough. In between, we bent over at our waists, trying to suck in as much air as we could, dangling our hands down near our toes. We focused on pulling ourselves together for the next effort. At every break, the older guys tried to get the float building location out of us. We hadn't even known it was a secret, but it was clear now that we best not tell.

The Homecoming theme that year was breakfast cereals. That meant that each class had to incorporate a cereal into its float design. A slogan might be something like "It Won't Take Lucky Charms to Beat the Wildcats!" and for the design you'd have some kid dress up like a Leprechaun like on the Lucky Charms box, except wearing a football helmet. Or your slogan might be "I Go Cuckoo for a Victory" with the crazy brown Cocoa Puffs bird on your float, also wearing a football helmet. Heady stuff.

Our float that year was constructed in the barn of Mr. Wilfred T. Lamberth. His granddaughter, Becca Lamberth, was the freshman class secretary. Becca looked like a farm girl ought to. She was pretty in a non-sexy way, which actually made me question what sexy was at its core.

If Becca wasn't sexy, it seemed sexy had something to do with being dumb or trashy or crazy, because Becca was pretty, but she wasn't any of those things. Maybe it was that she dipped Skoal that kept the fire in my loins from burning hot when I was near her. Maybe it was because when she laughed she sounded like a mule braying. In any case, Becca was sturdy as a kitchen chair, had a healthy yet chubby face, and liked to chew to prove she didn't care what anyone said. She could also throw a sixty-five mile an hour fastball underhanded.

"This is awesome!" I said as I walked into the Lamberth barn for the first time. The pleasant smell of hay was strong. Large hooded lights hung from the roof of the barn far overhead. It felt like a small, rustic indoor stadium.

Our flatbed was already prepped with the skeleton of our float. It was made with two by fours, the chicken wire into which our colored "pomps" would be stuffed, vaguely out- lining the shape of mini-bleachers and a field with goalposts at each end. "What's the plan?" I asked Becca.

She spit a brown blob in her styrofoam cup she carried for the purpose. "I'm gonna dress up like a tiger," she said. "We're Frosted Flakes. It's gonna say 'The Snappers are GREAT!' on the side." She spit again into her cup. "It's gonna be cool."

"Maybe," I said, "we ought to spell it GRRRRRRR-REAT!" I emphasized the growl as Tony the Tiger did in the commercials.

Becca thought about it. "Sure." She gave me a patronizing smile that suggested that I was goofy yet harmless. "That'd be good."

There must have been seventy or eighty kids there that night. It was a party. There was a table covered with pizzas, a bunch of two-liter bottles of soft drinks, and a lined trash can full of popcorn that Grandpa Lamberth seemed determined to keep full, as he brought out bowl after bowl from the little white farmhouse and dumped it in.

It was a kind of fourteen-year-old heaven—staying out late on a school night on a beautiful fall evening, the stars shining above, a yellow harvest moon hanging in the sky... Until the attack, that was.

The first egg hit the hard-packed and swept dirt floor of the barn with a thump, the bright yellow yolk splattering like paint. The second egg hit a girl in the shoulder, the yolk and the clear, sticky albumen splattering the side of her face. Then it seemed to rain eggs.

Pandemonium ensued when the maniacal buzzing of a chain saw fired up. We ran and hid, leaving the barnyard empty.

The kid who ran into the barn with the chain saw wore a black ninja suit, his face obscured by a black mask and hood. His appearance suggested quickness and stealth, except for his shoes, which were big clunky Nike basketball shoes—Air Force Ones. And, of course, there was absolutely nothing stealthy about his weapon of choice.

As he cut into our float, buzzing right through the goal posts and destroying the chicken wire sculptures we'd crafted, eggs flew in from the darkness surrounding the barn and provided cover. I can't imagine anyone rushing out to try to stop him, however. He had a chainsaw, for crying out loud.

Our float was in shambles when he finished. It looked like a shipwreck.

The chainsaw sputtered away as the ninja hopped off the flatbed. He picked up a stray can of spray paint and wrote something on the side of our ruined float. The chainsaw continued to growl as he ran back into the darkness and disappeared. As soon as he was gone, the eggs stopped coming.

The barnyard was silent then. It was the kind of silence you only hear after a truly loud and terrifying noise has suddenly ceased. There was an emptiness to it.

We freshmen slowly made our way back to inspect our ruined float. Becca picked up half of a goal post. "He did a good job," she said.

Seniors Rule was scrawled in red spray paint across the side of the trailer.

"I know who did this," said Leonardo quietly.

I knew who did it, too. But that didn't mean I intended to tell anyone. Or do anything about it, for that matter. Leonardo, however, was made of sterner stuff than me.

"We will get revenge for this," he said gravely as he stared up at Becca, who was half a foot taller than he was. "I promise."

"That's what I'm talking about," said Becca. She spit in her cup for emphasis.

THE PERPETRATORS - CULTURAL IMPLICATIONS CONCERNING REVENGE - SQUID THE PROBLEM SOLVER - PROMISE ROAD, PART II - OUT IN THE FIELD - CHARISMATIC OBJECTS

If there was any doubt that Swart, Bowden, Slade, and Yost were involved in the murder in its infancy of our first attempt at a float, it was dispelled the next day at practice.

"How's your float looking?" Yost asked, a slimy grin sliding across his greasy face.

"Hey," said Hyter. "How come the only time you seem happy is when someone else isn't?"

Yost's grin widened. "Just the way God made me, I guess," he said smugly. "By the way," he added. "You recognize the shoes that Ninja was wearing?" He held up a clunky pair of Nikes.

Slade and Bowden also couldn't help themselves from

divulging the secret of their involvement in the attack, if they'd ever intended to keep it a secret. "What'd you guys do when we left?" asked Bowden. "What'd people say?" He was giddy. It wasn't a good look for him. My substantial respect for Bowden was quickly eroding.

"You can tell us," said Slade conspiratorially.

I was certainly tempted just then to swap allegiances, to transition between loyal freshman float builder and loyal freshman runner, and confide in Bowden and Slade. Logic suggested I side with power. However, the steely gaze of Leonardo Chavez stopped me.

Some say that North Americans are soft when it comes to our responses to personal slights and signs of disrespect. Some say we live in such a civilized time and place that we've lost our taste for anything close to real revenge. The American way is to let bygones be bygones. We're too busy for revenge. It's too sloppy and the repercussions too great. At its most intense, we sic our lawyers on our transgressors and let a proxy do our dirty work. However, if you want to witness revenge done old school, you need only travel south. A few thousand miles south. The hot-blooded miens found in South and Central America are not so quick to forgive and forget. Exhibit A, Leonardo Chavez, second generation El Salvadoran, was stony in his silence that day.

Swart noticed and spoke up. "C'mon Leonardo," he said, a sly grin on his face. "It's tradition."

"We'll start a new tradition. You'll see," Leonardo told them calmly.

"You just try coming after the senior float, little man," said Slade. "We've got an army waiting for anyone who tries."

Leonardo glared at him.

It was just us Bluebirds together that day on our fifty-minute run. I knew better than to try to talk Leonardo out of his quest for revenge. Our saving grace seemed to be that, first of all, we didn't know where the senior float was. Second, we didn't have any way to get there even if we did. Squid screwed up both those blessings within minutes.

"I know where their float is," he huffed as we ran through the brilliant afternoon sunlight, our shadows stretching out across the street before us. "It's out at Johnston's farm. It's just past the little bridge on Moontown Road."

"We still can't get there," I said, thankful we weren't old enough to drive.

"I can drive," said Squid. "I got my license. Last week. I barely passed because my parallel parking was so bad, but—"

"You're a sophomore!" I nearly shouted. "They didn't wreck your float!"

Leonardo shot me a look. "What do you care?" His voice was quiet and steely like a razor.

"I'm just saying," I fumbled, "it seems like Squid wouldn't want to get involved."

"Oh," said Squid, "the sophomores don't like me much anyway. Consider me a mercenary."

"What do we have to pay you?" asked Hyter.

"Nothing," said Squid.

"You don't really know what a mercenary is, do you?" said Hyter.

Suddenly, Leonardo stopped running. We all slowed to a walk and turned back to him. "Let's turn around," he said.

"Why?" asked Keane. "I thought we were gonna go run in the park."

"Let's go run out on Promise Road," Leonardo suggested. "I wanna see something."

One thing about Leonardo, when he was in that kind

of mood, people just did what he said. It didn't matter that he was just over five-feet tall.

We turned and began running out towards the Hinterlands. My stomach was churning. I couldn't figure a way out of what was sure to be a bloodbath, without looking like the complete wimp that I was, so I went along and kept my mouth shut.

It's true—the greatest of all fears is not death, the greatest of all fears is looking bad in front of other people. That was the only reason I didn't speak out.

It was still there, exactly as I had expected, and it took my breath away. It took all of our breath away. It confirmed two things—that Bowden's story about the man with the gun and Slade that he'd told us at the start of the season was true, and that Leonardo Chavez was very serious about revenge.

The corn was brown and dry and loomed overhead. It crackled and whispered as we shouldered through it. The skid marks on the road had indicated to us the spot where Slade had taken the shotgun from the man and logic dictated, although applying logic to any of Slade's actions seemed a risky proposition, that he would have thrown it into the cornfield not far from where he finished beating the man's truck with it. We spread out and walked into the corn and, within five minutes, Keane shouted out, "I found it!" And there it was.

It was a twelve-gauge shotgun—a Remington. It was old and looked to have been well-used. It was heavy, the blue-steel of the barrel cool to the touch. The walnut stock was scarred.

Keane, who seemed to know something about guns, slid the chamber open with a metal clack and a red plastic shell popped out.

Leonardo picked up the shell. He tapped on the brass bottom. "How's it work?"

"There's shot, like, little lead balls, in there," explained Keane. "When you shoot it, the plastic shell stays in the gun and the little lead balls spread out. So you can shoot a bird." He pinched open the top of the plastic shell and poured some shot in his palm. "It would be nearly impossible to shoot a bird with a rifle. The shot spreads out, like, five or ten feet as it moves away from the gun." We all touched the gun, treating it like some strange magic.

A gun is a truly charismatic object. Guns simply draw one's attention. Think of it this way—you bring a gun into a room full of guys, and they know you're not nuts and gonna use it on them, and set it on a table, everybody shuts up and stares at the gun. Pretty soon, somebody's holding the gun. It's only a matter of time before someone shoots the gun. Guns are absolutely first on most boys' list of charismatic objects. Numbers two and three are typically motorcycles and pornography.

As we stood in a circle, reaching out and touching it, there seemed to be an almost palpable buzz surrounding us. The whispering of the corn stalks and the drone of the insects seemed to rise in volume. Everything about the moment was heightened.

"We can't run back with it," said Leonardo, breaking the spell. "Somebody'll take it away from us."

For a second, I foolishly believed we were saved. There was no way anyone would allow us to hang onto that weapon, should they spot us with it. And it was two miles back to the school, some of it through the busy streets of town. Then Squid opened his mouth again.

"I can get it," he said. "We'll just leave it here and I'll come get it when it gets dark. Then I'll come get you guys."

I couldn't think of a way to argue against that plan. Especially not with Leonardo, whom I'm certain was beginning to think me a potential hiccup in his plans for revenge, staring daggers at me.

LAND ROVER DEFENDER, THE BADDEST TRUCK YOU EVER SAW - THE FALKLANDS WAR - MOONTOWN ROAD - A PLAN? - GRANDPA LAMBERTH - ROCK SALT

"Where have you guys been?" I shouted as Hyter and I ran out our front door to meet Squid. We'd been waiting for what seemed like hours. It was dark.

Squid's truck looked like it ought to be part of a safari in the African veldt rather than sitting in front of our quaint Victorian house in our Midwestern town. Its back end consisted of a tailgate and, above that, an army green tarp. Leonardo brushed the tarp aside and leaned out. "We got the gun," he said, "and check out this badass truck!"

Hyter and I hopped into the back to find Leonardo and Popeye on one side and Adam Keane sitting across from them. They sat on metal bench seats and they faced each other, a steel floor between them. I understood quickly why Squid's dad spent over $50,000 on the beast. As I climbed in, I felt like a member of the Foreign Legion about to be driven to the front lines of some heroic battle.

Squid leaned over and looked back at us from the passenger seat. He waved, a big smile on his face. Where was the driver? Why wasn't it Squid? I saw it then. The steering wheel was in front of Squid—on the wrong side. "This thing's from England," Squid shouted happily, explaining the steering wheel's odd placement in a rather abstruse way.

"Is it even legal to drive?" I asked. Nobody seemed to care. I didn't get an answer.

"I feel like I'm going to fight Argentina," said Hyter as he inspected the inside of the Land Rover.

"What?" asked Keane.

"You know," Hyter said as he sat down next to Popeye, his knees nearly touching Keane's who sat directly across from him, "Argentina. They fought the British in the Falklands War."

He was met by impatient silence.

"You know, the war over the Falkland Islands …"

"K2," said Leonardo. "Shut up."

The gun lay across Leonardo's lap. Hyter shut up.

If we looked like a paramilitary squad, the senior float site looked like a prison camp. We drove through the darkness along country roads to get out there, and then, just over a bridge and small hill, Squid was stopped by two boys with tin buckets in their hands. There were eggs in the buckets—ammunition.

"Who goes there?" asked the boy on the right side of the truck as he leaned in toward Squid. He was all business. He wore a black knit skullcap and an army jacket. He even had a little face black smeared on his cheeks.

"It's Sydney Porter," answered Squid.

"What the hell are you doing here," said the other boy in a heavy flannel shirt and a Cincinnati Reds hat. He didn't seem to take his job as a sentry quite as seriously as his partner did. "And why's your steering wheel on the wrong side?"

While Squid talked, we looked out the small rectangular windows in the back of the truck. The senior float site was well guarded. The barn where their float must have been was set back nearly a quarter mile from the road. Along the dirt two-track that led to it were a series of small campfires. It looked like the entire senior class, nearly two-hundred kids, were either building the float or had been charged to protect it.

Squid put the Defender into reverse. With a whine, it backed up. He did a quick T-turn, and we were making our way back towards town. "We're not getting in there," Squid shouted back. "No way."

I could almost feel the heat coming off of Leonardo. He was frustrated. But he wasn't done. "We just need a plan," he said quietly.

And I thanked God for that. I hadn't had a clue what we were doing as we drove out there. Did we intend to shoot their float? Did we intend to shoot their Ninja? Our teammate—Chad Yost? Sure, he was a jerk, but I didn't want to spend any time in jail over him. I breathed easier on our way back to the Lamberth's barn. A disaster had been averted. Or so I thought. But then we got to the freshman float and Grandpa Lamberth got involved. Things got weird.

"You boys, don't park over there!" Grandpa Lamberth shouted as Squid pulled into a soft patch of earth, sinking down to the axels. "Damn it all!" Grandpa said. "You're stuck now sure."

"No we're not," bragged Squid. And he put the Defender into four-low and, sure enough, it popped right out back onto solid ground.

"Pretty impressive vehicle," I heard Grandpa say. We were all still in the back of the truck. He didn't even know we were back there. "Steering wheel's on the wrong side," he said.

"It's British," I heard Squid reply proudly.

"I know it's British," grumbled Grandpa Lamberth. "I was telling a damn joke. You just didn't get it."

I motioned for Leonardo to hide the gun, as Grandpa's creaky old voice seemed to be getting closer, but just then the cloth hanging down hiding us from view was torn to the side and Grandpa's wrinkled old prune of a head poked in. His gaze immediately fell on the shotgun in Leonardo's lap.

"Say now," he said. "What're you boys about here?"

I was about to try to come up with a good lie when Hyter stepped in.

"We were going to shoot some of those seniors who wrecked our float. Or maybe we were just going to shoot their float."

"Shoot 'em, eh?" Grandpa Lamberth didn't seem nearly as worried at the prospect as I did. "How come you didn't?"

"We couldn't get in," said Keane.

"Well," said Grandpa, "What's Plan B?"

"We didn't really even have a Plan A," I admitted.

"Well," said Grandpa slowly. I was pretty sure he was going to lecture us on the futility of violence, the idea that everyone loses in war, all that stuff. Instead, he said, "I'd like a piece o' them boys myself." His eyes grew glassy in the moonlight. "Coming on my property without my permission, scaring you good kids half to death …"

He looked at Leonardo, then nodded at the gun in his lap. "I say we load that son of a bitch with rock salt. I say we lure those bastards in here, and shoot 'em in the back when they're running to get away from us, and I say we listen to 'em scream while that salt melts in their very flesh." His eyes suddenly switched back to those of a contented old man again. "How's that sound?" he asked with a perfect smile that displayed his dentures nicely.

"That sounds very, very good," said Leonardo, his white teeth shining, his smile seemingly taking up half his face.

A "GREAT" FLOAT - THE NINJA COMES TONIGHT - SLEEP DEPRIVATION - MISPLACED PRIORITIES? - THE PLAN - THE EFFECTS OF ROCK SALT WHEN SHOT FROM A TWELVE-GAUGE SHOTGUN UPON A PIECE OF CARDBOARD - A FEEBLE ENEMY - NINJA VS. GRANDPA - A RIDICULOUS RATIONALIZATION

"Our float looks great," said Adam Keane loudly across the locker room. "Doesn't it?"

"Yeah," said Popeye, "it does. It looks really great."

"I agree," said Hyter. "It's great."

I was sure one of the seniors was soon to sniff out our plot. It was hard to listen to my fellow Bluebirds prattle on. They were the worst actors I'd ever seen.

"I'm glad we worked so hard on it," said Leonardo. "It looks very good now."

"I think you mean 'great,'" said Popeye nervously. "Great," had been the adjective we'd agreed upon.

I was cringing. It turned out, however, that I had nothing to fear. The seniors were far too interested in the thrill of destroying another of our floats and they were far too dismissive of Leonardo's potent drive for revenge. And, of course, they didn't have a clue about Grandpa Lamberth.

While a handful of freshmen had reconstructed our float to make it a passable entry in the Homecoming Parade (although certainly not a winning one), the rest of us, nearly fifty in number, had taken orders from Grandpa Lamberth until late into the night. We'd turned his farm into an absolute booby trap. The seniors were going to die. Unless such awful acting caused one of them to smell a rat.

"It doesn't look *that* good," I said hoping to balance things out a little.

I looked at Swart, the most likely candidate to catch on that something was amiss. I smiled and shrugged my shoulders. "They're just talking it up."

Swart stared at me then. I was suddenly certain that I'd screwed up, that it was me that somehow subconsciously sounded the alarm. "How good does it look then?" asked Swart, suspiciously, I thought.

"Not as good as yours," I said meekly.

His eyes bored into me. "You haven't seen ours. Nobody but the seniors has been within a quarter mile of our float."

"Well," I said, "I'm sure it's not as good as yours."

I believe Chad Yost's monomaniacal focus upon causing pain and misery to those lower on the social scale than himself saved me then. "It's goin' down!" Yost cried gleefully as he came out of the bathroom, still pulling up his shorts. "You little freshmen worms got me? The Ninja comes tonight!"

He was so excited, his grin so big, that his face looked like it was going to split in half.

"You should've just stuck with our plan and said it looked great," said Hyter during our run.

"Shut up," I said. I didn't like being chastised by my brother.

We were doing a five-mile tempo run that day. We were running along a paved trail that ran beside the river. Coach had marked all the miles with a can of spray paint. The plan was to run three miles at six minute pace, hit the fourth in 5:30, and be under 5:15 for the last. "But not all out," said Coach. "Nobody's under five on that last one. No racing, got it? We're saving the racing for Saturday."

Saturday was our conference meet. It was a big one and was only two days away. It was our last race before Sectionals.

It seemed to me as we jogged to the river trail that we'd spent most of our week thinking about things other than running. We'd been up late every night, too. I'd fallen asleep in math class that day, something I never did. Forget sleep deprivation though, the night before us promised greater damage to our team than a lack of sleep ever would.

Our varsity seven had solidified. Chambers had been coming on, but he had developed a stress fracture, so our varsity now consisted of three freshmen (me, Hyter, and Keane), three seniors (Slade, Swart, and Yost), and a junior firmly aligned with the seniors (Victor). It seemed to me a bad idea for almost half our varsity to be shooting the other half of our varsity (minus Victor) with a shotgun loaded with rock salt less than a week before the sectionals. But hey, that was just me.

The problem was, I didn't see a way out.

"They'll be here," Leonardo said to Grandpa in an attempt to ease his nerves as we sat in the darkness outside the barn.

"They wouldn't miss a chance to ruin our float for the world."

Grandpa held the gun. We'd decided he would be the one to shoot Yost. "It'd be a bad idea for you to shoot him," he'd said earlier. "I'll do it." We didn't protest.

It was nearly ten o'clock. The float was done. It wasn't much.

Green tissue paper made up a football field, white tissue paper made up the yard lines and end zones. Two yellow field goals stood at each end. In orange and pine green across the side of the float were the words *The Snappers are Great!* My suggestion to add Tony the Tiger's *grrr*, had been ignored. It was complete, or it would be when Becca dressed up like a tiger and pranced around on it with a football under her arm and a helmet on her head during the drag through town. Now we were just waiting for the seniors to come to try to destroy it.

The plan was to lure the Ninja and the egg-throwers in, then pull up a net Grandpa had rigged to two tractors behind them. In the darkness, they wouldn't be able to see the netting. When they got stuck in it, all us freshmen still there, willing and able, were to give them a taste of their own medicine. Grandpa had purchased the eggs himself. He'd provided the net as well. Gung-ho is an adjective I rarely use, but it applied to Grandpa Lamberth.

"I'll just shoot the Ninja," Grandpa repeated quietly to himself over the course of the evening. I could tell he wanted to blast away at all of them. We'd soon see if he was able to maintain his self-control.

To be sure we didn't accidentally murder Chad Yost, we'd done some tests that evening with the twelve-gauge. Grandpa had been packing rock salt loads all afternoon, emptying out shells of their shot and filling them with Morton's Ice Cream

Salt. "They're real, real light," he'd said worriedly before we tested them. "I don't know if they'll even work."

We tacked a piece of cardboard onto a tree behind his barn and set to find out.

"Let's see what happens from here," he said. Leonardo, Hyter, Keane, Popeye and I all covered our ears. He raised the gun and pulled the trigger from about twenty meters away.

The shotgun blasted. Blue gun smoke filled the air. The cardboard looked untouched.

"Dang," said Grandpa, "there was no recoil." This, apparently, was bad news.

We walked up to discover that our eyes hadn't deceived us. There was barely a mark on the cardboard.

"Let's get closer, see how close I'm gonna have to be to make it burn." It turned out, he was going to have to be close. Like, within ten feet.

"That's just fine," said Grandpa contentedly. "That way, they'll think I'm gonna kill 'em." He smiled a smile that was just this side of sane. I was glad, for many reasons, that I wasn't Chad Yost.

The moon was yellow and full that night. A light breeze blew in from the west, causing the acres of corn surrounding the barn to shimmer and roll in the moonlight like the surface of a vast dark green lake. Ten brave freshmen had agreed to serve as bait, pretending to pomp and hammer on our completed float in order to lure the seniors in.

By midnight, we were sure they'd decided once was enough, that they would allow our float to live. The disappointment was tangible on Grandpa's face, although he was saying it was probably for the best that they hadn't attacked. He'd been mighty riled up. He wasn't sure what he'd a done if "them boys" showed their faces again.

It was then that we heard the siren.

The siren was surprisingly loud, and although we were expecting an attack of some kind, it still sent shivers down my spine. I felt, perhaps a tiny bit, what soldiers must feel when the moment of truth arrives.

"Freshmen," said a crackly, amplified voice. "You have proven yourselves a feeble enemy. You are worthless and weak. We must teach you. We do this for your own good." The voice echoed through the barn and out across the misty fields. "Move away from the float. We don't want to hurt you physically. Emotionally and psychologically, we intend to crush you."

"Here we go boys," said Grandpa as the amplified voice echoed over us. He gripped the shotgun tightly to his chest.

The roar of the chainsaw moved my heart into my throat. A flurry of eggs spattered on the empty barnyard floor. Chad Yost in his ninja suit stormed past us, totally unaware that we were hiding in the tall grass. I could see the outlines of other seniors in the darkness standing and throwing eggs.

Grandpa stood and placed the whistle hanging around his neck between his teeth. He breathed in deep and let loose a long high shriek. It was our signal.

Becca Lamberth and another farm kid fired up the tractors, their bright floodlights coming on and blasting the seniors caught in front of them. They backed the tractors up quickly. The net rose between the two tractors and was nearly invisible in the darkness. All of us hidden in the high grass, nearly thirty of us, rose and began throwing Grandpa's eggs from the buckets full of them he'd provided. The seniors caught in the middle of our crossfire began to scream. I saw one drop to the ground, holding his head.

"Why aren't the eggs breaking?" shouted Leonardo, a triumphant grin on his face.

"I kept 'em in the freezer. They hurt more that way," said Grandpa just before he made his way between the Ninja and his path of escape.

Yost hadn't noticed what was happening behind him. In the euphoria of destruction, he had been both deaf and blind to our doings. I'm sure the roar of the chainsaw distracted him as well. When he turned around to find Grandpa standing in the empty barnyard within talking distance, the shotgun pointing right at his chest, he immediately dropped his instrument of destruction. It landed with a thud and died almost instantly. He froze.

Some said, after the fact, that Yost actually pooped his pants when he saw that old man with a shotgun before him. Some said he only peed them. Whatever the truth, I can say with certainty that Chad Yost did one or the other. Or both. He was that scared.

His hands raised, Yost shuffled to the side, trying to edge his way around Grandpa without setting him off. Grandpa was muttering things we couldn't hear, but I'm certain I wouldn't have wanted his words directed at me.

By this time, most of the seniors had worked their way free of the net and had escaped, scrambling on their hands and knees in terror, back to their cars parked along the road in front of the farm. The only sound was the sound of tires squealing to get away. The egg throwing had stopped. Now it was just Grandpa and Yost, center stage.

"I hope he doesn't shoot him," I said quietly as I peered through the dry grass.

"Not from *too* close," said Hyter.

"I hope he blasts his balls off," said Leonardo.

Popeye and Keane just stared.

Grandpa let Yost get all the way around him, etching out a semi-circle like he was trying to walk away from a grizzly he'd bumped into on a hike.

Then, as soon as Yost turned to run, the shotgun blasted. Yost jumped, covered his behind with his hands, and then continued his sprint. He slammed into the net pulling it free from one of the tractors. He tripped, rolled, and then seemed to regain his feet almost instantly. He disappeared into the darkness yelping.

"The float's ruined," said Grandpa as we sat on the flatbed, eating starchy popcorn, our adrenaline still working its way through our veins. It was nearly one in the morning.

"That's okay," said Leonardo. "It was worth it."

Grandpa chuckled and threw his arm around his fourteen-year-old soul mate.

FIVE HOURS LATER - SLEEP-DEPRIVED - ALL-OUT-WAR - DOOMED

Five short hours later, we all sat in the U in the locker room. Darkness reigned outside. A cold wind blowing that morning suggested that our Indian summer had come and gone. Nobody said a word about the previous night's adventures. We didn't even look at each other.

There was no tension, there was no taunting, and there was no finger pointing. We were just tired. The seniors were a little beat up, too.

Bowden's right eye was swollen nearly shut. He'd taken a frozen egg to the cheek. Slade's arms and thighs were covered in raw pink rope burns from when he'd run into Grandpa's net. Of course, Yost was the worst off.

He pulled down the back of his shorts to reveal a peppering of bloody splotches. He said he'd been up past three picking the salt out, scrubbing his ass with water and a soft washcloth.

"That net," said Bowden sleepily, "I didn't even see that thing."

"Grandpa set that up," said Keane. "He was our secret weapon."

"Was that dude a Navy Seal or something?" asked Slade as he stretched his arms over his head and yawned.

"He's just a farmer," said Popeye.

"Remind me not to mess with any farmers," said Bowden as he rubbed at the lump under his eye.

Nobody said anything then. There was the flush of a toilet. Someone else yawned. Swart stood up from the wooden bench where he sat and crawled under it, curling up in a ball. He was asleep and snoring gently when Coach walked in at about ten after six holding a piece of paper in his hand—his notes for the next two days.

"Okey dokey," he said, all chipper and hale and ready to go. He still hadn't looked up and seen Bowden's face or Swart asleep on the floor. He hadn't yet registered the fact that we looked like a bunch of zombies due to a week's worth of late night guerilla warfare. "We're going on an easy five this morning, we'll ride in the parade this afternoon, then you guys do your date thing, whatever, but leave the game at halftime." He continued staring at the white sheet in his hand. "I'll be walking 'round the stands checking up. They'll be big trouble if you're still around in the third quarter. You need your sleep this time of year."

It was then that he felt something amiss. Perhaps it was that there were no groans of protest upon being told to leave the game at half, maybe it was just too quiet, but he looked up, looked around at each of us, and saw what there was to see.

He jutted his head forward, his eyes squinted. "Leonardo? You go to bed last night?"

Leonardo's head was lolling around, resting on one shoulder then the other. It seemed he had no control over it. He opened his eyes from the slits they'd been. Barely and with what seemed like much effort. "Yes," he said dreamily.

"What time?" asked Coach.

"Two thirty," said Leonardo.

Coach glanced around again. "Bowden, what happened to your face?"

Bowden rubbed his swollen cheek. He smiled sheepishly. "Leonardo hit me with a frozen egg."

"When'd that happen?" asked Coach.

"About midnight last night."

Leonardo giggled. He seemed almost drunk.

"Swart," said Coach, looking down under the bench. Swart's ribs were gently rising and falling. He was truly asleep. "Swart," Coach said again. But Swart wasn't waking up.

"You guys," said Coach to all of us, "look awful."

"It was all-out war, Coach," explained Hyter. "The seniors wrecked our float Tuesday night; we had to get them back so we booby-trapped Grandpa's farm." He seemed to believe Coach would find all of this amusing. "We found that shotgun Slade took from that guy this summer out on Promise Road and we filled it with salt and we shot Yost, who was dressed up like a Ninja with a chainsaw." He paused. "Well, he was dressed up like a ninja and he *actually* had a chainsaw, there was nothing fake about that chainsaw. That chainsaw was the real deal for sure."

"How many of you guys were involved in this all-out war business?" Coach asked.

I was thinking, somewhere deep down, that now would

be a good time for all of us to lie. But at that point it seemed our cards were all on the table, face up. I raised my hand along with the rest of our varsity seven, excluding Victor, and several of the jayvee guys.

"So," said Coach. "You guys've been getting three, four hours sleep pretty much all week."

We nodded sleepily.

"And we got Conference tomorrow and Sectionals Thursday," he added.

We all nodded that yes, this was true as well.

"We're doomed," he sighed.

And he was right.

GRAVITY - THE HANGOVER - ATTITUDE IS EVERYTHING - THE KID IN THE GREEN JERSEY - HATE

Gravity seemed to be working particularly well that Saturday morning. Like, twice as powerfully as normal. My legs, my arms, even my head, all felt heavy. My spikes, when I took them from my bag, felt like they were full of loose change. My gray cotton sweats with the number two inked under the chin seemed lined with lead. I felt, should I lie down on the cool grass under our tent, as if I would sink, gradually, into the earth. I wished I could. If I disappeared, absorbed into the dirt, I wouldn't have to race.

"You all made your beds," said Coach as we moped around our camp like the walking dead, "now you're gonna have to lie in them." It was a particularly cruel metaphor.

As we stretched in our circle of seven before the race,

the mood was bad. The day before, there had been a neutral emptiness following the drama of our epic clash out at the Lamberth farm. Now the ugly hangover had truly begun.

Yost's behind was bruised and raw. Bowden's eye and cheek were turning yellow and purple. All the seniors save Yost rubbed their necks and shoulders and complained of soreness from slamming into Grandpa's net. The day fit our mood as well. It was cold and gray and windy. It was a great morning to spend at home in your own bed under the warmth of your blankets. It was an awful morning to strip down nearly naked and push your body to its limits for sixteen or seventeen minutes of agony.

"I wish I was dead," said Slade.

"I wish you guys weren't such a bunch of idiots," said Victor bitterly.

He was mad. The only one of us who'd had anything approaching a normal week, Victor resented our sleepy sullenness. "I wish you'd pull your shit together. We had a chance to win this before you guys acted like a bunch of tools all week."

"We can still win it," said Swart. But a huge yawn escaped him as he said it, which suggested otherwise.

"Right," said Victor. "And you got laid last night."

Attitude is everything is the saying. You may not be able to control anything else, but you're always in charge of your own mental approach to the task at hand. I kept telling myself that, but it seemed, when I attempted to force myself to be upbeat and to get aggressive, I couldn't control how much my eyelids seemed to weigh. They kept shutting on me.

Coach stood, hands on hips, at the first mile mark. He didn't say a word. He didn't have to. His face said it all. I'd never seen the man look angry before then. I'd seen him happy, sad, frantic, insane, worried, excited, and on and on . . . never angry. That day, I swear, there was actual steam coming out of his ears.

Victor led us through the first mile in a slow 5:10. The problem was, the rest of the contenders in the conference ran a quick 4:57. We were never even in it.

I have to admit, I let Slade beat me that day. We were both running like crap somewhere in the middle of the pack. It was clear we weren't going to win the race and it was clear I wasn't going to come near a PR In that last mile, when it feels like a grind in any race, if you're running poorly it's tempting to just take your foot off the gas and cruise home with as little pain as possible. And that was exactly what I did. That was why I saw it all unfold before me.

The kid in the green jersey was a complete victim of circumstance. How could he know the guy sprinting to the finish line beside him was a completely certifiable nut job? How could he know that the guy had been up and down, getting no sleep, plotting and planning violent deeds all week and was now at the end of his rope? How could he know the guy came from a long line of psychos? He couldn't.

That's why I don't blame him for pushing Slade in the finish chute after they'd crossed the line together. He couldn't have known that he was playing the role of the smoking line of gunpowder to Slade's pile of TNT. He couldn't know he was the pin and Slade was the grenade. In the end, it didn't matter. He lost his teeth just the same.

Blood sprayed on my chest and throat when the kid's head snapped back. A long red streak stretched across my white singlet from where his face had brushed against me as he fell backwards. I nearly tripped on him as he sat dumbfounded in the chute in front of me spitting out his own teeth. And then I did fall as I was pushed hard from the side.

I looked up from my spot on the ground to see a tall man with black hair and a gray beard. The man wore jeans and a brown leather jacket and big heavy boots. The man had taken my spot in the chute. He was punching Jeff Slade in the face, and Slade was punching him back.

I was scrambling to get away when Slade kneed the man in the groin. I was several feet away from the fight when the man got Slade in a headlock and punched him repeatedly in the face, holding him there, punching him over and over again. Even though I was doing my best to evacuate the scene, I was still close enough to hear Slade's shouts. And I was close enough to realize Jeff Slade, tough-guy psycho and team captain, was crying like a four-year-old. And I was close enough to see the bright red blood on the man's fist, Slade's blood, from where he'd broken Slade's nose with one of his punches. I was close enough to hear Slade screaming, over and over again, "I hate you, Dad! I hate you!"

BACK ON THE BUS - SLADE'S DAD - DINNER AT HOME - THE NICKEL PLATE - SOME GUYS LIKE FIGHTING - THREE WARNINGS - OUT THE WINDOW - NAILS IN THE COFFIN

"Okay," said Coach from the front of the bus, shouting back at us, "we're gonna eat at this restaurant and I wanna see you guys on your best behavior."

They were the first words he'd spoken to us since we'd left the conference meet. We hadn't stayed for the awards. As soon as Coach had us all together back at camp, he'd told us to break down the tent and to get on the bus as quickly as we could. It was just us guys that day, the girls' meet had been held elsewhere. Thankfully.

We nodded at him from our seats. The ride up to that point had been grim and silent. Slade sat holding a bloody rag wrapped around some ice to his face. Without the girls along, we each had our own seats. Most of the rest of us had our foreheads pressed against the seat in front of us. That position kept us from staring at Slade's screwed up face. Also, we were low and that posture, eyes down on the scuffed floor of the bus, shoulders slouching, fit our collective mood perfectly.

We'd taken next to last, yet that seemed a minor disappointment compared to the shock of watching Slade's father beat him up in the finishing chute. The surreal event had continued when Coach jumped into the chute and wrapped his arms around the much larger man, Slade's dad, from behind. They'd both fallen to the ground then, Slade's dad kicking and yelling and Coach struggling to pull him away from his son.

I'd heard about Slade's dad before. I'd never seen him until that day, but I'd heard of him. My father, aside from being a grocer, served as the town judge one day a week. He knew Tom Slade. He'd had him in court before. Knowing Tom Slade gave my dad a certain insight into Jeff Slade. Back when he was still talking to me, before my attempt to get coach fired, he told me and Hyter a story about him.

"His dad's the meanest man in town," Dad said at the dinner table. "I don't doubt the kid's dangerous. I'd guess his dad's been beating him up for years." Hyter had told the story of Slade and the man with the gun. "I wouldn't get involved with that boy if I could help it. Tom Slade's currently *not* in jail only because we don't know everything he's done. I'm sure of that." Dad salted his peas. "Most men, their barks are worse than their bites. Tom Slade's the opposite."

"What'd he do?" I asked. "To make you say that, I mean."

"Well …" said Dad.

Mom spoke up then. "Dear," she said, "I don't think this is really good dinner conversation." Mom liked things to be pleasant. Especially at dinner.

Dad set the salt down. "Okay, then," he said. Hyter and I groaned with disappointment. "I'll tell you later." And he did.

After we moved our conversation to the living room, Dad continued the story. Tom Slade had been in the bar in town one night, our only bar, The Nickel Plate. The place was full of people, as it was a Saturday. Two guys from a neighboring town came in. One of them knew Slade from back when they'd both been in high school.

The man had a few drinks and started talking about Tom Slade, how he once kicked a girl out of his car out in the middle of nowhere and made her walk home because she wouldn't give him what he wanted. He talked about how Slade's first wife left him for a dentist and then he laughed loudly about how funny that was. "A dentist!" the guy had shouted.

"I guess the guy was after a fight," said Dad. "I don't know why, but some people seem to like fighting."

Hyter and I waited for the rest of the story. Dad turned on the television. It seemed he was done. Hyter went up to the TV and turned it off. Dad smiled. "You want to know what happened?" he asked.

"Yes!" said Hyter. I nodded too.

"Well," Dad said, settling back into his chair. "Slade finally hears the guy. He's been playing pool, minding his own business. But once he hears him, his business turns into shutting this guy up and teaching him a lesson. I'll give him credit: he gave the guy a chance. Tom Slade, according to several people who were there, said, 'One more word ...' and he left it at that. Didn't even look up from his pool shot."

"What'd the guy do then?" I asked.

"He said one more word," said Dad, "and before he knew it he was on the floor, blood running out of his ear from where Tom Slade had hit him with his pool cue."

"Man," whispered Hyter.

"Oh," said Dad, "that's not the end of it. Once he's on the ground, Slade doesn't give him a chance. He hits him in the head three or four times with the pool cue until the guy's pretty much out of it. Then, he ruined his knee."

"With the pool cue?" I asked.

"With his big steel-toed work boots. He dropped the pool cue and jumped up and down on the guy's knee until it was almost flat."

I wanted to retch at the picture that had formed in my mind.

"The doctor who testified in court said the guy nearly had to have that leg amputated, the knee was so bad."

"I guess that's where Slade gets it," said Hyter.

"Could be," agreed Dad, and he said it one more time for good measure: "I'd be careful around him."

Remembering this story, I looked to the back of the bus in spite of my fear of being caught looking. Slade no longer had the bloody rag to his face. He was staring out the window blankly. His long bleached blond hair was matted on one side with blood. His nose had an angry black crease in it just between his eyes.

As we silently filed off the bus into the restaurant, none of us wanted to be there. We just wanted to be home. We just wanted the season to be over. Forget Sectionals, forget Coach's tearful hopes that we might move on this year for the first time. We all, at that moment, wanted it to be done.

VICTOR'S STEAKHOUSE - COACH'S NEW PLACE - KEANE'S NOT WEIRD - FREAKS - ONE OF US - THE CHECK - A SEEMINGLY FATAL ERROR

Victor's Steakhouse in Anderson, Indiana wouldn't make anyone's list of great dining establishments. It was the kind of place with video games in front and one of those cranes where you attempt to grab a stuffed animal out of a glass box for twenty-five cents. It was the kind of place you expect the toilet not to work. It stank of hot grease.

Coach thought it would be fun to eat there only because it was called "Victor's." He had called ahead, in an unusual display of forethought and organization for him, and reserved a table. A cloudy miserable day, it was already growing dark outside as we quietly lined into the restaurant.

"Coach," said Bowden, "Maybe this isn't a good idea. We're all pretty fried, I think."

Several of us stood behind Bowden in support of his motion that we simply go home and try to forget the day. Coach wouldn't have it.

"We get one meal on the athletic department per year, goddammit," he said. "And this is it. We ain't saving it for after Sectionals. I'm gonna be so depressed after we don't make it again I'm just gonna wanna go home and drink."

"You're back at home?" asked Victor.

"Nahh," said Coach, waving that thought off as nonsense. "My marriage is over. Home for me is now the Grand Hotel."

This gave me a jolt. The Grand, just off the town square, was a huge old fleabag joint for alcoholics, drifters, and, rumor was, the occasional small-town hooker. He had mentioned it that morning in the wrestling room, but I thought he was joking. The place was downright squalid.

"What?" said Coach in response to the looks on several of our faces. "It ain't that bad. I got cable." He scratched his chin thoughtfully. "Don't got a television, but I got cable when I get one."

Our waiter, dressed in cowboy gear complete with a fake holster and six-shooter, lethargically led all sixteen of us to a back room. Four tables had been pushed together. Our waiter appeared to be sick. His skin was a weird vampire shade.

"How's your nose?" said Coach from the middle of the table where he sat.

"Broken," Slade said.

Popeye laughed twice. Victor, who sat next to him, stared at him like he was going to kill him. "I can't help it," said Popeye. "I laugh when I'm scared."

"That's weird," said Swart.

"I know," said Popeye apologetically. "I'm a weird kid."

"You're all weird," said Coach. "How could you not be weird with me as your coach?"

"Keane's not weird," said Hyter.

We all looked at Keane and considered him. Keane just took it in, blinked his movie star blue eyes once, and looked back at us.

"You're right, Champ," said Coach after a moment. "Keane ain't weird. How do you suppose that happened?"

Slade set his bloody rag down on the table and took a drink of water. "He doesn't say enough to seem weird, but he's weird, too," he said. "It's like in that movie *Freaks*."

I was happy to hear him talk about something other than his nose. I half expected him to never speak again and then one day just start killing people after what his dad had done to him.

"I ain't seen that one," said Coach.

"We'll come and watch it with you," said Victor. "We'll come over to The Grand, score a trick, then watch *Freaks*. I own the video. It'll be a big night."

"Tell me about the movie," said Coach. "Sounds like something we all ought to watch together."

Slade and Victor regaled the table about the movie *Freaks*. "It's the scariest movie ever made," said Slade, who seemed to be forgetting about his broken nose.

"It's absolutely got the greatest scene ever in it," said Victor.

"Well, start at the start," said Coach. "None of us knows what the hell you're talking about."

Above the clinking of glasses and through the process of giving our orders to our pasty cowboy waiter, Slade and Victor described *Freaks*.

"There's this circus, see? Like, back in the twenties or thirties," said Victor.

"That's when it was made," added Slade. "It's black and white. And it's not really a circus. It's a freak show. They've got a bearded lady, these creepy as hell pinheads, midgets galore, and a guy with no legs who scrambles around on his hands."

"And there's this woman, right?" said Victor. "She thinks the midget who owns the freak show is rich. She acts like she loves him, but instead she loves the strong man. She just wants the midget's money."

"They used real midgets?" asked Coach.

Slade leaned forward. "They used real *everything*. That's what makes it so damn scary! No way could anybody make that movie now. It would totally offend freaks, retards, and cripples everywhere."

"So," said Victor, "this one night the freaks all get together, with this lady who marries the midget for money, and they all get trashed. They're all drinking wine and partying, and then the freaks do this 'freak wedding' thing. They start saying this lady is 'one of us.' Then they start chanting it, saying, *One of us! One of us!*"

Popeye started chanting it along with Victor. *One of us! One of us!* Leonardo laughed and joined in. Pretty soon we were all laughing and chanting, *One of us! One of us!*

Victor raised his hands to silence us. "Jesus," he said, "shut the hell up. Anyway, the lady goes bonkers. She's like, 'I'm not one of you, you freaks!'"

Slade took over. "So, now everybody sees what she and the strong man are up to." His voice was nasally and high, his nose clogged with blood. "And then comes the greatest scene in the history of movies."

Victor stole the spotlight once again. "It's this rainy, nasty night. The wagons are going down this muddy road because the freaks are moving on to another town. You think it's just showing them moving, but then you see a freak, like, sharpening a knife in its nasty little room."

"Then you see the other freaks, and they're getting ready to go get this lady," said Slade. "They got pipe wrenches and ropes, they're fixing to teach that lady a lesson."

We were all leaning in towards the center of the table, totally sucked in.

"The best," said Victor, "is when this little thing with no legs puts a knife in its mouth. It drags itself through the mud, grabbing onto the bottom of the wagons as they move." He shook his head at the thought. "It's so twisted, dude."

"And then," said Slade, "they all get to the lady's wagon at the same time. And they start chanting, *One of us! One of us!*"

The cowboy waiter began sliding plates of pink and gray meat in front of us, potatoes wrapped in aluminum foil on the side along with some brownish green beans. Although we'd ordered different things, our plates all looked the same. Nobody paid dinner any attention.

"The movie ends," said Victor, "with a circus announcer talking to a crowd of people. It's like, they didn't show you what happened to the lady, they just ended with all those freaks bearing down on her with their knives and wrenches and shit. And the announcer says to the people that they're about to see the craziest freak of all …"

Victor dramatically stared at us in our seats. None of us made a move toward our food. We were all listening.

"And he pulls a cover off of this cage to reveal the woman . . . but she's totally messed up. Like, she doesn't have any arms or legs, and one of those freaks cut her tongue out so all she can do is make this crazy clucking noise."

Slade smiled and got the last word in himself. "She's one of them!" he said, a smile on his ruined face.

"I'd like to see that," said Coach. He shrugged. "I ain't got no VCR though."

"We can bring one over," said Victor.

"That'd be swell," said Coach. "Can you bring a TV too?"

"Swell," said Popeye. He began to laugh.

The meat was raw or burnt, even both in some cases. The green beans were cool and mushy, and the potatoes were room temperature and butter wouldn't melt on them. We didn't care.

There was laughter at the table. Slade told the story of the kid in the green jersey, how he'd popped him without even thinking about it, how shocked he'd been to see that blood. He didn't mention his dad. Victor taunted us, holding the number one on his sweatshirt up for us all to see repeatedly, chanting, *I'm number one! I'm number one!* Bowden told the story of being hit in the cheek with the frozen egg on Thursday night, blaming Popeye, who laughed in response. Squid told about the farmer who saved him from the telephone pole where he'd been duct-taped back on the first day of school. I was almost brave enough to tell the true story behind my black eye. But not quite.

It seemed we'd turned a corner somehow. Just by sitting down together at that table we'd come to terms. Even with ourselves.

Then the pasty cowboy brought the check and set it before Coach. I didn't even see it happen, we were all talking and carrying on. The next thing I knew, Coach's face was stricken with anxiety. And then, suddenly, he was whispering loudly at all of us, saying "Let's go! Let's go!"

Up we stood, confused and disorganized. A chair clattered as it fell over.

"We gotta go," Coach said in a hoarse whisper. "We gotta go, *now*."

As we hustled out the door, I looked back at our table. The waiter was searching for something, moving plates, picking up napkins. "Hey," he said as Coach pushed us out the door toward the bus. "Hey!"

"Run!" said Coach. "Get on the bus, hurry!"

We ran. The bus driver, an old slow-witted man, was totally confused, but he did as Coach said, limping along as fast as he could on a bad hip. We piled on, the bus engine fired up.

"Go! Go! Go!" shouted Coach at the confused driver.

The waiter was pounding on the bus door as the bus lurched out of the parking lot like some drunken dinosaur. He stopped running alongside us as we bounced roughly out into the street.

"What was that about?" shouted Slade from the back seat.

"I ain't got no check!" said Coach as he stared back at us. "I don't know where it went, but I ain't got it!"

"WE WON'T WANT TO BE THERE WHEN IT HAPPENS" - DR. BILLINGS - GOING FOR A RUN - THE GRAND HOTEL - SEE ELEANOR - DON'T GO - FINISH, PART II

"I don't think we'll want to be there when it happens," said Bowden, his eyes tired and his face sad. "Because there's no way we'll change anything."

"That's a bullshit way to go," said Victor viciously.

Bowden raised his palms in supplication. "You want to see him crucified, you go ahead and go. I don't want to watch. I didn't go when my family put our dog down, and I'm not going to go see this. It's the same thing."

Swart nodded his agreement with Bowden.

Slade was lying flat on his back under a bench, his eyes shut. He wasn't sleeping. "You act like it's already a done deal," he said.

"It is," said Swart. He sounded exhausted.

Coach, when we had arrived that cool fall Monday morning, had been nowhere to be found. It was like him to be a little late, but only a little.

Soon, we began searching. Coach wasn't in his office curled up on his ratty couch. He hadn't been in the wrestling room asleep on the rubbery floor.

Our concern grew when the school principal, a quiet scholarly man called Dr. Billings, came clicking into our musty locker room in his maple-colored wingtips and gray suit. He wore round wire rimmed glasses and had a ring of silver hair that went around the back of his head from just over one ear to the other. He wore a bow tie. He removed his glasses before he spoke to us in a calm, quiet voice.

"Your coach," he said quietly with a trace of a Southern accent, "has been suspended indefinitely. A substitute coach," he went on over our gasps, our obvious confusion and anger, "will be selected, and you will meet said substitute coach tomorrow afternoon." He put his glasses back on. He looked at Swart, whom he seemed to know. "Do you have a practice scheduled for tomorrow morning Devin?" Swart nodded. "Then that practice is cancelled as well."

"What's gonna happen to our coach?" Victor asked. "What'd he do wrong?"

Dr. Billings had already turned to leave. He did, however, turn and dignify Victor's question with an answer. "There will be a school board meeting tonight to determine exactly what is to be done concerning Mr. Viddstein's future employment at Pennsgap High School. As far as what he did wrong …" He sighed. His eyes seemed tired. "I would imagine all that will come out at the meeting."

Dr. Billings removed a handkerchief from his front

pants pocket. He seemed about to blow his nose, but then put it back without using it. I got the impression he didn't like having to talk to us. "To be frank, I think you ought to prepare yourselves to run for a new coach at Sectionals this year. And in the years to come, for those of you not graduating. I'm sorry." Then he turned and left, a sandy echo coming from his leather-soled shoes as he walked away.

We'd been reeling since he'd left—fighting about what to do next.

"Are we gonna go on a run this morning?" asked Popeye in a rare moment of silence.

"Shut up," Leonardo whispered.

Popeye shrugged. "What?" he asked.

Suddenly, Slade sat up, knocking over the bench he'd been lying beneath. He hadn't moved once during Dr. Billings' announcement. "Popeye's right," he said. "Let's go for a run." He gathered himself and stood. And in less than fifteen minutes, we were all standing in the lobby of the infamous Grand Hotel.

The place was worse than I'd heard, and I'd heard it was bad. It had been a railroad stop on the way up to Chicago in years long past. There must've even been something romantic and actually grand about it way back when. The marble floor must've been impressive once upon a time. But the floor was now cracked and filthy, the cracks packed with a black oily sticky substance. There was a vintage cigarette machine with fake brass pulls under a tiny TV bolted to the wall. The little TV had a wire cage around it, as if anyone would ever want to steal it.

The marble check–in counter was covered with plaited metal blinds that were pulled down. A battered piece of cardboard had the words SEE ELEANOR TO CHECK IN—ROOM 301 scratched out in blue ink.

The lobby smelled of stale tobacco smoke. The two skeletal chairs sitting before the television looked small and insufficient in the vast lobby. The place was lonely and forlorn, and I felt vulnerable standing there in my running shorts and long-sleeved T-shirt, like some of the bad luck and morbidity of the place might rub off on me.

"This place must have more than hundred rooms," said Swart as he took in the twelve-foot high ceilings. "It's big."

"Three floors," added Victor.

"And about three people staying here total," added Bowden.

"How are we gonna find him?" asked Swart.

Victor started down a gloomy hallway without looking back to see if we were following. "We're gonna knock," he said. And with that he began shouting, *Coach!* over and over as he banged on one door after the next.

"How many people'd you wake up?" asked Coach as we sat on the curb in front of the hotel, the sun just coming up, the sky before us red and gray. It had been too small and dingy in his room—too sad to stay in there to talk.

"I don't know how many we woke up," Bowden said, "but you were the only one who answered the door."

Coach, sitting on the curb, wore a pair of worn jeans and a college sweatshirt, INDIANA, his alma mater where he'd been a member of a national champion 4-by-800 team back in better days. Although the morning was cold and damp, he wore only a pair of dirty white socks. His feet stretched out onto the street in front of him.

Coach smiled. He put his arm around Slade. "You boys're all right in my book," he said. His smile disappeared. "Just so's you know how I feel though. You oughtn't to be there. At the meeting tonight." He glanced around at us all. "If that's what you're thinking, I mean ... that you oughta go."

A garbage truck rounded the corner, grimy and hulking, like some kind of monster out of *The Terminator*. Two men, black silhouettes against the red sky, hung off the back. Popeye waved at them. They didn't wave back.

"That's what we heard," said Victor as the garbage truck disappeared back into the gloom with a roar. He was glaring at Bowden. "That we shouldn't be there."

"We'll be there," said Slade.

"I promise," added Victor.

Coach smiled again. He stared at the empty street in front of him. He seemed to be searching for something to say.

"I'll be there too," said Bowden, his eyes hard on Victor. "If that's what you want, Coach."

"Me too," said Swart quietly.

Coach glanced up at all of them in turn. "You know it won't change anything."

"We know. You're getting fired," said Swart matter-of-factly. "There's no doubt about that. Dr. Billings as much as said it twenty minutes ago."

Victor rose as if to kick Swart as he sat there on the curb, but Coach reeled him in by the tail of his oversized number one sweatshirt. "Swart's right, as usual," said Coach as Victor sat back down on the curb. "He's a touch insensitive sometimes, but he's right. It's a done deal."

"We'll go anyway," said Victor. "We'll make it hard for them at least. Make 'em feel like the assholes they are."

It was quiet for a few seconds. A streetlamp tinged off and a dishwater color of gray bled up from the horizon, the red began to fade to pink.

"I know you're behind me," Coach finally said, breaking the silence. He sighed and glanced around at all of us. "But I'd really rather none of you went."

Victor began to protest, but Coach raised his hands for silence. Victor shut his mouth. "I appreciate that you want to support me. But when you run a monkey up a tree, you're gonna see its ass."

Popeye's eye squinted in confusion. Swart put his finger to his lips to keep him from talking.

Coach took off his glasses and wiped his sleeve across his eyes. "I surely appreciate that you boys wanna go ... but there's gonna be nothing you can say that'll change anything." He sighed. "I'm gonna look bad. Real bad. If they even agree to let you say anything, they'll just end up asking you questions that'll sound awful when you answer 'em and then you'll feel bad when you shouldn't ... besides, your season ain't over. Don't think just because they're canning me you can give up on me."

Silence filled the street until Slade spoke up. "Finish," he said, his eyes hard on Coach. "Finish the job."

"That's right," said Coach, a real smile on his face. "You gotta finish, right Slade?"

Slade nodded. "You gotta finish," he repeated. He looked around at all of us. "Finish," he said. And there was nearly a snarl on his face. It was the first time I felt like he was actually our captain.

I'd like to say that we all banded together that night and stormed the school-board meeting and gave such passionate and heartfelt testimony that Coach kept his job. I'd like to say that we told Coach we loved him and everyone there cried, even Dr. Billings, at the heartfelt emotion swirling through the room. I'd love to tell about Slade threatening the entire school board, doing something crazy and full of good intentions. But none of that happened.

As is sometimes the case, your best teachers and coaches, your best *people*—the unusual ones, the ones that make a difference—sound like lunatics and frauds to those not familiar with them. The gems of experience they provide sometimes come off as wrongheaded or worse in the retelling. You have to know the whole story for the anecdote to work, and there's never time enough to tell the whole story.

So, that night, Coach was fired, and none of us were there because that was the way he wanted it. We cared about him enough to do what he asked of us, whether we agreed with him or not. And we, at least us Bluebirds, were still just kids. What could we do? That's what we told ourselves at least.

I see now that the protective harbor of childhood allowed us Bluebirds to sit by and not say a word while Coach was given his death sentence, and that's the only thing I truly regret about that season. Although we all had things we could have said on his behalf, at least things we should have said to him, we felt no urge and no duty to do so. That's the luxury of being a child.

But the story doesn't end there. As Coach said to Slade and Slade said to all of us that morning we sat on the sidewalk outside the Grand Hotel while the sun rose:

We still had to finish.

THE HAMBURGLAR - INCOGNITO - MERE LAWS - WHY COACH GOT FIRED - SLADE STEPS UP - LEGIONS OF SALUKIS AND A VISIT FROM BIG, BAD, BALD MOATS - 1, 2, 3 - A ROAR FROM THE DEPTHS - BALING WIRE

"You look like the goddamn Hamburglar," said Slade, a grin cracking his face for the first time all week. It may have been the first time he'd spoken since Coach was canned.

It looked strange, Slade's smile did, on a face with two black eyes and a freshly crooked nose. It looked a little painful. But it brought warmth to all of our chests to see it there on Slade's battered mug. And the cause of it brought on even more of a glow—one that warmed us from deep inside.

"Coach, Slade's right. You do look like the Hamburglar," agreed Bowden. He was laughing and shaking his head. "Man, Dr. Billings is sure to spot you in that crazy getup."

"That's why I'm hiding in the woods here! The disguise is just in case anyone sees me." He cracked a crooked grin and assumed a crouching ready-for-anything stance as his voice dropped into a whisper. "I'm incognito." He seemed in high spirits for a man who'd just lost his job, his family, and his home.

Coach had jumped out at us on our warm-up before Sectionals from behind a tree in a forest loop on the course. He wore black pants, a black shirt, and a big black hat, some strange affair somewhere between a bowler and a fedora that he had pulled down low to hide his face. He also had a navy windbreaker tied around his neck for some crazy reason. It looked, at first glance, like a cape.

"Rubble-rubble," said Victor.

"Aren't you supposed to stay away from us?' asked Hyter, his toe digging into the ground. "I mean, I'm glad to see you . . . it's just . . . isn't there some kind of court order or something saying you can't be within a thousand feet of us or talk to us?"

Coach waved that off. "Mere laws," he said. "This moment transcends any laws made by the fallible minds of men. *This*, my boys, is the Sectional."

Coach was downright swashbuckling that day.

"Love," he proclaimed, "is the root of all courageous acts." He paused to let us soak that in. He paused a little too long, and Swart started nodding impatiently, circling his hand. Coach got the hint and fired back up. "And I've found the courage to be here."

My heart quickened a touch to hear such grandiose language and such tender sentiments from the lips of Coach. I wondered if he'd been drinking.

He then grew quiet, his mood shifting. He grew very sober. "Truth is," he said, his brown eyes glancing around sheepishly, "I didn't know how much you guys meant to me until I didn't get to see you all week." He looked down at the ground. "Truth is, you boys are family."

We all looked at the ground at this confession. Not because we were embarrassed by it, but because we felt the same.

In that silence though, I had an epiphany. Not the good kind either. A flash of psychic lightning seemed to strike me, and I was suddenly certain that it was I who had been the impetus of coach's firing. The possibility, I realized later, had been gnawing at me all week. The truth was, I hadn't slept well since Victor's restaurant. It was at that moment though, standing there before Coach as he expressed his love for us, that I remembered with sudden force and vividness that night back in early September at the dinner table when I'd spoken so disparagingly of him. The night I'd begun my attempt to get Coach fired which ended with my dastardly lie about him punching me.

I remembered the looks of concern on my mother's face as I described Squid's being taped to a pole and Slade's eating of his Walkman while we all cheered him on—at Coach's insistence no less. I remembered Dad's eventual call to Dr. Billings to tell him my coach had hit me. That conversation had lasted nearly half an hour. Surely the discussion had been about things true as well as my giant lie. Coach was right: you run a monkey up a tree, you are gonna see its ass. And I was the guy who had run him up the tree to begin with. It seemed the effects of my lie would ripple on throughout my high school years. Maybe even my life.

As I stood there, I thought of Squid, who hadn't told anyone about being duct-taped to that telephone pole. Squid, whom all of us agreed was generally a spineless, lazy, spoiled brat. I remembered him saying to me, when I'd asked if he was going to tell, which felt like planting the seed and nearly telling myself now that I thought of it, that he would *never* tell. That he had more spine than that. A look of utter disgust had crossed his face when I'd even mentioned the idea.

So Squid was, and had always been, more of a man than I. After all, it had been me, not Squid, who had ultimately ratted. It had been me who'd been walking the tightrope of loyalty all along. And who had fallen off.

I suddenly found that I couldn't look Coach in the face.

The seven of us who were running that day—me, Hyter, Keane, Victor, Slade, Bowden, and Yost—had, out of deeply ingrained habit built by hours in that musty locker room, formed a horseshoe with coach filling in the open space at the top. We fell quiet quickly and waited for Coach's final words. I was sure he would begin by pointing at me. He would then explain to our varsity seven how it was me who had gotten him fired.

I decided to confess it, right then and there, rather than be called out.

"Coach," I stuttered, unable to look at him and near tears.

Coach put his index finger to his pursed lips. "Shhhhh," he whispered, his brown eyes boring into mine. He knew. "You just shut the hell up about me and what happened to me, because today ain't about me and it ain't about Dr. Billings or the School Board or nothing like that."

I nodded.

Coach spoke to us in a quiet, calm voice as we shuffled our spikes in the damp orange and yellow and brown leaves at our feet. Our bare ankles shooting from the bottoms of Coach's gray sweatpants were thin and delicate like the legs of racehorses. I know because I was staring at them the whole time.

"This day is about you," he said. "It's about the seven of you." He was firm and in control. He was in no way the man who ran out of Victor's restaurant screaming for us to hurry and get on the bus. He wasn't the man who broke down in the driver's seat of his car on that hot August morning in the corn field. He didn't apologize or cry. He looked us all in the face, and by the time he was done, I'd steeled myself inside. I'd made up my mind about how I was going to run the race. And I was going to do it for Coach. I would make up for my sins as best I could.

Just a minute before the gun we were stripped down, standing out past the start line with all the other teams. Interim Coach Willie Davis—yes, that Willie Davis, the man who had once upon a time told me I was a runner—pulled Slade over, gave him a few words, and then allowed the seven of us our own moment before the race. Willie was smart enough not to mess with us. Slade took over.

We'd never done a chant or a cheer or a prayer before a race. Coach didn't believe in it. "If you still need to talk about it a minute before you're supposed to do it, you ain't ready to do it," he'd say. But on that day, we did.

"Get in here, guys," said Slade. We automatically formed a circle. "Coach's never been to Regional. And it looks like he'll never go. But we can go there, and he'll be with us. He'll know it." Slade's black eyes were glinting as he spoke. He looked ready to attack. He looked ready to race. "Shit, maybe he can hide in the goddamned woods again, and be even happier than he just was."

My eyes flicked around the circle—Victor, Swart, Bowden, Keene, my brother, Yost … they all looked ready, their eyes steady and calm, their mouths firmly set.

"We can run with him in our hearts today," continued Slade. "We can carry him with us."

Just then Moats, the big bald runner from Ridgeline, sauntered by. It felt like a lifetime since Slade had gotten into it with him on that hot summer afternoon back in September. The Salukis' other varsity runners were surrounded by fifty or sixty jayvee runners in spotless matching warm-ups who were chanting, *It's great—to be—a Ridgeline—Saluki!* Over and over, clapping three times in perfect unison between each chant. I expected them to start goose-stepping.

Moats leaned into our circle, shoving his way in between my brother and Keane.

"Howdy boys!" he shouted in his best hayseed accent, grinning at us all like the fool he was. "Farm work all done and you Snappers ready for a little jogging?"

I was sure for a moment that Slade was going to jump on him then and there and pummel him into the ground. Half of me wished he would, the other half prayed he wouldn't. We couldn't afford to lose Slade.

Slade ignored him. Totally. It was as if Moats didn't exist. I knew then that Slade was going to have the race of his life.

Moats' gloating skeletal grin shifted a little. His eyes lost a bit of their mischievous gleam. "Get out of here," said Hyter calmly and quietly. He sounded like a mean old dog roused from a nap by a careless child—as if he was seconds away from going for Moats' throat. I'd never been more proud of him.

"Well," Moats said, shifting gears after not getting the desired response, "good luck today then." He was trying to save face, acting like he'd always intended good will.

"Are you done?" asked Victor coolly.

"Yeah," said Moats, his smile totally gone, a look of

confusion and embarrassment taking its place. "Yeah," he repeated, "I'm done."

"Goodbye then," growled Yost.

On that day, we would not be distracted. On that day we were one. We were truly zoned in—all of us. There would be no stupid kamikaze first miles and there would be no self-doubt when the pain set in halfway through the race. There was coach and there was, flowing through all of us, the bond he had, in his own crazy way, created in us.

The starter called us back to the line, his voice formal and electric through the megaphone. Slade put his hand in the center of the tight circle we'd formed and we all did the same automatically, placing our hands on top of each other's. "Okay," said Slade. "On three, 'Coach' is the word."

I'd never felt such a powerful surge inside me in my life before. As he chanted *one, two, three!* it was as if the energy of all my teammates was in me and mine was flowing out into that stack of hands and into them. "Coach!" we shouted on his signal.

I jumped, roared, and pounded my chest as we jogged back to the start. I had to. If I'd kept what I was feeling inside me entirely, I would've exploded. While they may not have let loose as I did, I saw the same look, the same glaring intensity, on the faces of my teammates.

As we high-kneed it back to the line, I glanced at Ridgeline two boxes over from us. Moats was staring. He was staring at me.

His eyes were wide and his brow registered some crinkly kind of confusion. He looked scared. He should have.

I was locked and loaded and ready to rock and roll. I was ready to cut some heads and eat some glass and any other cliché you can think of concerning readiness to compete.

Nothing was going to stop me from running as hard as I could run.

But Moats should've been even more scared of Leonardo than he was of me. Because Leonardo was carrying eight feet of baling wire and was hiding in the woods, waiting for Moats' big, bald moon of a head to come around a dark corner. And I should've been as scared of Leonardo as Moats, because I would not be where Leonardo thought I would.

BALING WIRE - IGOR - HYPER-REAL - BEING IN THE PRESENT TENSE - THE WOODS - A SUDDEN FALL - SLADE AND MOATS - THE FINISH - SECRETS IN THE BACK OF THE BUS - A DUTY

It's always piano wire. At least one murder in every great murder story involves piano wire. It's genre-fiction grammar for tooth-grinding, strangulating death. If you want your reader to feel murder's edge cutting into their windpipe, just say piano wire.

Well, piano wire was hard to come by in Pennsgap, Indiana. But baling wire was everywhere. I find it pleasingly ironic, even poetic, that just minutes after his disparaging comment about "farm work," Moats was going to encounter a staple of farm life in a most unpleasant way. Unfortunately, so was I.

None of us knew of Leonardo's plan. In fact, none of us knew that Leonardo felt he needed to take revenge for the disrespect the Salukis had shown us two months before by jogging to our place and whipping us, then jogging home, but Homecoming had made revenge concrete for Leonardo. And Leonardo liked it. "I feel like an angel sent from Hell to do justice," he told me later on the subject. I had no idea Leonardo had such dark poetry in him.

Of course, Popeye was to be his accomplice. Popeye didn't have enough brains to make a decision about what to eat for lunch without some serious mental grinding. A complex moral decision involving revenge was way beyond his simple circuitry. Because of this, he would serve as Leonardo's witless Igor. His job would be to hold the other end of the wire.

As the starter called us to the line, Leonardo and Popeye were scrambling through the dark woods searching for the perfect spot to hijack Moats. I didn't know this. By then I didn't know much of anything except that I was going to run a race as hard and fast as I could. I'd gone completely internal. When the starter said "set" it sounded to my ears like he was speaking from the bottom of a well. He raised his starting pistol in what seemed like slow motion. I don't remember hearing it go off. I ran on the cue of movement to my left and right.

But then everything became very clear and definite and simple and direct—the sensation I had throughout that race was hyper real. I was aware of everything happening around me at once. I heard a kid take an elbow in his ribs and sigh ten feet or so to my right. I felt the vibration of spikes hitting the soft ground. The cool moist air felt like a buzzing living thing. I swear I could've counted my individual heartbeats I was so tuned in.

Everything was moving in real time, flowing along easily, and I was comfortably running in the first quarter of the pack as we hit the half-mile mark. There was no nervousness, there was no anxiety, there was no past and no future. There was just the ten feet in front of me, the runners to my immediate right and left, and the air that filled my lungs.

By the mile mark I was in the top fifteen, along with all seven of the Ridgeline runners, my brother, Keane, and Slade. A coach with a royal blue hat and a large, round head held his fogged pair of glasses raised up off the tip of his nose with one hand and held a stopwatch up to his face in the other. He shouted out the mile split—*four fifty-eight, fifty-nine, five, ohh-one, ohh-two.*

Slade, just to my left, looked like he was working hard, but his face, the two black eyes and the scab across the bridge of his nose, showed pure determination. Hyter and Keane, both floating right in front of me, seemed zoned in as well. I felt fine. I felt within myself.

The jayvee runners stationed at the mile clapped hard for us, shouted our names, then sprinted off to the next spot on the course where they might cheer us on. I noticed them only in passing, like driving by an exit sign on the highway that's not your exit. I focused only on what was necessary for me to run as fast as I could.

In the end, I believe the point of all art—all sport, all work—is to be entirely in a moment. It's the place we human beings are most comfortable. It's what we strive for. In making love, in listening to music, in scaling a rock wall, or surfing a wave … the point is to be where you are, one-hundred percent, and to be nowhere else. It's what we shoot for every time out. That's where I was on that dark, misty autumn day.

By the two-mile mark the spectators, my jayvee team-mates, my parents, all the girls watching our race, might as well have been mist. All I knew was the runner in front of me, the runner beside me, and the next turn ahead.

The two-mile mark was just before a short loop through a small dark, dripping, woods—the setting where coach had been hiding that afternoon waiting for us to jog by so he could see us before our race.

By that point, three Ridgeline runners had clearly broken free of the pack. Two runners, strong individuals on weak teams, one wearing white and blue and the other in gold and green, had chased after the tight maroon and silver pack of three. They were the top five. Then it was Moats. Moats and me.

Somewhere along the way I'd dropped my fellow Blue-birds, barely noticing. I'd decided to stick on Moats until I had to make a decision of some sort. Through the second mile mark in 10:18, it registered somewhere in the back of my mind that I was on my way to a personal record. I didn't think much of that either. I thought only of the next twenty steps, the next ten seconds.

The dropping sun, the heavy air, and the lateness of the day conspired to make the woods a ghostly place. The grayness of the early evening turned darker under the trees. The branches and leaves, yellow, green, red, and brown that afternoon, were now muted gray, purple, and black. Misty figures stood alongside the course, their handclaps muffled by the atmosphere. The trees seemed gauze-covered. The sound of our spikes on the leaves of the hard-packed dirt path was muted. There was the smell of smoke from some long dead campfire or some faraway cookout where people didn't know anything about running races.

Moats and I, side by side, made our way. His breathing heavy and labored, mine controlled. It was my world complete.

Then I saw it. He had a hitch in his stride. His right hand flopped a little after each time his left foot hit the ground, the fingers curling up as if to snatch something invisible out of the air. I was noticing this, thinking that he might be getting tired, thinking he might be tightening up because I, a lowly freshman Pennsgap Snapper, was hanging onto him, thinking of the move that I would make and crush him, when both of us slammed into the ground. The mulch of the forest floor suddenly filled my mouth.

I looked around, dazed. Utterly surprised. "What the . . . " Moats said breathlessly.

From behind us, a pack including Keane arced around the corner and was upon us almost immediately. A Ridgeline runner dodged to our left and slipped and fell in a pile of wet leaves that had been raked off the course. Keane hurdled between us instinctively. My ankles suddenly felt as if wrapped in burning rope. Moats grabbed at his ankle as well. "Shit!" he yelled.

"Get up!" yelled Keane as he hurtled down the path.

Hyter passed me then, glaring at me as he breezed by, seemingly confused at why I might choose that spot to sit and rest and chat with Moats.

Then Slade arrived. He stopped running and leaned over and pulled me from the ground. The cotton tongues of my spikes, I saw, were bright red. "We need you," he said clearly. "We need you up front." And he pushed me onward in front of him.

By that time, Moats too had risen. We took off together. Slade just behind us. There was a mile left in the race.

As we found our strides again, Slade stuck hard on our heels. After about a quarter mile, he began talking in a quiet low voice. "You're done, Moats," he whispered like the devil he'd once claimed to be. "This little bastard is faster than all us old guys."

Moats turned and glared at him. He looked scared. I remembered those words from somewhere back in my shared past with Slade. I remembered them and felt a jolt of energy. I almost laughed out loud. Moats was toast.

"You're fucked, Moats," Slade whispered. He inhaled and exhaled hard, finding the breath to speak one last time. "With a chainsaw."

I left Moats seconds after that and never saw him again.

With eight-hundred to go, I caught Hyter. With a quarter left, I caught Keane. I kicked and passed one of the two individuals who'd broken away with the Ridgeline three.

I'd placed fifth overall. My last mile, if you add in the ten long seconds on the ground, was just over five minutes. My overall time was a personal record of 16:23.

Keane was right behind me, Hyter right after that, all three of us in the top ten. Slade and Victor were in the teens.

We'd moved on with a second place finish. And we had broken up Ridgeline's pack—placing three freshmen in front of their fourth. We had actually run with them. It was the first time any team had done that to them all season.

At the awards ceremony, we sat shivering on some aluminum benches before an empty football field. Ice on both my ankles, my shins were marked by a bloody gash just above the tops of my trainers. I barely noticed. I kept admiring the number up high on my chest. The number that looked the same right side up or upside down. Number One. I'd finally earned it.

As we rode back home, Leonardo and Popeye apologized profusely about having caught me up in their wire. Slade attacked them both for their stupidity, but the secret of why

Moats and I had gone down would always stay in the back of the bus. We'd all learned to keep our secrets to ourselves, it seemed. Still, that brought up certain thoughts. Those things I had failed to keep to myself. And worse, the secret I had kept from my coach and teammates. They were thoughts I didn't like thinking. But I had no choice. That's just the way a conscience works.

MISERY LOVES COMPANY, PART II - PRAISE - HYTER IN THE BIG TUB WITH HIS WASHCLOTH - CAIN AND ABLE - THE PLUNGER - UNWRITTEN RULES - ANYTHING GOES - THE CRACK OF THE SKULL - LIKE PENNIES

Misery loves company. I believe that was a theme of a previous chapter—something about me hiding in a barn with Squid way back when it was still hot and summer seemed like it would go on forever. Well, with winter on the horizon, that particular cliché reared its ugly head again. Maybe misery truly does love company. Maybe all clichés are accurate.

At home that night, I was praised for my race as was Hyter. We even got a call from our Grandpa, my father's father, which was a rare luxury as my grandfather had thirty-two grandkids. That phone call was something my father was truly proud of. I could hear it in his voice as he spoke on the phone after I had accepted Grandpa's congratulations. It meant the world to me, to hear him talk about me with actual pride in his voice again. Unfortunately, something sour turning in me made it impossible to enjoy.

I was restless and grouchy that night. I was spiteful, even. There was something poisonous within me, something I had yet to expel. It showed itself in my mood at the table.

My dad had to tell me to thank my mother for dinner and my mom stared at me with big sunny-side-up eyes when I refused to answer her question about my pleasure at finally having earned the number-one sweatshirt. I had shrugged off several comments from all three of my family members designed to lead me to tell of my race, how I responded to my fall, what I thought it had been that had tripped up Moats and me.

Eventually, Hyter spoke up, saying "How come you're being such a jerk?"

Dad raised his eyebrows after he said that, and not at Hyter. A yellowish-brown wash of acidic guilt was bathing my brain. I felt like I couldn't inhale. I felt cheated out of my triumphant moment. Of course, I took it out on Hyter.

He liked to take baths after races. We had a big claw-footed tub and he would fill it with bubbles and sit in there until his hands and feet were as wrinkled as a monkey's. He was in there soaking, a washcloth covering his face, when I went in and sat down on the toilet next to the tub. He pulled the washcloth off his face. "You're not taking a crap when I'm in here," he said.

That wasn't my reason for being there, but I didn't like being told what to do. "I might," I said.

"No, you're not," he said, raising his body up out of the sudsy water with a gentle slosh.

"I will if I have to crap," I said.

He gave me an eye and slid back down into the water when he saw that I had no intention of actually using the toilet.

"You know," I said, finally spitting it out, "Coach got fired because of us."

Hyter put the washcloth back over his eyes. "Because of *you*," he said without any emotion. "If it was you at all."

The grinding in my head that had been going on all night ceased and something cracked and gave. I nearly leapt up from the toilet. "It was both of us and you know it! It was Dad's call."

Hyter didn't even move the washcloth from his face. "It was you if it was either of us," he said in a monotone. "I never said anything about him. Nothing bad."

It is a mark of brotherhood, a stain going back to Cain and Able, to want to murder your brother on occasion. And not just your identical twin because he looks like you and people mistake him for you. Cain and Able weren't twins.

While your friends may make you fist-clenching mad, and while you may scuffle with strangers to stave off embarrassment or in the face of injustice, only shared blood has the power to generate flashes of anger so profound as to create the temporary insanity necessary for murder. At least in normal people. Serial killers excluded, obviously.

The plunger next to the toilet was the most weapon-like object available to me. I suppose I could've tossed the plugged-in radio that sat next to the sink into the tub and done the job with the use of electricity, frying him. However, an old-fashioned beating to death with a wooden stick appealed more to me for some reason.

The first blow was to his sternum. Washcloth covering his eyes, he didn't even see it coming. The sound was like a bat hitting a baseball, a dull crack.

The air was full of water then. My left foot slipped out from under me at the same time his fist hit my right shoulder. I slammed onto the hard tile floor, my left buttock taking the brunt of my weight. A wave, several gallons of bathwater, slopped out of the tub onto my legs as I wriggled on the tile floor like an upended turtle. Hyter, completely naked, was then on top of me. My anger evaporated as quickly as it had developed.

"Get the hell off me, you homo!" I squealed.

I wasn't actually afraid that my brother was gay. I had no real fear that he was incestuously attracted to me, or that he wanted to express anything but hatred for me when he jumped on me the way he did. It was just that his murderous temper had exploded on me at the same time my murderous and mysterious anger evaporated completely.

I was no longer angry. I was scared. Calling him a homosexual was a survival tactic, the only one I could think of. I hoped to make him self-conscious of his position—naked and on top of me. It didn't work.

"I'm gonna kill you!" he yelled.

He jammed his hand in my mouth and scraped at my gums with his fingernails. The coppery taste of blood gagged me. My anger erupted again. I attempted to hit him, I'm not proud to admit, where it hurts the most. I mean, there it was, dangling in the air. In doing so, however, all unwritten rules concerning fights between us were rescinded. I would soon regret my decision.

Our fights, and we had a good blowout at least once a month for many years, were governed by some basic rules: 1. No damage to the face. 2. No blows to the balls. With one hard shift of my knee, I'd opened up a world of potential pain upon myself. After Hyter dodged my shot between his legs, he made this clear to me by screaming, "You're dead!"

Terror shot through me again. I took him at his word, and I immediately started apologizing. Profusely.

"I'm sorry! I'm sorry! I'm sorry!" I shouted. But I couldn't break the rule and then apologize and expect to get away with it. And I didn't.

Hyter slammed my nose with his wet forehead. The dull echo of my skull bouncing off the tile floor filled my head for the next several seconds. Then things slowed way down.

The hot, wet creep of blood, like warm milk spilling over my face, was the only sensation I registered for a hazy space of time. Then there was the weight lifted off my chest, the distant voice of my Dad, his voice confused and a little frightened, the sound of Hyter crying and explaining and the blurred image of him still standing there still dripping wet and naked.

Then the warmth of the blood and the taste of it was my world entire. I lived in a world of pennies. Liquid pennies trickling down my throat.

DAD MADE ME - BLOOD - CALL ME STUPID THEN - THE EMPTINESS OF THE GRAND HOTEL - A RED ROBE, GOLDEN SLIPPERS, A CIGAR, AND A BEER - GUESTS/FREAKS - A TOAST - CONFESSION - WHAT THE WORLD SPINS AROUND - WHAT I REMEMBERED

Hours later, I awoke to find Hyter sitting at my bedside. He was reading. He looked very mature, sitting on a hard little wooden chair. He looked calm.

He sensed my open eyes and raised his own from his book—some huge Stephen King apocalyptic disaster. He shut the book.

The reading lamp next to him spread the only light in the room. It made a cone through the darkness down to the wooden planks of the floor. Hyter's face was shaded dramatically and his brown eyes were bright. "The only reason

I'm sitting here is because Dad made me," he said, his voice tight as Leonardo's wire.

"I'm sorry," I said. "I'm really sorry." My voice was nasally and high.

"It's okay," he said, shutting his book.

I felt my nose to find it bandaged. It felt like there was a weight on my face. I tasted blood. Sitting up, I quickly wished I hadn't. My head ached and throbbed.

"Sorry about your nose," he said.

I grabbed a bloody white towel that had clearly been used to swab my face. It was sitting on my bedside table. I pressed it to my nose and blew. Blackish red chunks. Small, but still chunks. My stomach did a forward roll.

I folded the cloth so I didn't have to look at whatever it was I'd blown out. My brains, maybe. "Sorry I went after your balls," I said. I wanted it to sound funny but it didn't.

"That's okay, you were really mad."

I'd started to lie back down, but when I remembered why I'd been mad, I straightened up again. Blood rushed into my head like some kind of cranial tide. "I've got to go see Coach," I said. "What time is it?" I gingerly touched my temples.

Hyter glanced at the bedside clock, the red digital numbers glowed 9:48.

"Mom and Dad aren't going to let you leave. They're going to take you to the hospital. They almost already did but you said you were okay."

"I said I was okay?" I didn't remember that. "Well, I need to talk to Coach. That's why I was so mad. I have to tell him it was me."

"That's the stupidest thing I've ever heard," said Hyter. "You didn't run out of that restaurant without paying. You didn't let the seniors tape Squid to that telephone pole."

"Call me stupid then," I was out of bed then, picking up my brown corduroys and my green sweater I'd worn that day to school.

"If you're going, I'll go with you."

"You don't have to." My head ached, badly, to the point that I felt I might throw up.

"I know," he said. "I'll go anyway."

I washed my face and went into Mom and Dad's room. They were both reading and in bed. Dad had his glasses on. Mom too. She had a pen in her hand and was marking sections of her Bible. Dad was reading a Louis L'Amour western.

"I'm okay," I started. Mom put down her pen and Bible. Dad laid his book spread open next to him on the bed. Neither spoke. "I know you're worried about me, but I feel okay. I'll go to the hospital if you want me to, but I need to stop and see Coach first."

It was raining hard when our car slid up to the curb outside the Grand. The gutters along the streets were swollen. Black water dripped off rooftops and the streets shined. My skull felt full of poisonous, sloshing water.

Hyter and I walked in the cavernous old building. Dad drove home. On the way I had explained what I had to do. "Call when you're ready to come home," he said. And he smiled at me for the first time in a long, long time. It felt good. But I still had to find the courage to do what I had to do. I had to finish.

The place was even more desolate at night than it had been in the morning. The smell of ancient cigarette smoke filled my nostrils and I nearly puked. "Where's his room?" I asked.

"It's on the third floor," said Hyter. "I don't' remember the specific number."

"Let's go find it."

As we made our way to Coach's room, I half expected to see translucent spirits floating in the echo-laden stairwells and above the musty, spotted carpet. The place was straight out of a bad ghost story. It smelled of evil doings. Like crimes not truly washed away yet forgotten. I gagged about every ten seconds.

He was standing in the hallway in a red robe when we turned the corner that led to his room. He had a cigar in one hand and a brown bottle of beer in the other. He wore a pair of fancy gold leather slippers and reminded me of a genie.

Pointing his orange tipped cigar at us, he shouted, "Hey!" as if he'd been expecting us. "Great races! I was just celebrating with my guests in this fine residence." He ashed his cigar on the maroon hallway carpet. "Sorry I didn't stick around to shake your hands, but the principal was starting to sniff me out. Perhaps you'll join us."

He nodded towards his open door and tipped his beer in that direction. The tinny sound of a television blared out the door.

"We can't stay long," said Hyter. He nodded at me. "He has to go to the hospital."

"I guess so," Coach said, leaning in towards me, his eyes squinting, a look of sympathetic pain spreading across his face, his big black eyebrows furrowing. "What happened to your nose?"

"Hyter head-butted me," I said, feeling stupid. Coach's fresh cigar smelled of earth and spices and didn't make me want to puke. The blue-grey smoke spiraled up and disappeared.

"Why'd you head-butt him, Champ?"

"He tried to knee me in the nuts," Hyter replied, matter-of-factly. With good humor, actually. One thing about my brother and me, our fights might be vicious, but once they were over, they were *over*.

Coach stared at me for a second. "You earned it then," he said, decisively but not cruelly. "A man shouldn't try to get to another man's jewels."

We three pondered that truism for a moment. "Well," Coach said, "moving on, come in here so's I can introduce you to my friends, even if you can't stay long."

"Coach," I started. I had to get out what I had to say. I didn't think I could do it with an audience.

"Just come in here!" he whispered loudly, waving his cigar for us to hurry. "You'll hurt their feelings if you don't say hi."

Hyter shrugged. It didn't seem that I had a choice.

If I wanted to confess my sins and absolve myself, I needed to do it that night. I knew that. And I supposed I didn't get to pick and choose my perfect moment. "Just for a second," I said. "And then I've got to talk to you."

The room was dingy and small and almost entirely filled by a large iron-framed bed covered by a thin mattress smack in the middle of it. A crooked little picture of a red, yellow, and purple sunset over a northern lake hung on the wall. Two large windows at right angles in the corner of the room were streaked with rainwater. The night outside was black. A threadbare chair sat beside the bed, wedged between it and the far wall. The chair was empty. Sitting on the bed were Slade, Victor, Swart, Keane, and Bowden.

"Look who's here!" shouted Victor who sat cross-legged with what looked like a beer in his hand. He pointed his brown bottle at me and Hyter. "Number One and Number Three!"

A black and white movie flickered on the television Coach had set up on a dresser. There was an image of circus animals, black and white elephants, a giraffe, and chimpanzees, all parading across the screen.

"Freaks!" said Hyter, pointing at the TV. I noticed an unwieldy VCR, bigger than the television, had been hooked up.

"One of us! One of us!" chanted Swart as he bounced up and down on his butt like a happy four-year-old, the bedsprings squeaking and complaining under him. He took a belt of whatever was in those brown bottles. Several empty pizza boxes covered the few square feet of floor available.

"Glad you fellas could make it to our humble little soirée," said Bowden. He also had a cigar in his hand.

"I propose a toast!" said Coach as he moved to his chair, taking it by the arm and dragging it out from behind the bed.

"Hell yes," said Bowden. "I like mine with butter and jam."

Swart bounced off the bed and snatched two bottles out of an icy chest under the little TV. He cracked them open, each with a pop and a hiss, and handed one to me and one to Hyter. I sniffed at it. It was root beer.

"Here's to Bluebirds!" said Slade, imitating Coach's East Coast braying. "Without 'em we wouldn'ta made it ta Regionals!" He grinned. "Gawddamnit!"

"Here, here," said Coach, nodding. He winked at Keane and nodded at my brother and me. "Although I was the one who proposed the toast so's I was supposed to be the one to make it."

"Hell with you," said Slade. "You old baahhs-tud." Slade could do a pretty good Boston accent. I'd have been impressed if I hadn't been solely focused on my impending confession.

When we all took a drink, my throat felt like there was

a golf-ball-sized tumor in it. I had come here to crumble before my coach. Instead, I'd been caught up in a celebration.

"Another toast!" said Bowden. "Here's to Coach! Without him, Slade would be dead by now!"

"That's the truth!" said Slade. "Remember that night I slept in your garage? That night my Dad was after me with his gawd-damned belt?"

"Buckle end hurts like a bitch," said Victor.

We clinked again.

"What about my toast?" whined Coach, although I could tell that he wasn't really upset. A grin had spread across his face.

"I think we ought to hear a toast from Number One himself," said Victor. He tapped his stogie, ashing right on Coach's bed covers.

"Here! Here!" shouted Coach, raising his Budweiser.

They clinked their bottles, and chanted *number one, number one* over and over, happy as they could be in Coach's nasty little dump of a room.

The joy in there ... the brotherhood ... well, it broke my heart. I couldn't help it. I started to cry.

The room slowly grew silent but for the blaring of the television, the dialogue of the old movie playing. Something about receipts for the circus. Money missing.

Coach was the only one who didn't notice the tears on my face. He shouted, "Okay! Okay! My turn! Finally! My toast is ..."

And then he noticed.

"K1? What's the matter, little man?" He set his beer down on the floor. "What're you crying for?" He clutched the top of his head. "Awww! For God's sakes! We made Regionals! Goddamnit, why does someone always gotta ruin my good time!" He glared at me. "Out in the hallway with it then! The rest of you, carry on, carry on."

"So, what's the problem buddy?" he asked me out in the hallway. "Your mom's good looking, your dad makes a lot of money, you got fifth in Sectionals as a freshman. What is it?"

I was sniffling now, trying to get through it.

"You're ugly," he said thoughtfully. "Especially with that messed up nose you earned yourself by trying to grab your brother's nuts, but you can't do nothing about that but get over it."

I laughed, even though his joke hadn't been that funny. "So … what's up?"

It all spilled out then. I got you fired, I told my dad, he told Dr. Billings, I didn't understand, I thought you were crazy, I thought I hated you, I am so sorry, I am so, so, *so* sorry. Then tears. Lots of them.

"You know kid," Coach said softly, his hand on my shoulder, "the world don't spin around you."

"What?"

"I said, 'The world don't revolve around you.' Well, actually I said, 'The world don't spin around you,' but it's the same thing, eh?"

"What do you mean?"

Coach smiled. "Look. I didn't get fired because of you. Okay?"

"What?"

"Yeah," Coach said grinning. He seemed so overjoyed at our advance to Regionals that nothing could upset him. "I ain't no teacher. Hell, I don't know nothing but running and

I make most of what I know about that up as I go. But," he sighed a resigned sigh, "I gotta teach a class to be a coach. They stuck me in health. So, I show the same movie about dinosaurs over and over, catch a few zzzzzs ... I'm a night person, you know? I don't do so good in the morning." He shrugged. "Anyway, I got caught sleeping for the third time while I was showing the same dinosaur movie I showed nearly every class, which don't got nothing to do with health but I figured it was kinda science-related, you know? Anyways ... I knew it was over after that. Straw that broke the camel's back, so to speak." He grinned. "It wasn't you, K1. Don't you worry about that!"

So it hadn't been Dad, and it hadn't been me. And the world, I was shocked and in a really small and weird way disappointed to realize, did not revolve around me. In fact, I didn't truly believe it. I continued to plead my case.

"Dad called Dr. Billings. About you," I said. "Remember when I found you asleep? It was the night before that. I lied."

"You never told anyone you found me sleeping in the wrestling room, did you?" He was smiling. It was as if he hadn't heard me properly. "You never told my secret, did you?" He had complete faith in me. Faith I didn't deserve.

"I didn't. Not about that. But listen. I lied. I made up something really bad. About you." His faced changed then. He lowered his cigar and stared at me. He was waiting. "Remember my eye, how it was black?"

"Yeah?" he said.

I started to hiccup a little. "I did that to *myself.* And I said it was you. I wanted to get you fired, Coach."

Coach raised his cigar to his mouth, sucked on it, and blew smoke over his shoulder. He stared at me for a few seconds. He reached toward my face and I pulled back. "I ain't gonna hurt you," he said gently. He touched my face near my eye. It was still a little yellow from the bruise. "You did that to yourself? To get me canned?"

"Yes," I whispered.

"Ha!" said Coach. And he did say it, he didn't laugh it. He looked about the hallways as if someone might be eavesdropping on us. "About this revelation, I ain't exactly sure how to respond. Except to say that it makes me feel better somehow."

I was confused. "How could that make you feel better?"

"Well, the truth is, my favorite thing, besides running a race or watching you guys run a race, is when I am reminded that I ain't the only fuckup in the room, you know?" He smiled and rubbed the top of my head. "You feel bad about it?"

"About the lie?" I sniffed.

"Yeah."

"Very."

"Good. Would you take me for your coach if you could?"

"Absolutely," I said. "You'll always be my coach."

He smiled a big smile then. "That's all I needed to hear."

He hugged me then. I was so surprised, I barely hugged him back. He shook me gently by my shoulders, affectionately, smiling at the shock on my face. "You just pull yourself together, buddy. Get that nose fixed, and be ready to run next Saturday. That's all you gotta do. Stop worrying all the time and stop worrying about me. I'm gonna crash and burn no matter what *you* do." He laughed. I smiled for the first time that night. I felt as light as the blue smoke floating upwards from the tip of Coach's cigar.

We lost at Regionals the next week. Overwhelmed and worn down by all we had been through, we ran as poorly as we'd run all year. I don't remember our place. It wasn't worth committing to memory.

I remember this. The bus ride home was nearly silent. There was the hum of spinning tires on the road beneath us. I remember the gold and brown fields spread out beyond my bus window in the late afternoon sun, how pretty they were. The corn stalks, tattered and twelve-feet high just days before, had been mown down and were now barren stubble. As I stared out, head against the cool glass, it almost seemed I could see the curve of the Earth in the clear, bright blue distance.

It's always been my favorite time of a race day—the ride home. The lungs wrung out and the chest clear, the legs a good sore, perhaps a calf or quad buzzing from a mild strain. The mind is airy and sensory perception is high after your system's been flushed with adrenaline, endorphins, and lactic acid. Even after a bad race, there's a pleasant emptiness that feels like a waking sleep somehow. It's the feeling of completely lacking any desire—as if you've run the need out of yourself. It's what Heaven must feel like.

As we rode, I remembered.

I remembered that first day of practice—how scared I'd been of Slade. I wasn't scared of him anymore. Knowing a person does that. I thought of Slade's father and how I'd come to understand the boy by understanding the man who had raised him. Then I thought of Squid, how I'd hidden in the barn with him on that August morning and how he never came close to earning that Land Rover, but how he got it anyway. And this made me think of unfairness, not with bitterness in my heart, but just the fact of it. How Coach could get fired and how it was inevitable, how no sane person could argue against it, yet how it was still somehow not right or fair. But, as Bowden said all those days ago on the first day of school, the fair was in August.

Looking down at my gray sweatshirt at Coach's "2" inked at the throat, I remembered how important wearing that "1" was to me. And how I had done it. I remember realizing that it didn't matter to me so much anymore, and how I was glad Slade had earned it one last time in the last race he ever ran. He wore it all that winter at school. I remember how he smiled and nodded at me, a lowly freshman, a Bluebird, when I passed him in the hallways. I remember the respect he gave me, just as Willie Davis had after that first race all those years before.

But what I remembered most of all was when I went back into that hotel room on that black October night after confessing myself to my Coach, the best coach I ever had. I remember going in there and sitting on that ratty old bed with my teammates—my brother, Bowden, Keane, Slade, Victor, Swart and Coach himself, all of us on that one bed. I remember those freaks in black and white on that tiny television chanting over and over, *One of us! One of us!* and I remember us, a bunch of freaks ourselves, chanting it along with them. Coach's big smile on his face and a tear in his eye ... I remember how he chanted it the loudest of all of us.

As I rode that big yellow bus back towards home feeling the beautiful emptiness of autumn fill me up, I thought of what it meant to be a runner—how good it felt to know what I was. I thought of the other things I was—a brother, a son, a coward, a liar, a friend, a rat, an angel and a devil, a victim, an accomplice, a winner and a loser, a convert, a student, a freak, a teammate ... I thought of all the things I was, and the list seemed long. But "child" wasn't on it anymore.

My insecurities and fears would return, as they always do. I would, over the next four years, lose myself again many times. But for at least an hour on that quiet bus ride home, I was content. I knew what I was.

And it was good to be me.

ABOUT THE AUTHOR

Bill Kenley earned a bachelor's degree from Miami University and a masters from Ohio State University. Twice voted the most inspiring and influential teacher at his high school, he's taught creative writing at the college and high school level. He's got a 2:47 marathon PR and a fifty-miler under his belt. For more information about Bill and his books go to www.BillKenley.com.

CPSIA information can be obtained
at www.ICGtesting.com
Printed in the USA
FFOW05n0110020415